Sonic the Hedgehog #11
"The Good, the Bad, and the Hedgehog"

The first appearance of Evil Sonic! Just as fast, powerful and all evil!
Finding a universe where everything is reversed, Sonic goes toe-to-toe
with someone who is his equal in every way!

"Beat the Clock"

Tired of being second banana and coveting a top slot on Robotnik's
Top Ten Badniks List, Coconuts does the unthinkable and captures the
Freedom Fighters. Will his monkey business lead to a slip up, or will
Coconuts be a great ape?!

"Food for Thought/You Are What You Eat"

After scarfing down a ton of chili dogs as a midnight snack, Sonic
dreams that everyone has turned into fast food: Sonic is a chili dog,
Sally is an ice cream cone, Tails is an order of fries, and they all
confront Chef Ivo Robo-Burger. Will our heroes put evil on a diet
or will they be deep fried?!

Sonic the Hedgehog #12
"A Timely Arrival"

Robotnik uses a time machine to send Sonic to the past! Sonic is trapped
in prehistoric Mobius where he meets Sonugh the Boghog, the caveman
Ivo Robotnik, and other Freedom Fighter ancestors. This may be one
dino-disaster even Sonic can't escape from!

"Bold-Headed Eagle"

Can Cyril, the last of the eagles, help Sonic defeat Robotnik before his
sanctuary is destroyed? Or will this elderly eagle's goose be cooked?

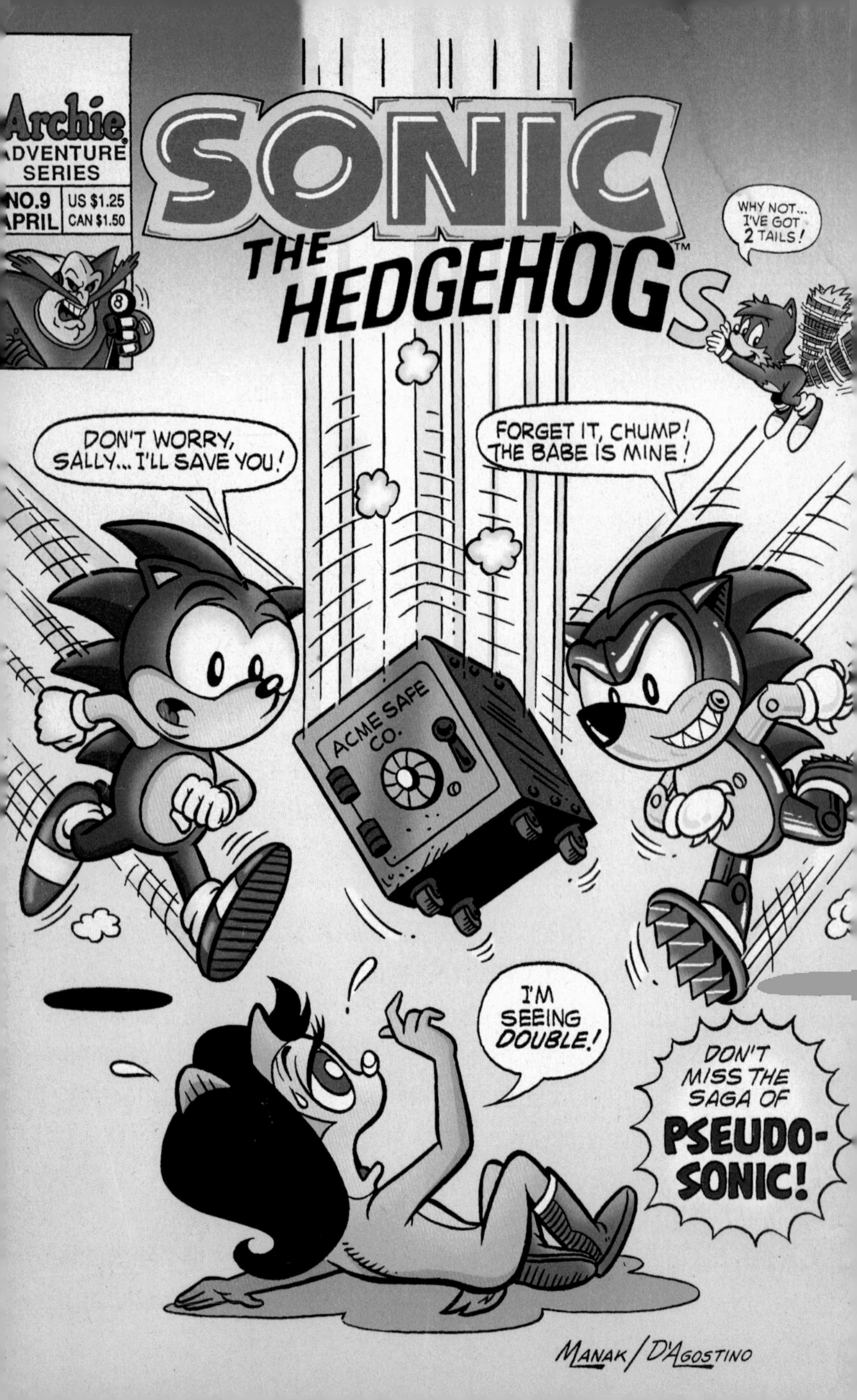

Archie ADVENTURE SERIES
NO.9 APRIL
US $1.25 CAN $1.50
SONIC THE HEDGEHOGs™
WHY NOT... I'VE GOT 2 TAILS!
DON'T WORRY, SALLY... I'LL SAVE YOU!
FORGET IT, CHUMP! THE BABE IS MINE!
ACME SAFE CO.
I'M SEEING DOUBLE!
DON'T MISS THE SAGA OF PSEUDO-SONIC!
MANAK / D'AGOSTINO

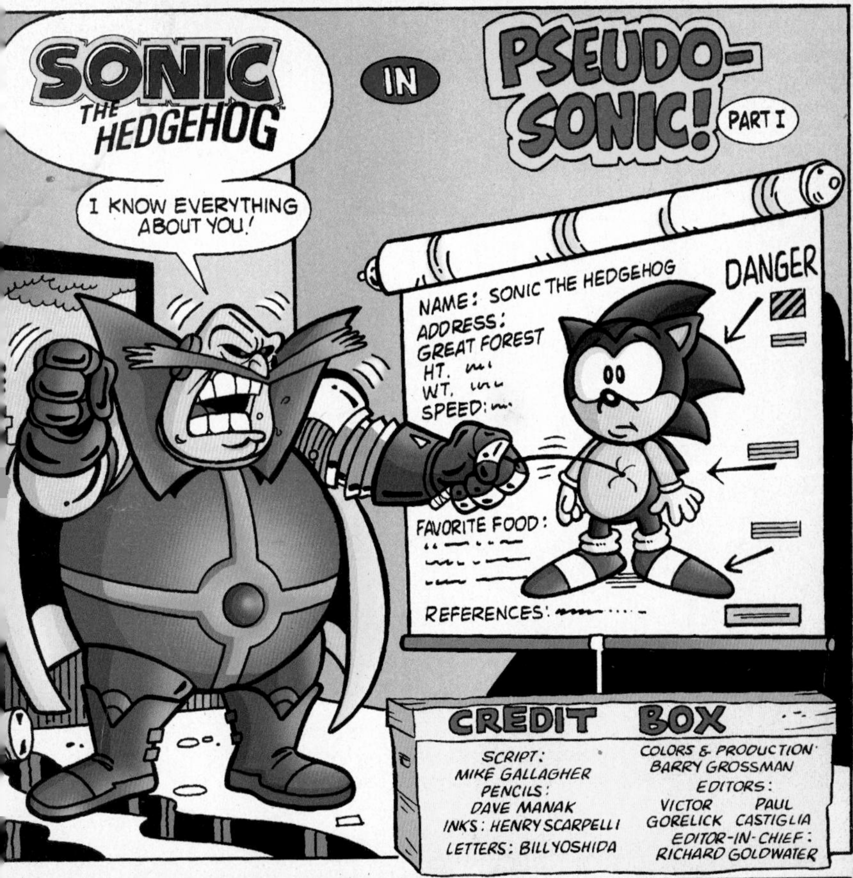
SONIC THE HEDGEHOG
IN
PSEUDO-SONIC! PART I
I KNOW EVERYTHING ABOUT YOU!
NAME: SONIC THE HEDGEHOG
ADDRESS: GREAT FOREST
HT.
WT.
SPEED:
DANGER
FAVORITE FOOD:
REFERENCES:
CREDIT BOX
SCRIPT: MIKE GALLAGHER
PENCILS: DAVE MANAK
INKS: HENRY SCARPELLI
LETTERS: BILL YOSHIDA
COLORS & PRODUCTION: BARRY GROSSMAN
EDITORS: VICTOR GORELICK PAUL CASTIGLIA
EDITOR-IN-CHIEF: RICHARD GOLDWATER

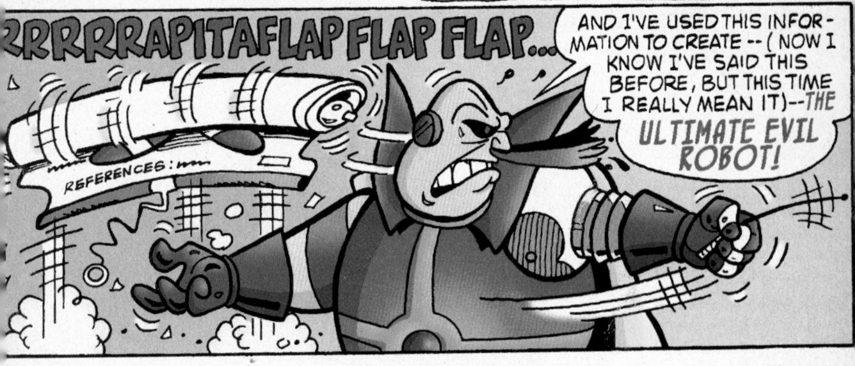
RRRRRAPITAFLAP FLAP FLAP...
AND I'VE USED THIS INFORMATION TO CREATE -- (NOW I KNOW I'VE SAID THIS BEFORE, BUT THIS TIME I REALLY MEAN IT)--THE ULTIMATE EVIL ROBOT!
REFERENCES:

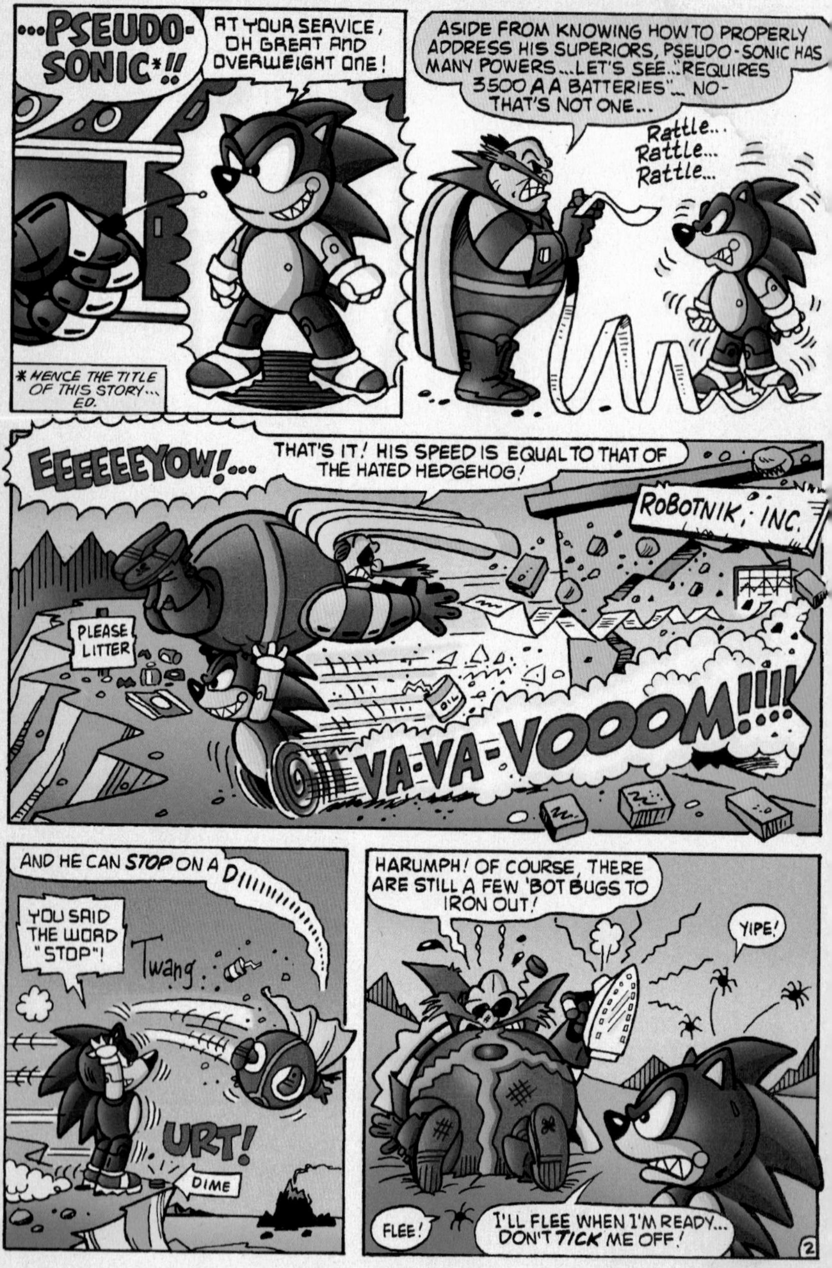
...PSEUDO-SONIC*!!
AT YOUR SERVICE, OH GREAT AND OVERWEIGHT ONE!
* HENCE THE TITLE OF THIS STORY... ED.
ASIDE FROM KNOWING HOW TO PROPERLY ADDRESS HIS SUPERIORS, PSEUDO-SONIC HAS MANY POWERS... LET'S SEE... "REQUIRES 3500 AA BATTERIES"... NO- THAT'S NOT ONE...
Rattle... Rattle... Rattle...
EEEEEEYOW!...
THAT'S IT! HIS SPEED IS EQUAL TO THAT OF THE HATED HEDGEHOG!
ROBOTNIK, INC.
PLEASE LITTER
OIL
VA-VA-VOOOM!!!!
AND HE CAN STOP ON A DIIIIIIII
YOU SAID THE WORD "STOP"!
Twang
URT!
DIME
HARUMPH! OF COURSE, THERE ARE STILL A FEW 'BOT BUGS TO IRON OUT!
YIPE!
FLEE!
I'LL FLEE WHEN I'M READY... DON'T TICK ME OFF!

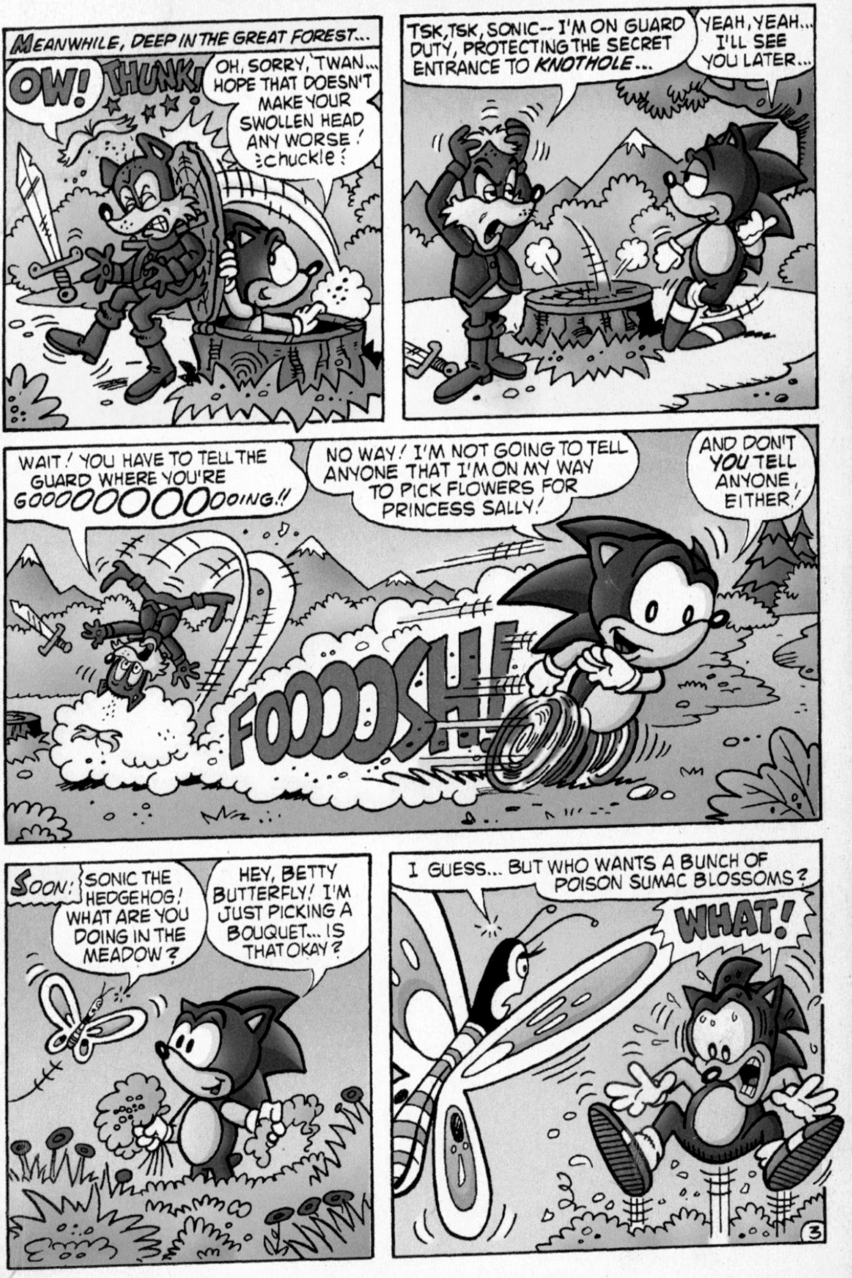
MEANWHILE, DEEP IN THE GREAT FOREST...
OW!
THUNK!
OH, SORRY, TWAN... HOPE THAT DOESN'T MAKE YOUR SWOLLEN HEAD ANY WORSE! chuckle
TSK, TSK, SONIC-- I'M ON GUARD DUTY, PROTECTING THE SECRET ENTRANCE TO KNOTHOLE...
YEAH, YEAH... I'LL SEE YOU LATER...
WAIT! YOU HAVE TO TELL THE GUARD WHERE YOU'RE GOOOOOOOOOOING!!
NO WAY! I'M NOT GOING TO TELL ANYONE THAT I'M ON MY WAY TO PICK FLOWERS FOR PRINCESS SALLY!
AND DON'T YOU TELL ANYONE, EITHER!
FOOOOSH!
SOON:
SONIC THE HEDGEHOG! WHAT ARE YOU DOING IN THE MEADOW?
HEY, BETTY BUTTERFLY! I'M JUST PICKING A BOUQUET... IS THAT OKAY?
I GUESS... BUT WHO WANTS A BUNCH OF POISON SUMAC BLOSSOMS?
WHAT!

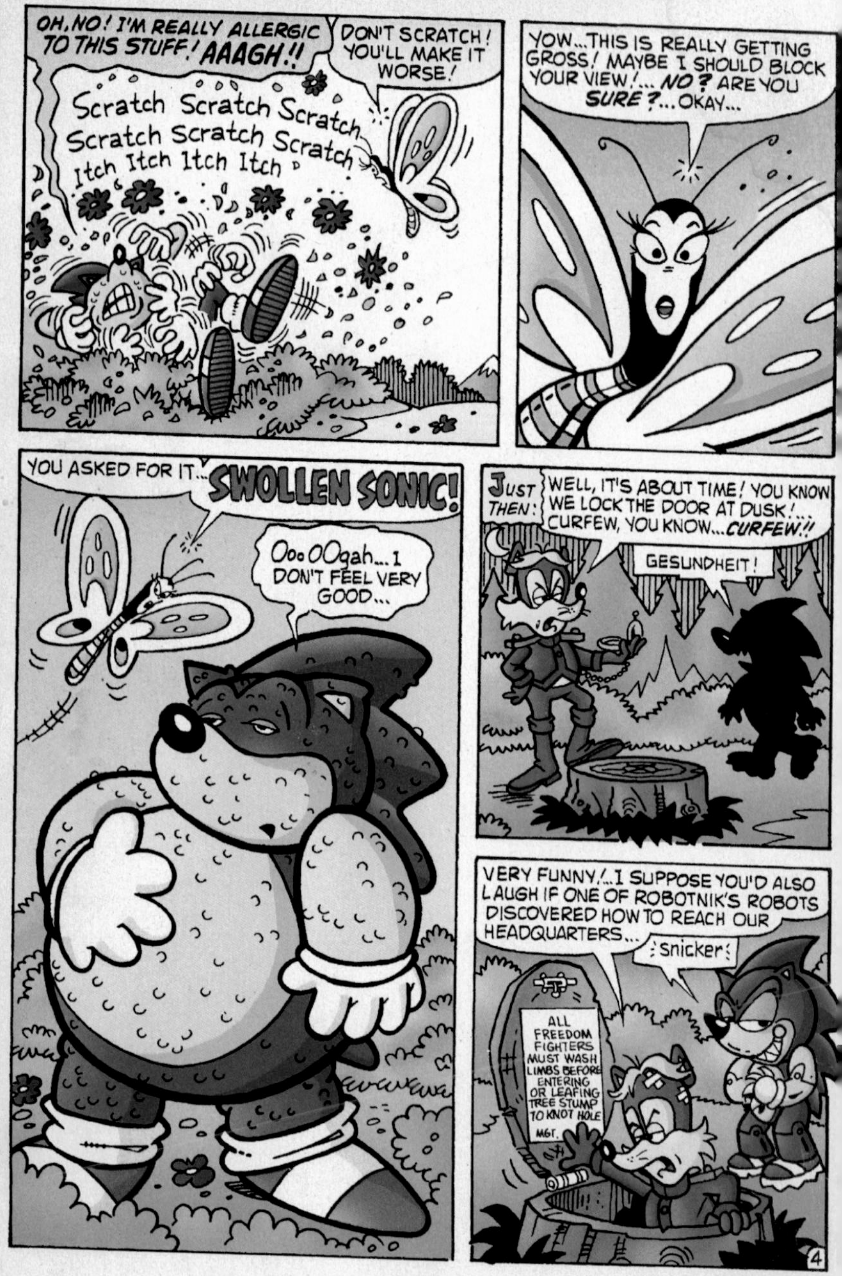
OH, NO! I'M REALLY ALLERGIC TO THIS STUFF! AAAGH!!
DON'T SCRATCH! YOU'LL MAKE IT WORSE!
Scratch Scratch Scratch Scratch Scratch Scratch Itch Itch Itch Itch
YOW...THIS IS REALLY GETTING GROSS! MAYBE I SHOULD BLOCK YOUR VIEW!... NO? ARE YOU SURE?... OKAY...
YOU ASKED FOR IT... SWOLLEN SONIC!
OooOOgah... I DON'T FEEL VERY GOOD...
JUST THEN:
WELL, IT'S ABOUT TIME! YOU KNOW WE LOCK THE DOOR AT DUSK!... CURFEW, YOU KNOW... CURFEW!!
GESUNDHEIT!
VERY FUNNY!...I SUPPOSE YOU'D ALSO LAUGH IF ONE OF ROBOTNIK'S ROBOTS DISCOVERED HOW TO REACH OUR HEADQUARTERS...
Snicker
ALL FREEDOM FIGHTERS MUST WASH LIMBS BEFORE ENTERING OR LEAFING TREE STUMP TO KNOT HOLE MGT.

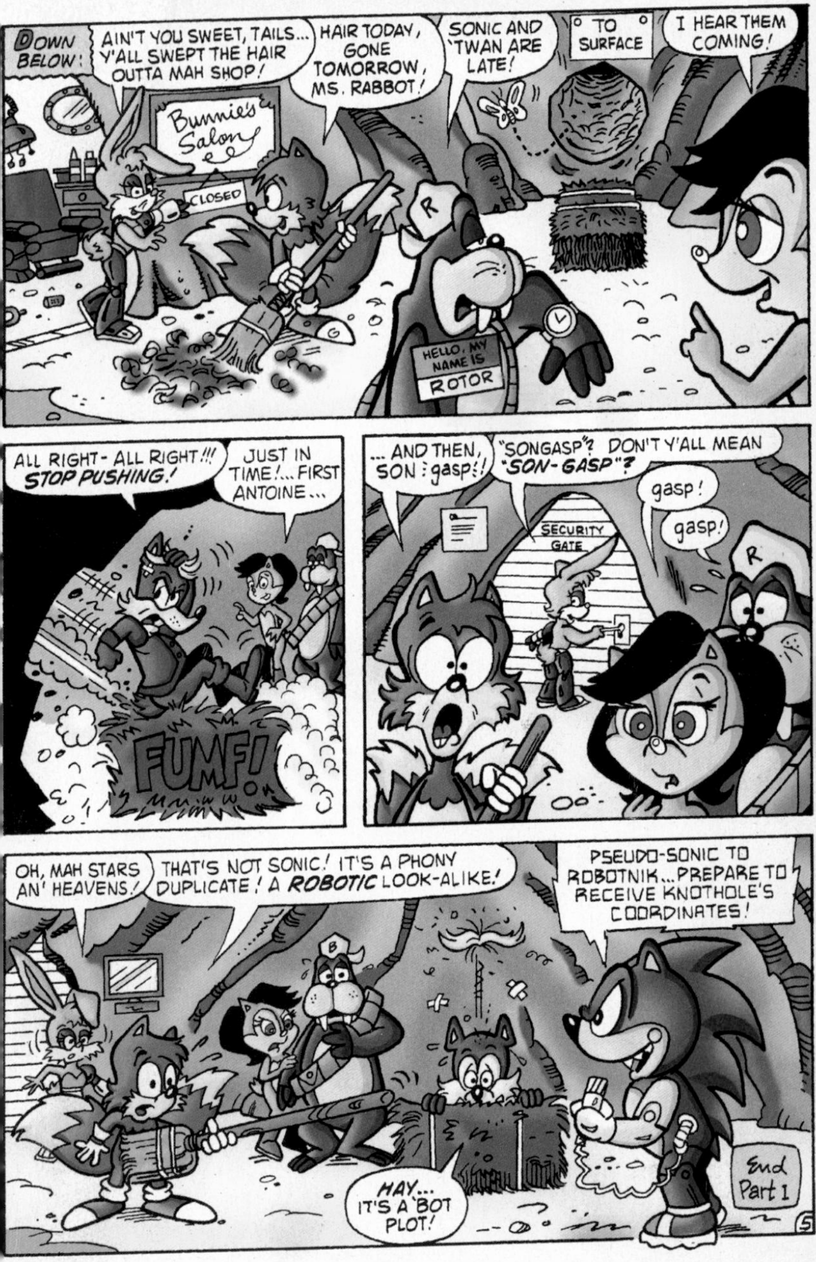
DOWN BELOW:
AIN'T YOU SWEET, TAILS... Y'ALL SWEPT THE HAIR OUTTA MAH SHOP!
HAIR TODAY, GONE TOMORROW, MS. RABBOT!
SONIC AND 'TWAN ARE LATE!
TO SURFACE
I HEAR THEM COMING!
Bunnie's Salon
CLOSED
HELLO, MY NAME IS ROTOR
ALL RIGHT- ALL RIGHT!!! STOP PUSHING!
JUST IN TIME!... FIRST ANTOINE...
FUMF!
... AND THEN, SON : gasp!!
"SONGASP"? DON'T Y'ALL MEAN "SON-GASP"?
gasp!
gasp!
SECURITY GATE
OH, MAH STARS AN' HEAVENS!
THAT'S NOT SONIC! IT'S A PHONY DUPLICATE! A ROBOTIC LOOK-ALIKE!
PSEUDO-SONIC TO ROBOTNIK... PREPARE TO RECEIVE KNOTHOLE'S COORDINATES!
MAY... IT'S A 'BOT PLOT!
End Part 1
5

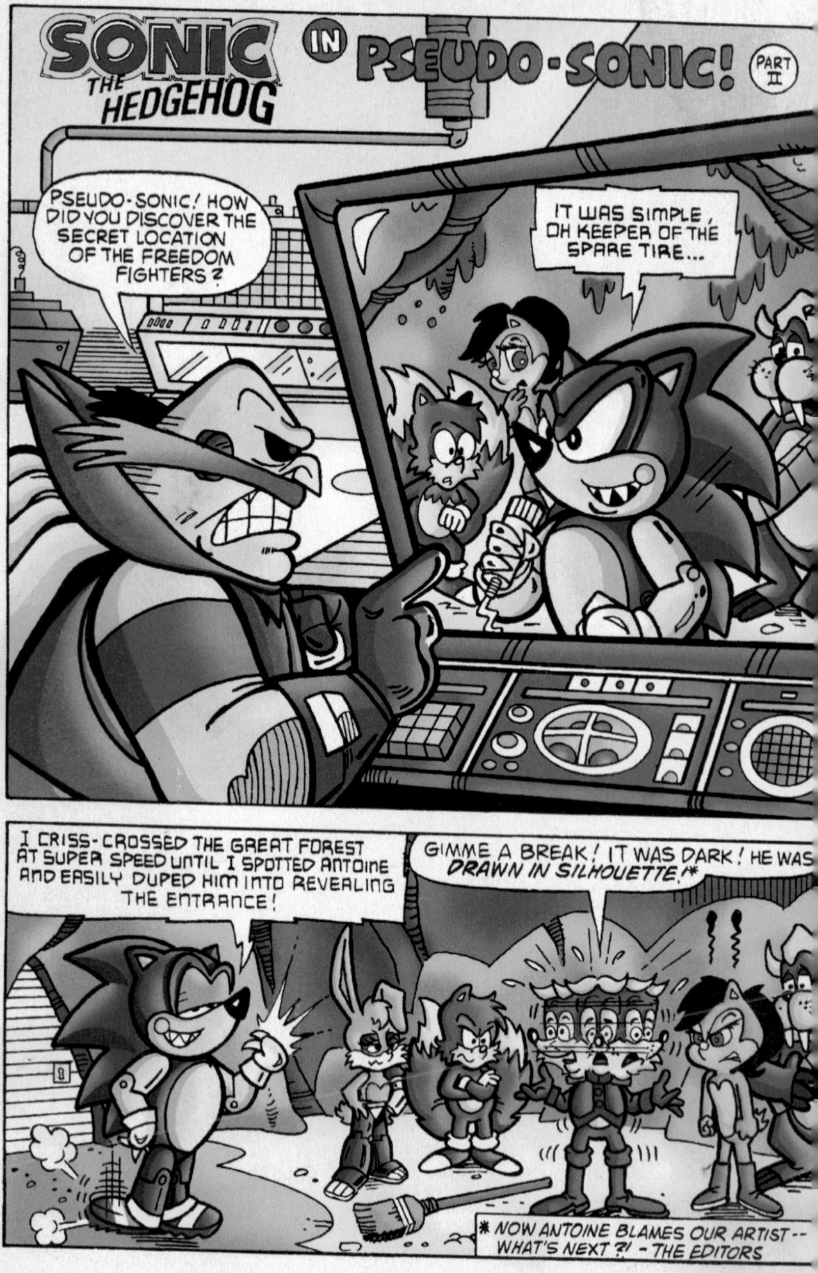
SONIC THE HEDGEHOG
IN
PSEUDO-SONIC! PART II
PSEUDO-SONIC! HOW DID YOU DISCOVER THE SECRET LOCATION OF THE FREEDOM FIGHTERS?
IT WAS SIMPLE, OH KEEPER OF THE SPARE TIRE...
I CRISS-CROSSED THE GREAT FOREST AT SUPER SPEED UNTIL I SPOTTED ANTOINE AND EASILY DUPED HIM INTO REVEALING THE ENTRANCE!
GIMME A BREAK! IT WAS DARK! HE WAS *DRAWN IN SILHOUETTE!**
* NOW ANTOINE BLAMES OUR ARTIST -- WHAT'S NEXT?! - THE EDITORS

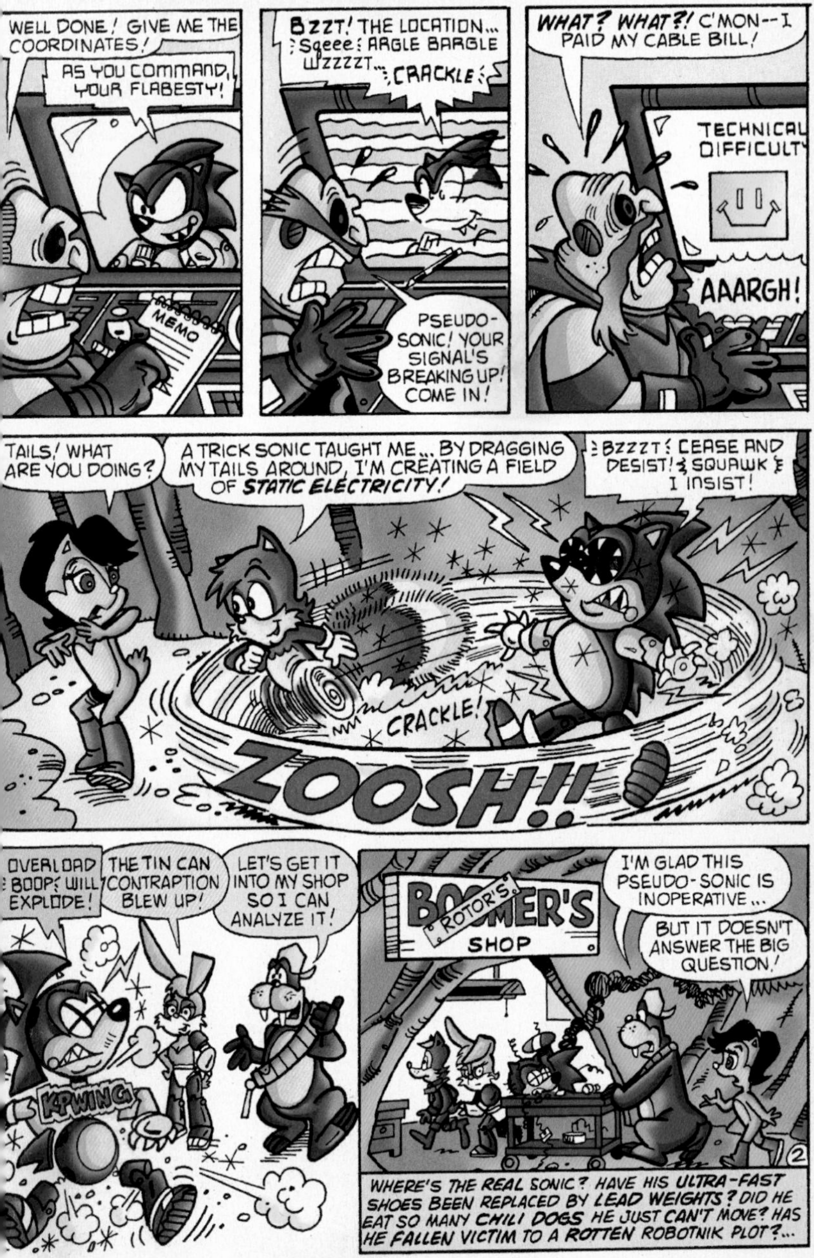
WELL DONE! GIVE ME THE COORDINATES!
AS YOU COMMAND, YOUR FLABESTY!
MEMO
BZZT! THE LOCATION... Sqeee: ARGLE BARGLE WZZZZT...
CRACKLE
PSEUDO-SONIC! YOUR SIGNAL'S BREAKING UP! COME IN!
WHAT? WHAT?! C'MON--I PAID MY CABLE BILL!
TECHNICAL DIFFICULTY
AAARGH!
TAILS! WHAT ARE YOU DOING?
A TRICK SONIC TAUGHT ME... BY DRAGGING MY TAILS AROUND, I'M CREATING A FIELD OF STATIC ELECTRICITY!
BZZZT CEASE AND DESIST! SQUAWK I INSIST!
CRACKLE!
ZOOSH!!
OVERLOAD BOOP: WILL EXPLODE!
THE TIN CAN CONTRAPTION BLEW UP!
LET'S GET IT INTO MY SHOP SO I CAN ANALYZE IT!
KPWING
BOOMER'S
ROTOR'S
SHOP
I'M GLAD THIS PSEUDO-SONIC IS INOPERATIVE...
BUT IT DOESN'T ANSWER THE BIG QUESTION!
WHERE'S THE REAL SONIC? HAVE HIS ULTRA-FAST SHOES BEEN REPLACED BY LEAD WEIGHTS? DID HE EAT SO MANY CHILI DOGS HE JUST CAN'T MOVE? HAS HE FALLEN VICTIM TO A ROTTEN ROBOTNIK PLOT?...

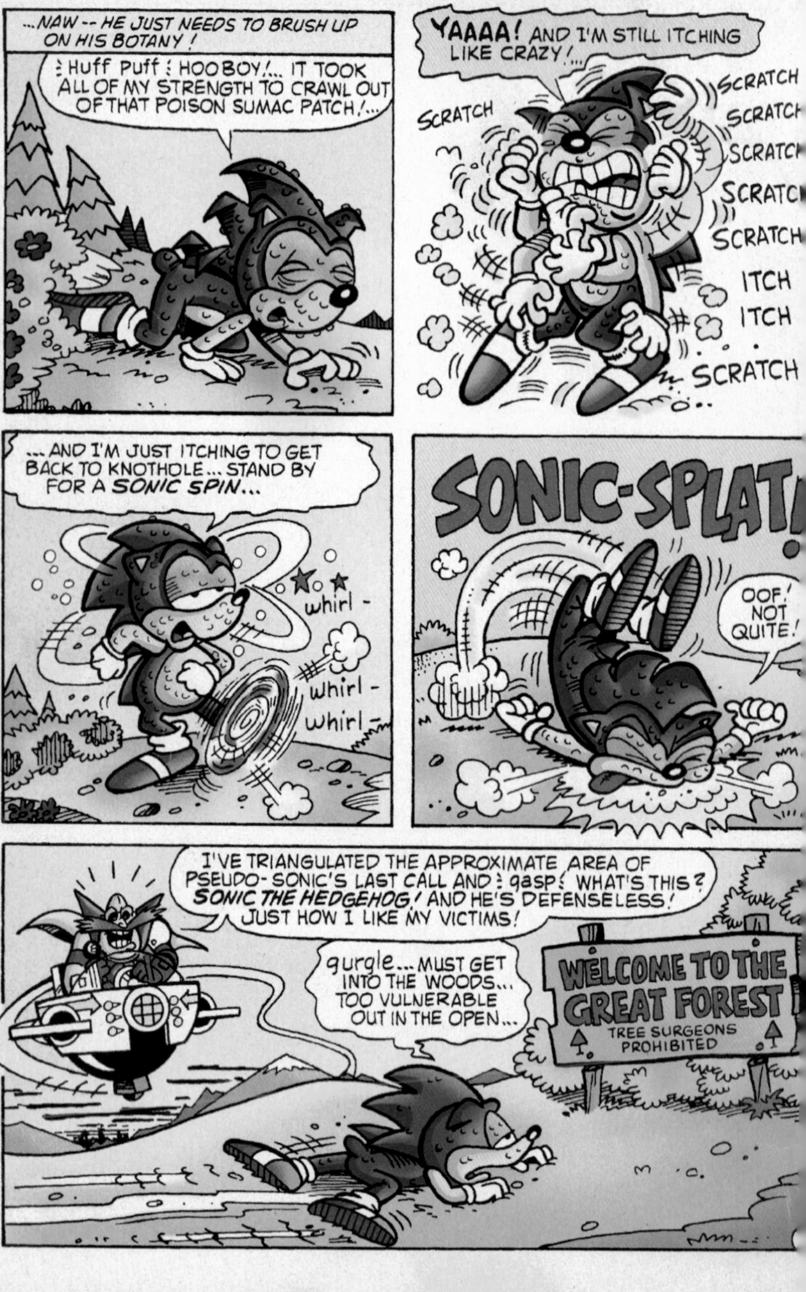
...NAW -- HE JUST NEEDS TO BRUSH UP ON HIS BOTANY!
Huff Puff HOOBOY!... IT TOOK ALL OF MY STRENGTH TO CRAWL OUT OF THAT POISON SUMAC PATCH!...
YAAAA! AND I'M STILL ITCHING LIKE CRAZY!...
SCRATCH
SCRATCH
SCRATCH
SCRATCH
SCRATCH
SCRATCH
ITCH
ITCH
SCRATCH
...AND I'M JUST ITCHING TO GET BACK TO KNOTHOLE... STAND BY FOR A SONIC SPIN...
whirl -
whirl -
whirl -
SONIC-SPLAT!
OOF! NOT QUITE!
I'VE TRIANGULATED THE APPROXIMATE AREA OF PSEUDO-SONIC'S LAST CALL AND gasp! WHAT'S THIS? SONIC THE HEDGEHOG! AND HE'S DEFENSELESS! JUST HOW I LIKE MY VICTIMS!
gurgle... MUST GET INTO THE WOODS... TOO VULNERABLE OUT IN THE OPEN...
WELCOME TO THE GREAT FOREST
TREE SURGEONS PROHIBITED

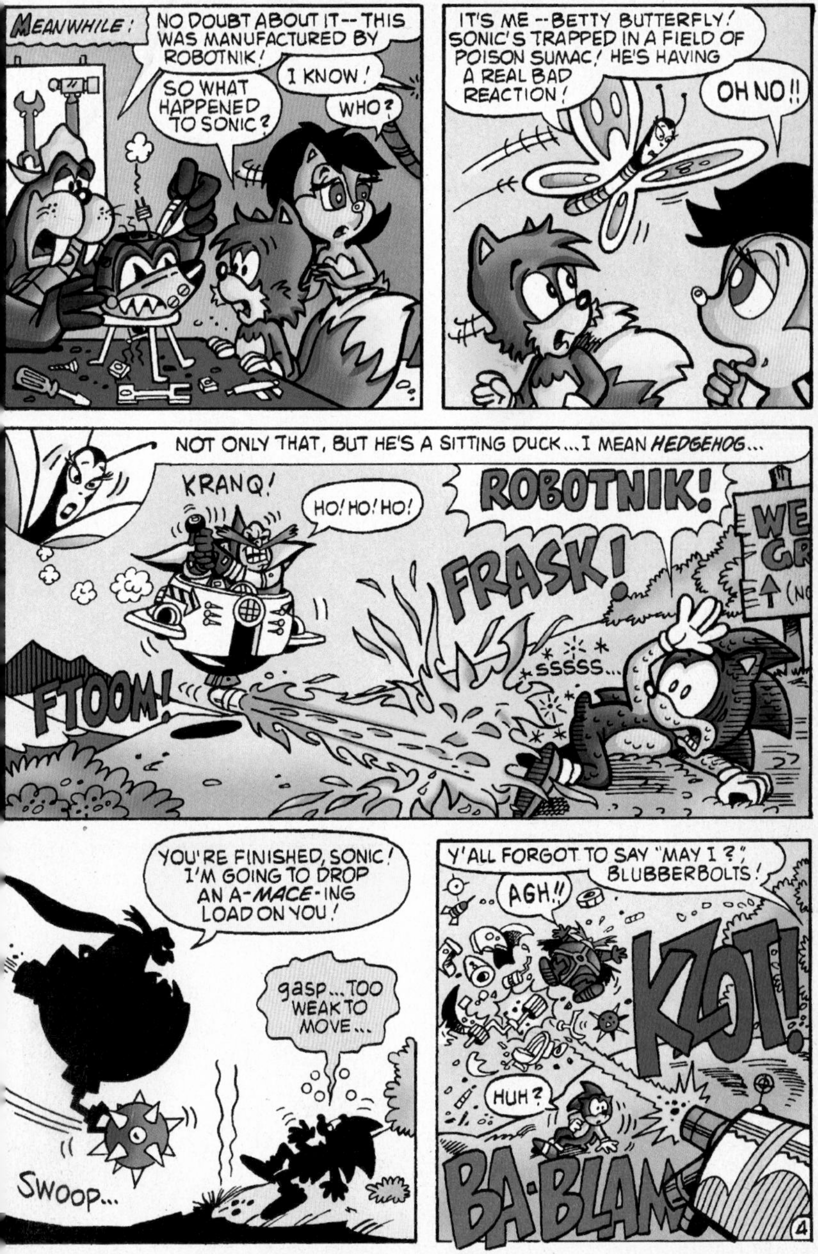

MEANWHILE:
NO DOUBT ABOUT IT -- THIS WAS MANUFACTURED BY ROBOTNIK!
I KNOW!
SO WHAT HAPPENED TO SONIC?
WHO?
IT'S ME -- BETTY BUTTERFLY! SONIC'S TRAPPED IN A FIELD OF POISON SUMAC! HE'S HAVING A REAL BAD REACTION!
OH NO!!
NOT ONLY THAT, BUT HE'S A SITTING DUCK... I MEAN HEDGEHOG...
KRANQ!
HO! HO! HO!
ROBOTNIK!
FRASK!
FTOOM!
SSSSS...
YOU'RE FINISHED, SONIC! I'M GOING TO DROP AN A-MACE-ING LOAD ON YOU!
gasp... TOO WEAK TO MOVE...
SWOOP...
Y'ALL FORGOT TO SAY "MAY I?," BLUBBERBOLTS!
AGH!!
KZOT!
HUH?
BA-BLAM

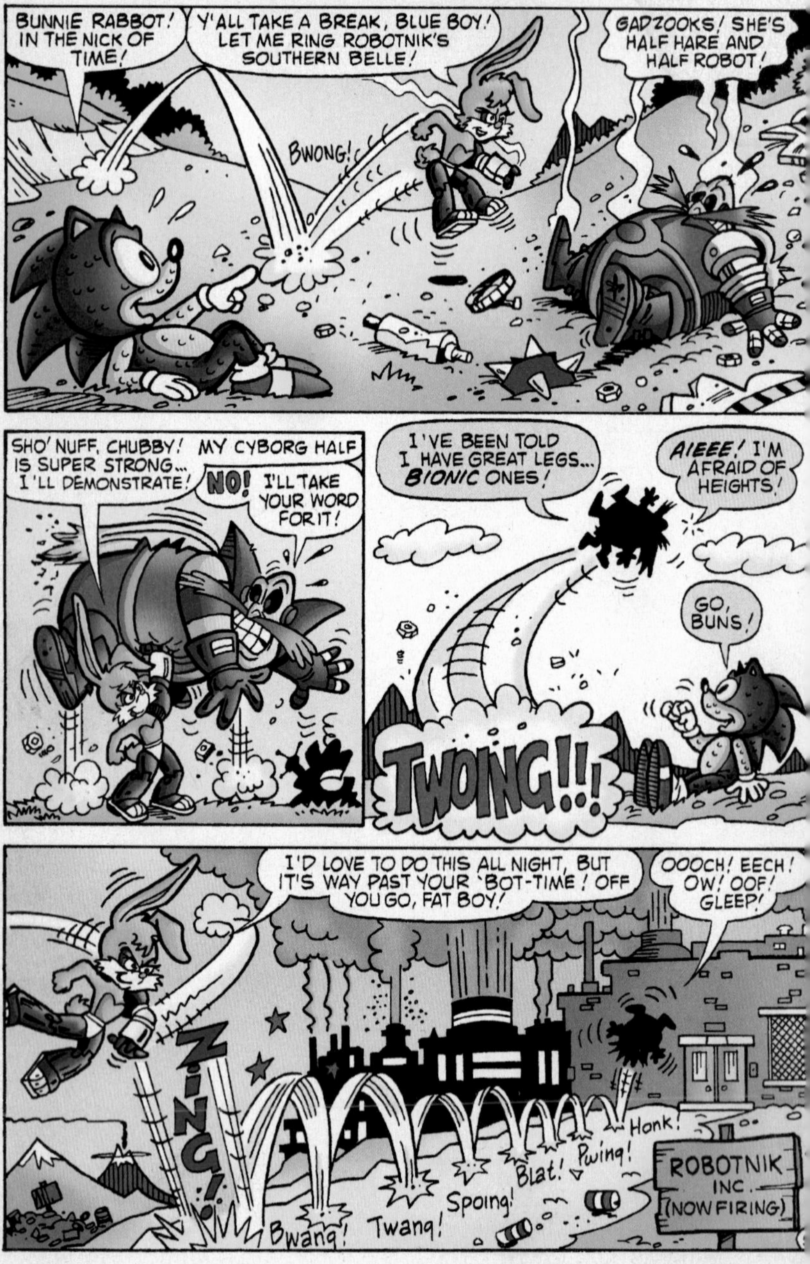
BUNNIE RABBOT! IN THE NICK OF TIME!
Y'ALL TAKE A BREAK, BLUE BOY! LET ME RING ROBOTNIK'S SOUTHERN BELLE!
GADZOOKS! SHE'S HALF HARE AND HALF ROBOT!
BWONG!
SHO' NUFF, CHUBBY! MY CYBORG HALF IS SUPER STRONG... I'LL DEMONSTRATE!
NO! I'LL TAKE YOUR WORD FOR IT!
I'VE BEEN TOLD I HAVE GREAT LEGS... BIONIC ONES!
AIEEE! I'M AFRAID OF HEIGHTS!
GO, BUNS!
TWOING!!!
I'D LOVE TO DO THIS ALL NIGHT, BUT IT'S WAY PAST YOUR 'BOT-TIME! OFF YOU GO, FAT BOY!
OOOCH! EECH! OW! OOF! GLEEP!
ZING!
Bwang!
Twang!
Spoing!
Blat!
Pwing!
Honk!
ROBOTNIK INC. (NOW FIRING)

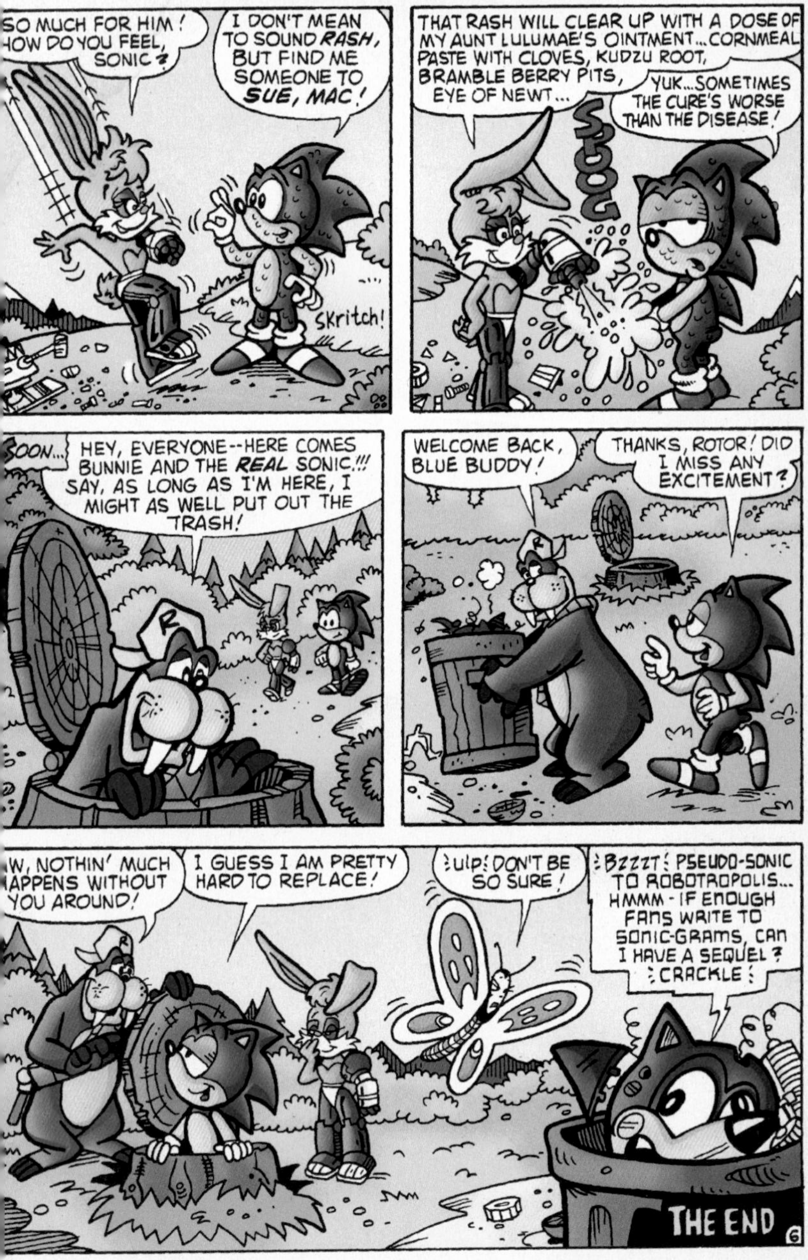
SO MUCH FOR HIM! HOW DO YOU FEEL, SONIC?
I DON'T MEAN TO SOUND RASH, BUT FIND ME SOMEONE TO SUE, MAC!
SKritch!
THAT RASH WILL CLEAR UP WITH A DOSE OF MY AUNT LULUMAE'S OINTMENT...CORNMEAL PASTE WITH CLOVES, KUDZU ROOT, BRAMBLE BERRY PITS, EYE OF NEWT...
SPOOG
YUK...SOMETIMES THE CURE'S WORSE THAN THE DISEASE!
SOON...
HEY, EVERYONE--HERE COMES BUNNIE AND THE REAL SONIC!!! SAY, AS LONG AS I'M HERE, I MIGHT AS WELL PUT OUT THE TRASH!
WELCOME BACK, BLUE BUDDY!
THANKS, ROTOR! DID I MISS ANY EXCITEMENT?
W, NOTHIN' MUCH APPENS WITHOUT YOU AROUND!
I GUESS I AM PRETTY HARD TO REPLACE!
ulp! DON'T BE SO SURE!
BZZZT! PSEUDO-SONIC TO ROBOTROPOLIS... HMMM - IF ENOUGH FANS WRITE TO SONIC-GRAMS, CAN I HAVE A SEQUEL? CRACKLE!
THE END

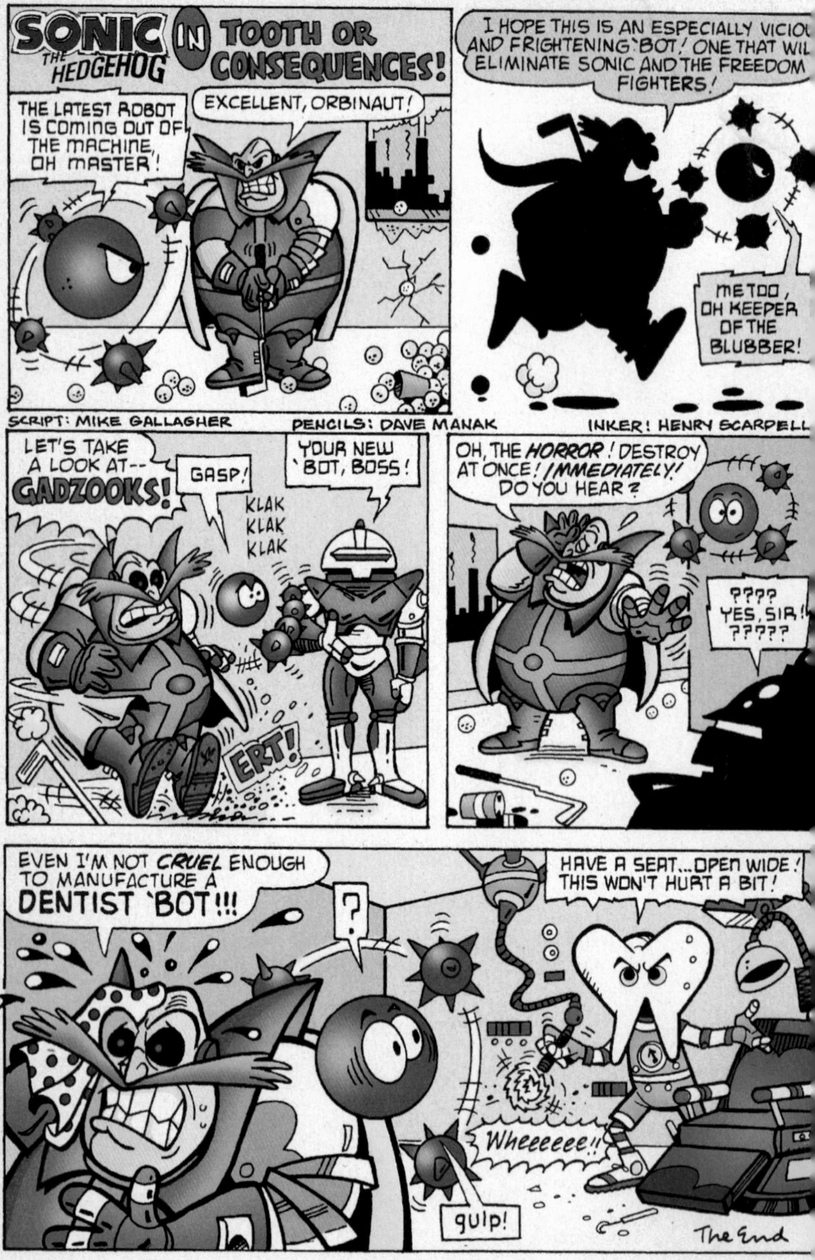
SONIC THE HEDGEHOG IN TOOTH OR CONSEQUENCES!
THE LATEST ROBOT IS COMING OUT OF THE MACHINE, OH MASTER!
EXCELLENT, ORBINAUT!
I HOPE THIS IS AN ESPECIALLY VICIOU AND FRIGHTENING 'BOT! ONE THAT WIL ELIMINATE SONIC AND THE FREEDOM FIGHTERS!
ME TOO, OH KEEPER OF THE BLUBBER!
SCRIPT: MIKE GALLAGHER
PENCILS: DAVE MANAK
INKER: HENRY SCARPELL
LET'S TAKE A LOOK AT-- GADZOOKS!
GASP!
YOUR NEW 'BOT, BOSS!
KLAK KLAK KLAK
ERT!
OH, THE HORROR! DESTROY AT ONCE! IMMEDIATELY! DO YOU HEAR?
???? YES, SIR! ?????
EVEN I'M NOT CRUEL ENOUGH TO MANUFACTURE A DENTIST 'BOT!!!
?
HAVE A SEAT...OPEN WIDE! THIS WON'T HURT A BIT!
Wheeeeee!!
gulp!
The End

SONIC THE HEDGEHOG in "QUICK SKETCH"

IN RESPONSE TO MANY LETTERS, HERE'S A LESSON ON "HOW TO DRAW SONIC"... START WITH A CIRCLE FOR HIS HEAD!

...THEN ADD A SMALLER OVAL SHAPE BELOW FOR HIS TORSO...

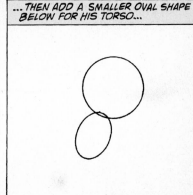

SCRIPT: MIKE GALLAGHER   PENCILS: DAVE MANAK   INKER: HENRY SCARPELLI

..NEXT, INDICATE HOW YOU WANT HIS ARMS AND LEGS POSITIONED...

DRAW IN HIS HANDS, FEET, NOSE AND QUILLS...

...NOW DEVELOP HIS LIMBS, EYES, EARS AND QUILLS!

OKAY-- REFINE THE SKETCHY LINES... FILL IN THE DETAILS AND YOUR SONIC THE HEDGEHOG IS ALMOST...

...FOOEY! THAT HAPPENS EVERY TIME!

ZOOM!

SONIC THE HEDGEHOG IN WHAT'S THE POINT?

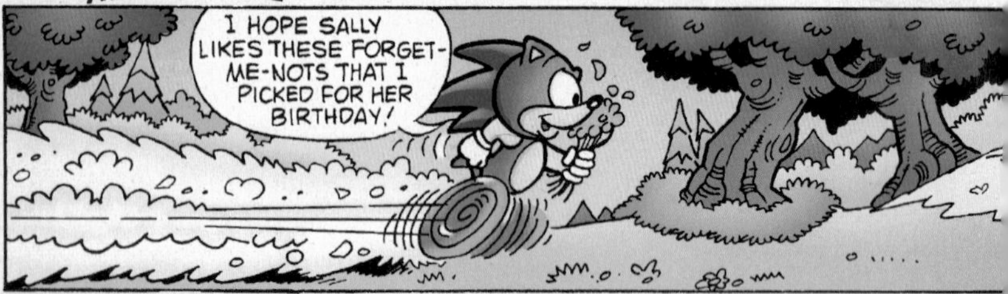
I HOPE SALLY LIKES THESE FORGET-ME-NOTS THAT I PICKED FOR HER BIRTHDAY!

SCRIPT: ANGELO DECESARE PENCILS: DAVE MANAK INKER: HENRY SCARPELLI

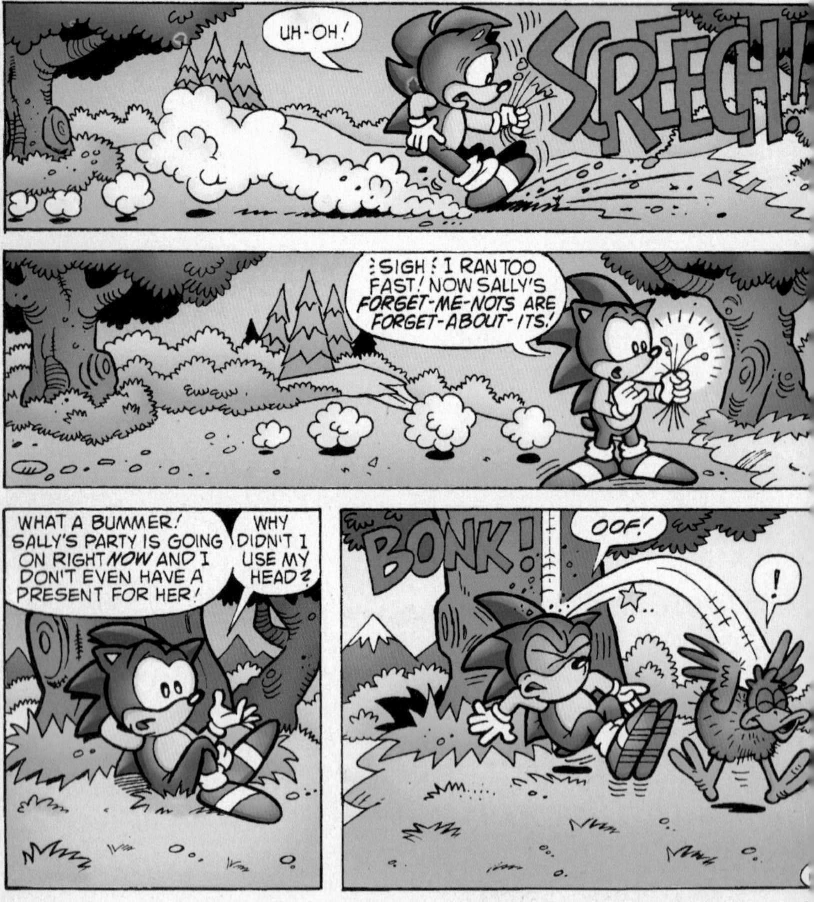
UH-OH!
SCREECH!
:SIGH: I RAN TOO FAST! NOW SALLY'S *FORGET-ME-NOTS* ARE *FORGET-ABOUT-ITS!*
WHAT A BUMMER! SALLY'S PARTY IS GOING ON RIGHT *NOW* AND I DON'T EVEN HAVE A PRESENT FOR HER!
WHY DIDN'T I USE MY HEAD?
BONK!
OOF!
!

HEY! THIS IS A *MOBIAN NEEDLE BIRD* ...HALF BIRD, HALF PORCUPINE! I DIDN'T THINK THERE WERE ANY LEFT AFTER ROBOTNIK TURNED THEM ALL INTO *ROBOTS!*

!!

IT MUST'VE FALLEN OUT OF A TREE TRYING TO FLY! LOOKS LIKE ITS WING IS INJURED! POOR LITTLE GUY!

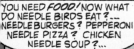

YOU NEED *FOOD!* NOW WHAT DO NEEDLE BIRDS EAT?-- NEEDLE BURGERS? PEPPERONI NEEDLE PIZZA? CHICKEN NEEDLE SOUP?...

~

I KNOW!

?!

ZOOM!

HERE YOU GO! SOME DELICIOUS BERRIES FROM THE NEEDLE BERRY BUSH! JUST REMEMBER THAT THE *BLACK ONE* IS MY NOSE!

ZIP!

SALLY LOVES ANIMALS! I'LL NAME YOU THORNY AND GIVE YOU TO SALLY FOR HER BIRTHDAY! SHE'LL BE *SO HAPPY!*

CHOMP!
CHOMP!
CHOMP!

2

SOON...

YOU GET THAT FLYING CACTUS PLANT OUT OF HERE *RIGHT NOW*, SONIC!

BUT, SAL...

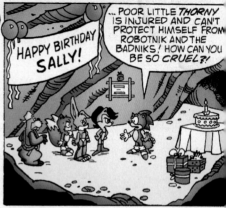

...POOR LITTLE *THORNY* IS INJURED AND CAN'T PROTECT HIMSELF FROM ROBOTNIK AND THE BADNIKS! HOW CAN YOU BE SO *CRUEL*?!

HAPPY BIRTHDAY SALLY!

CRUEL? MAY I REMIND YOU, SONIC, OF SOME OF THE OTHER *CUTE LITTLE ANIMALS* WE'VE FOUND IN THE FOREST?...

...LIKE THE BEAVER WHO TURNED OUT TO BE A VICIOUS ROBOT DESIGNED BY ROBOTNIK...

YOU WILL SURRENDER!

...OR THE SQUIRREL WHO WAS WEARING A *TRACKING DEVICE*...

??!

BOOP! BOOP! BOOP! BOOP!

...OR THE BABY DEER WHO TURNED OUT TO BE A *BOMBADIER*!

TWEEEEEEE EE... **BLAM!**

WE FREEDOM FIGHTERS CAN'T AFFORD TO TAKE IN ANY MORE PETS! IT'S BEEN TOO *PET*-RIFYING!

THORNY? WHERE'D HE GO?

③

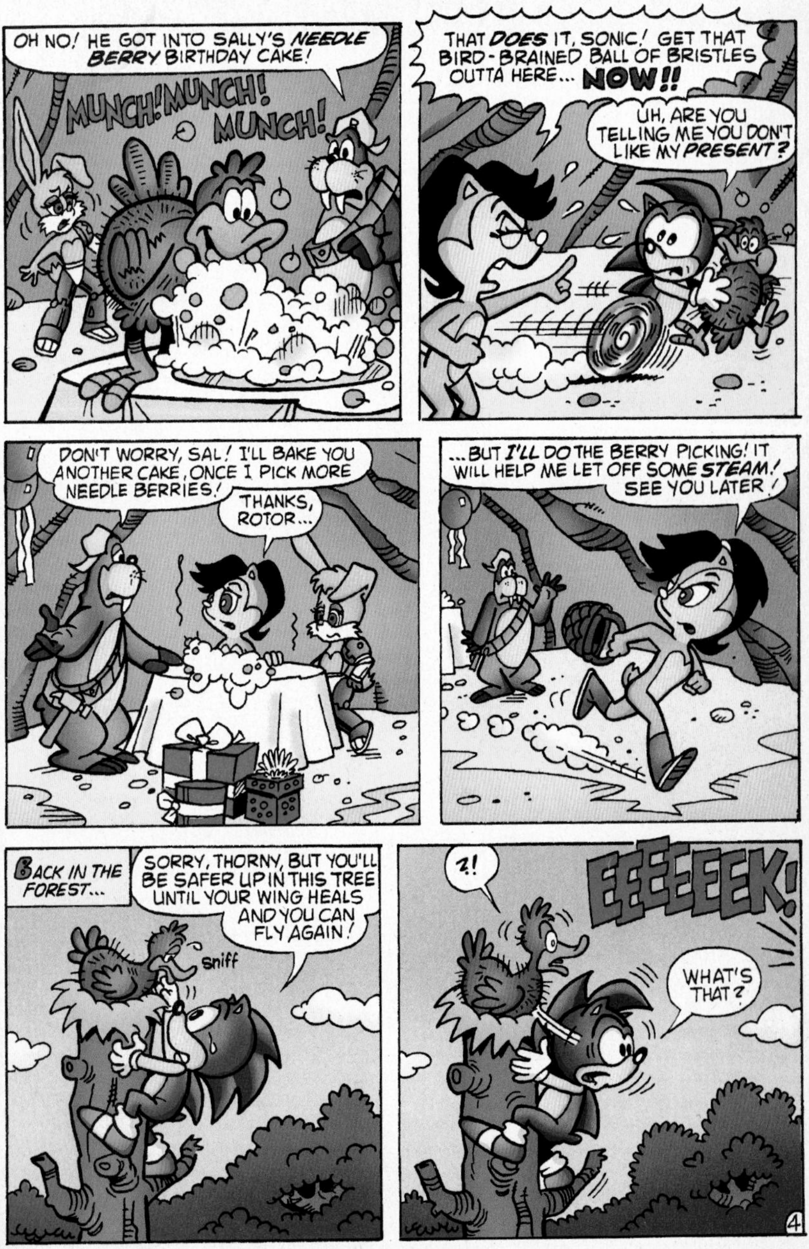
OH NO! HE GOT INTO SALLY'S *NEEDLE BERRY* BIRTHDAY CAKE!
MUNCH! MUNCH! MUNCH!
THAT *DOES* IT, SONIC! GET THAT BIRD-BRAINED BALL OF BRISTLES OUTTA HERE... **NOW!!**
UH, ARE YOU TELLING ME YOU DON'T LIKE MY *PRESENT*?
DON'T WORRY, SAL! I'LL BAKE YOU ANOTHER CAKE, ONCE I PICK MORE NEEDLE BERRIES!
THANKS, ROTOR...
...BUT *I'LL* DO THE BERRY PICKING! IT WILL HELP ME LET OFF SOME *STEAM*! SEE YOU LATER!
BACK IN THE FOREST...
SORRY, THORNY, BUT YOU'LL BE SAFER UP IN THIS TREE UNTIL YOUR WING HEALS AND YOU CAN FLY AGAIN!
sniff
?!
EEEEEEK!
WHAT'S THAT?
4

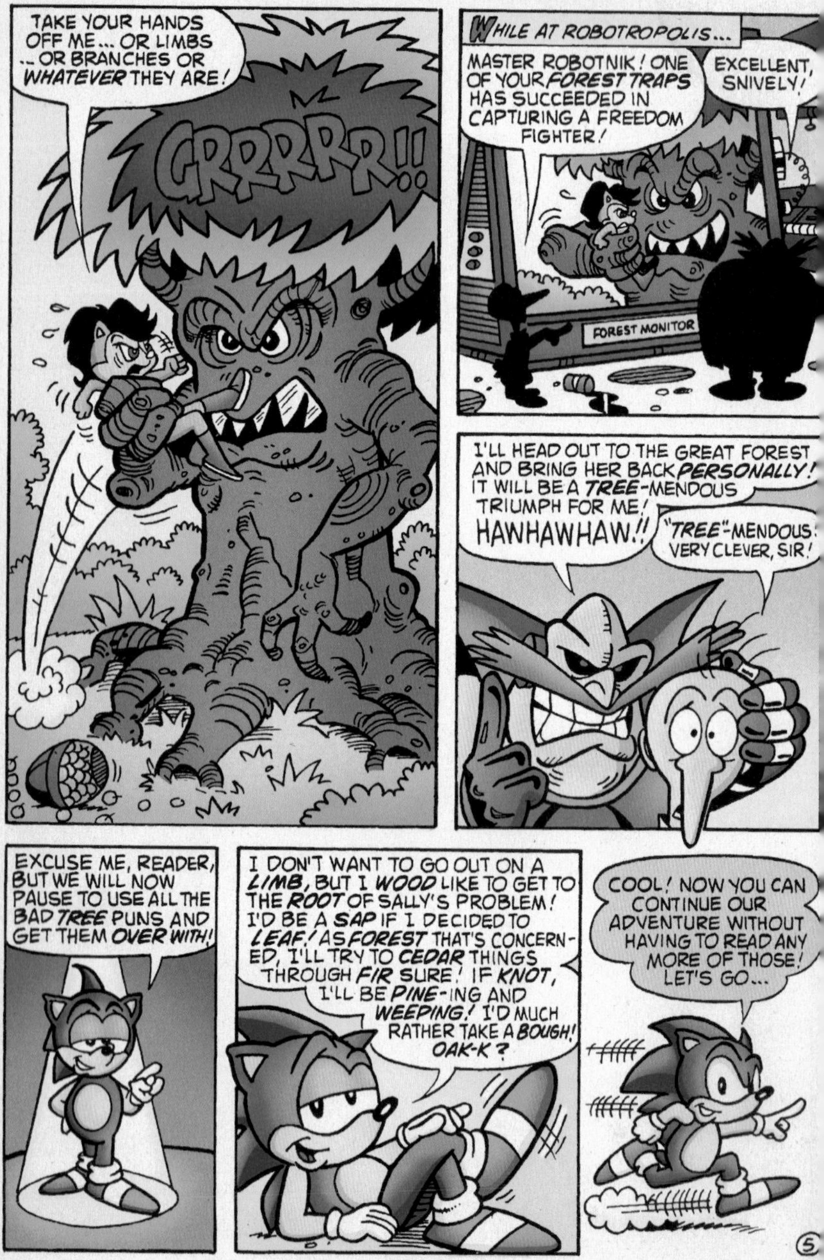
TAKE YOUR HANDS OFF ME... OR LIMBS .. OR BRANCHES OR WHATEVER THEY ARE!
GRRRRR!!
WHILE AT ROBOTROPOLIS...
MASTER ROBOTNIK! ONE OF YOUR FOREST TRAPS HAS SUCCEEDED IN CAPTURING A FREEDOM FIGHTER!
EXCELLENT, SNIVELY!
FOREST MONITOR
I'LL HEAD OUT TO THE GREAT FOREST AND BRING HER BACK PERSONALLY! IT WILL BE A TREE-MENDOUS TRIUMPH FOR ME! HAWHAWHAW!!
"TREE"-MENDOUS. VERY CLEVER, SIR!
EXCUSE ME, READER, BUT WE WILL NOW PAUSE TO USE ALL THE BAD TREE PUNS AND GET THEM OVER WITH!
I DON'T WANT TO GO OUT ON A LIMB, BUT I WOOD LIKE TO GET TO THE ROOT OF SALLY'S PROBLEM! I'D BE A SAP IF I DECIDED TO LEAF! AS FOREST THAT'S CONCERNED, I'LL TRY TO CEDAR THINGS THROUGH FIR SURE! IF KNOT, I'LL BE PINE-ING AND WEEPING! I'D MUCH RATHER TAKE A BOUGH! OAK-K?
COOL! NOW YOU CAN CONTINUE OUR ADVENTURE WITHOUT HAVING TO READ ANY MORE OF THOSE! LET'S GO...

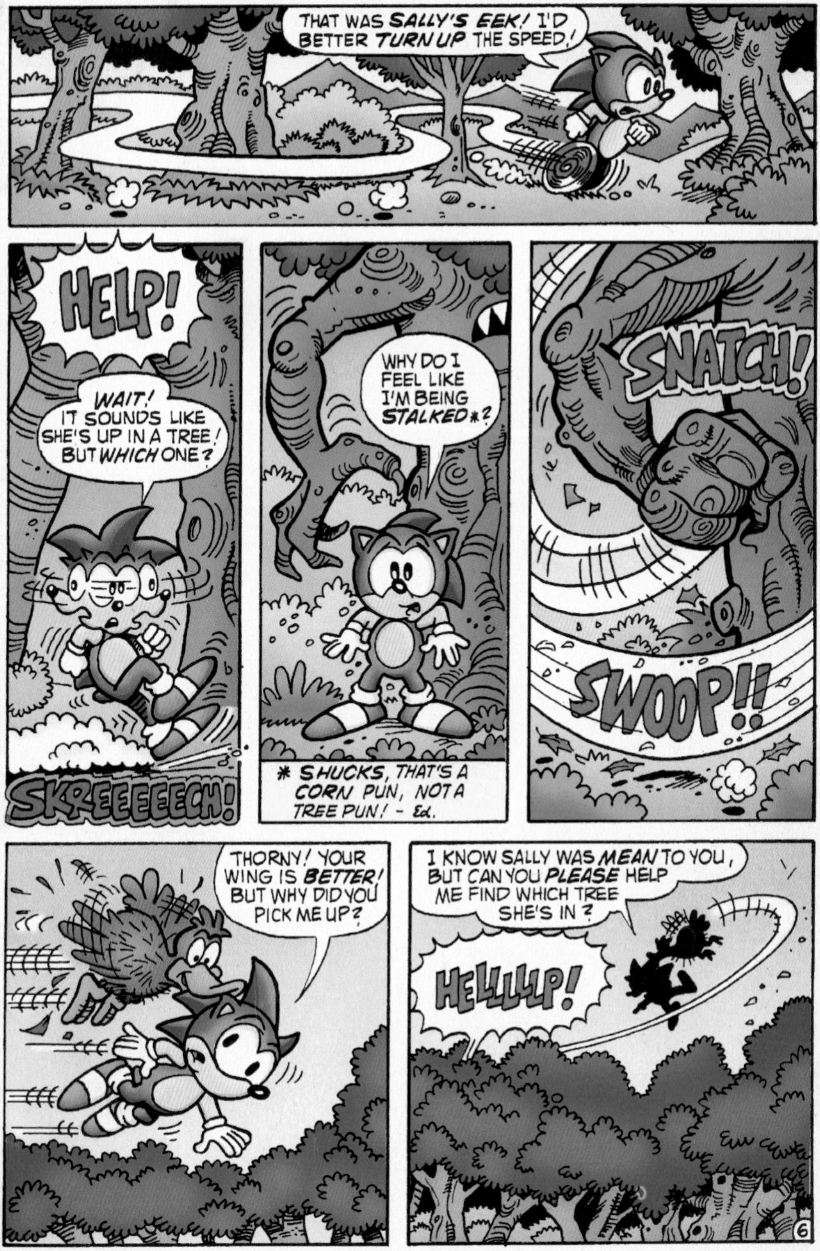
THAT WAS SALLY'S EEK! I'D BETTER TURN UP THE SPEED!
HELP!
WAIT! IT SOUNDS LIKE SHE'S UP IN A TREE! BUT WHICH ONE?
SKREEEEEECH!
WHY DO I FEEL LIKE I'M BEING STALKED*?
* SHUCKS, THAT'S A CORN PUN, NOT A TREE PUN! - Ed.
SNATCH!
SWOOP!!
THORNY! YOUR WING IS BETTER! BUT WHY DID YOU PICK ME UP?
I KNOW SALLY WAS MEAN TO YOU, BUT CAN YOU PLEASE HELP ME FIND WHICH TREE SHE'S IN?
HELLLLP!
6

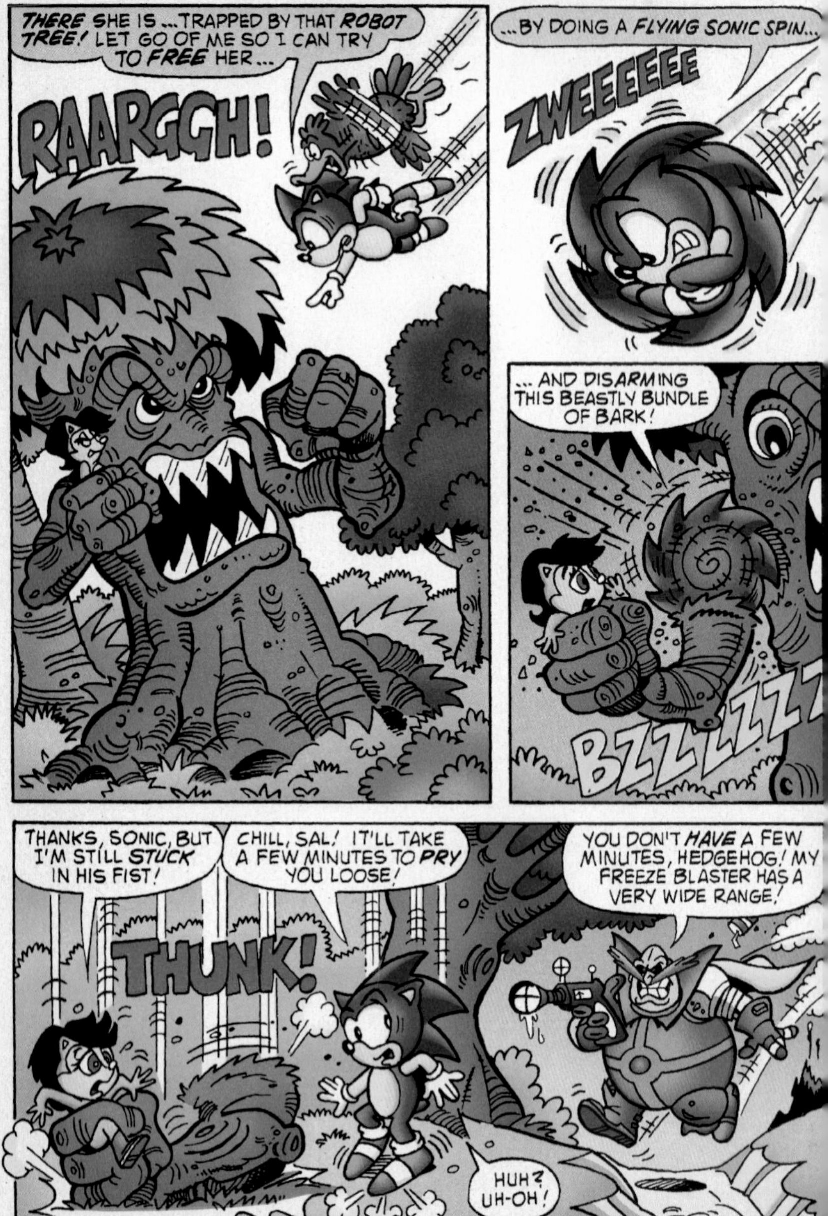
THERE SHE IS ...TRAPPED BY THAT ROBOT TREE! LET GO OF ME SO I CAN TRY TO FREE HER...
RAARGGH!
...BY DOING A FLYING SONIC SPIN...
ZWEEEEEEE
... AND DISARMING THIS BEASTLY BUNDLE OF BARK!
BZZZZZZ
THANKS, SONIC, BUT I'M STILL STUCK IN HIS FIST!
CHILL, SAL! IT'LL TAKE A FEW MINUTES TO PRY YOU LOOSE!
THUNK!
YOU DON'T HAVE A FEW MINUTES, HEDGEHOG! MY FREEZE BLASTER HAS A VERY WIDE RANGE!
HUH? UH-OH!

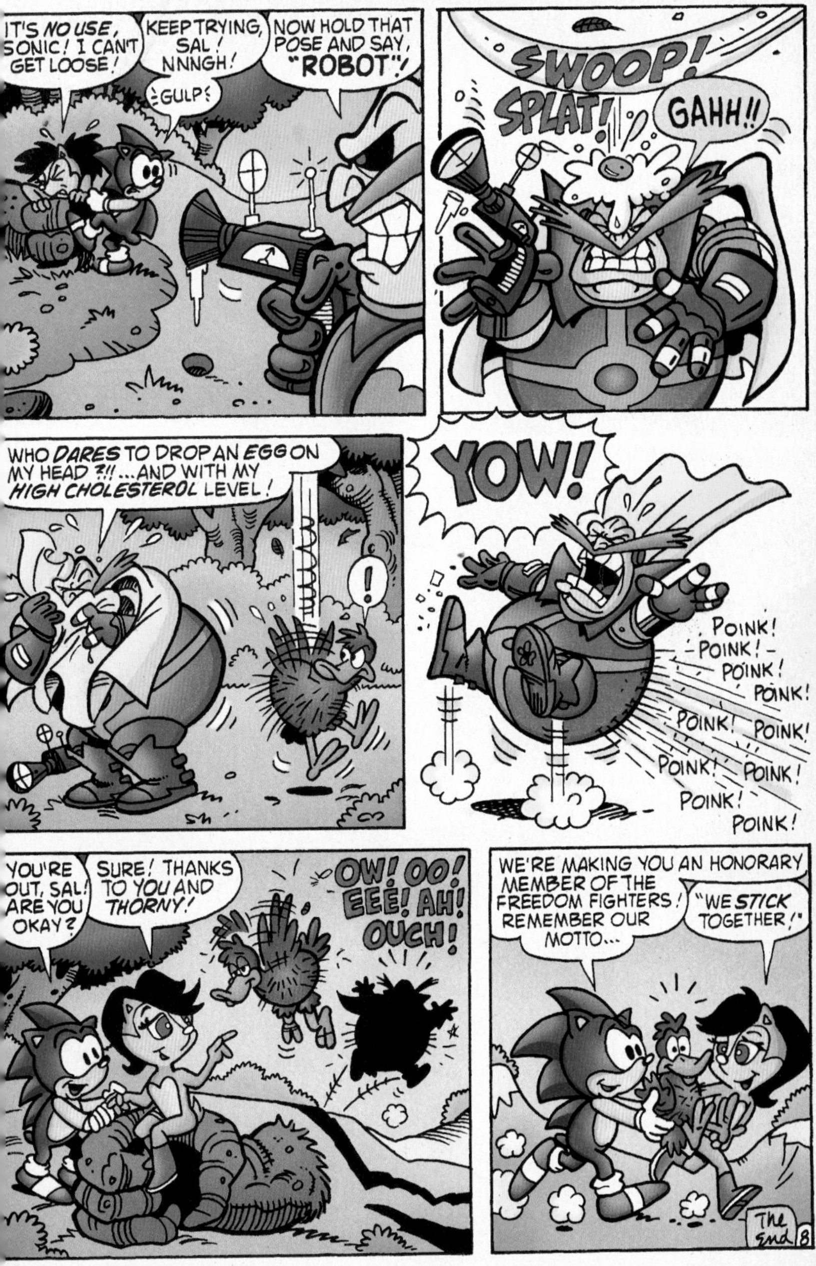

IT'S NO USE, SONIC! I CAN'T GET LOOSE!
KEEP TRYING, SAL! NNNGH!
GULP
NOW HOLD THAT POSE AND SAY, "ROBOT"!
SWOOP!
SPLAT!
GAHH!!
WHO DARES TO DROP AN EGG ON MY HEAD ?!! ...AND WITH MY HIGH CHOLESTEROL LEVEL!
!
YOW!
POINK! POINK! POINK! POINK! POINK! POINK! POINK! POINK! POINK! POINK!
YOU'RE OUT, SAL! ARE YOU OKAY?
SURE! THANKS TO YOU AND THORNY!
OW! OO! EEE! AH! OUCH!
WE'RE MAKING YOU AN HONORARY MEMBER OF THE FREEDOM FIGHTERS! REMEMBER OUR MOTTO...
"WE STICK TOGETHER!"
The End
8

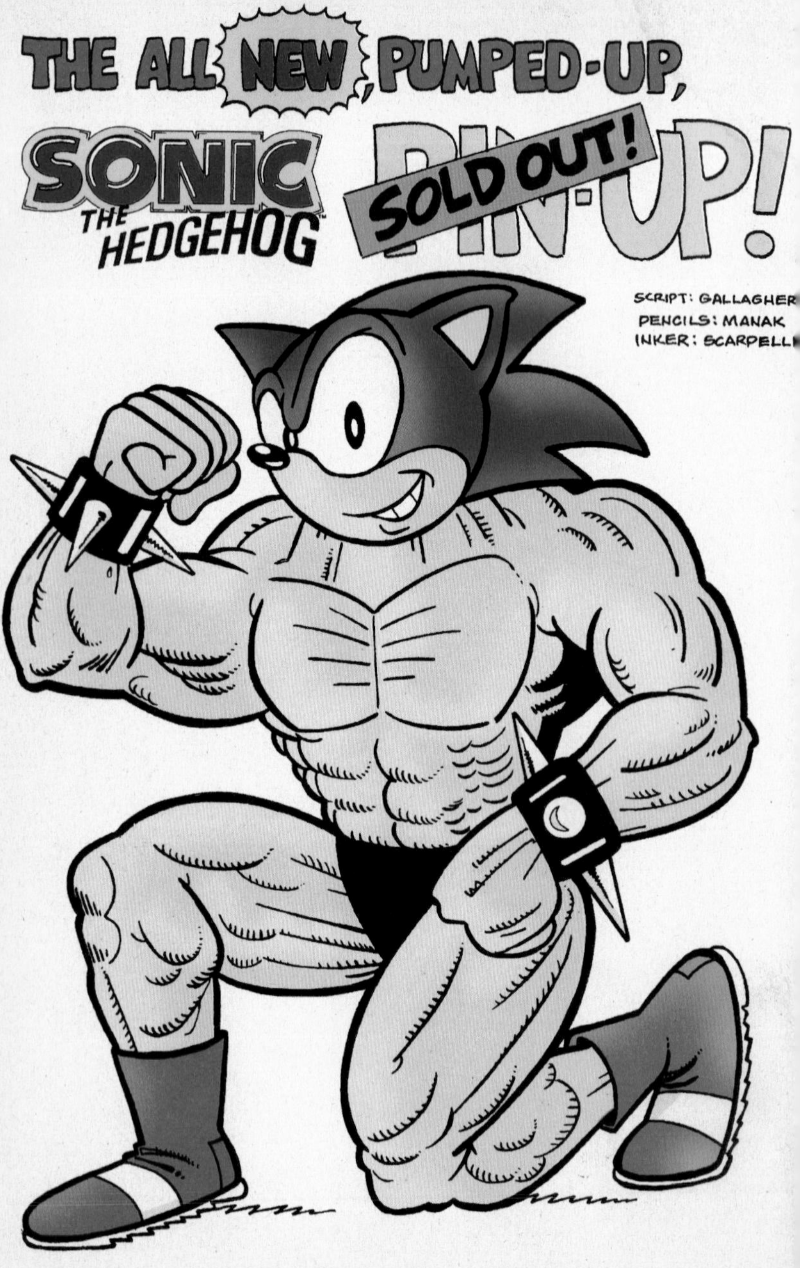
THE ALL NEW, PUMPED-UP,
SONIC THE HEDGEHOG
SOLD OUT!
PIN-UP!
SCRIPT: GALLAGHER
PENCILS: MANAK
INKER: SCARPELL

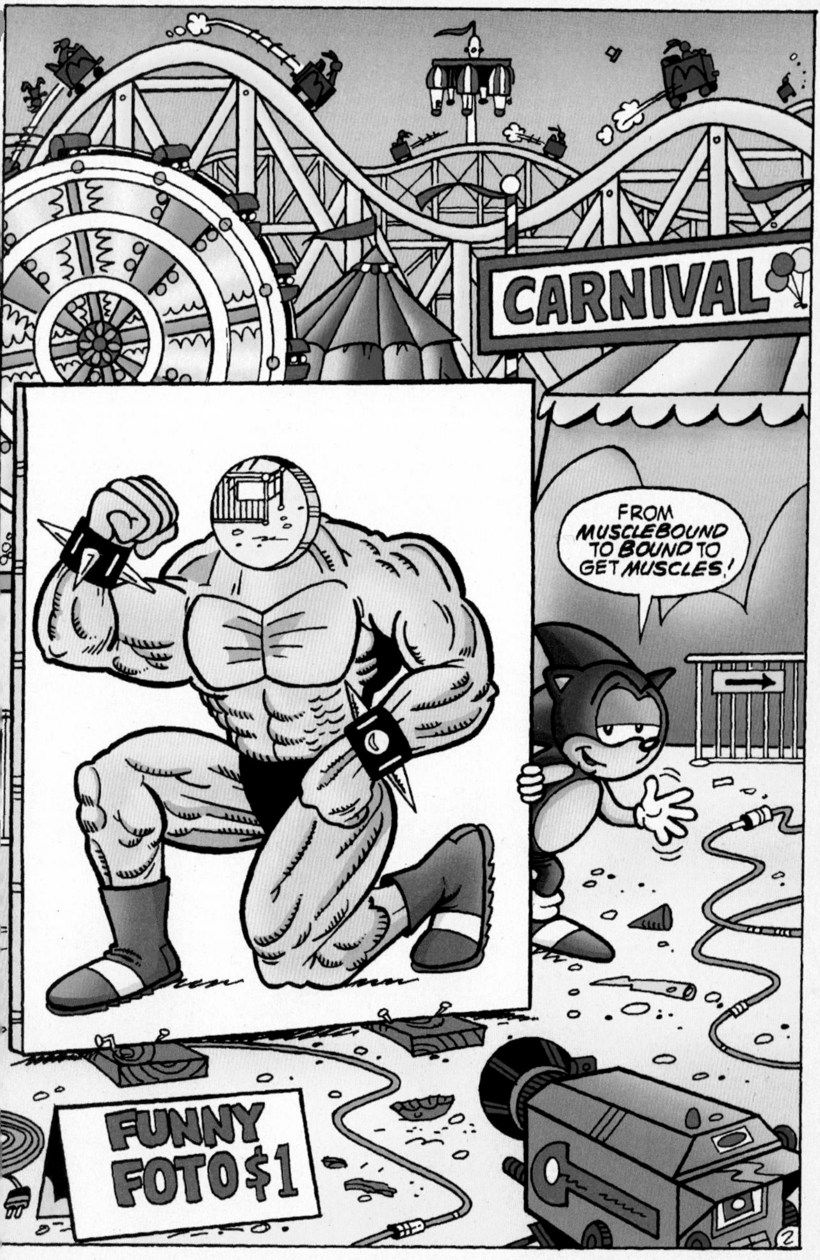
CARNIVAL
FROM MUSCLEBOUND TO BOUND TO GET MUSCLES!
FUNNY FOTO $1
2

Archie ADVENTURE SERIES
NO.10 MAY
US $1.25 CAN $1.50
CHILL, SONIC!
SONIC THE HEDGEHOG™
FREEZE FRAME!
FROST RAY
MANAK/D'AGOSTINO

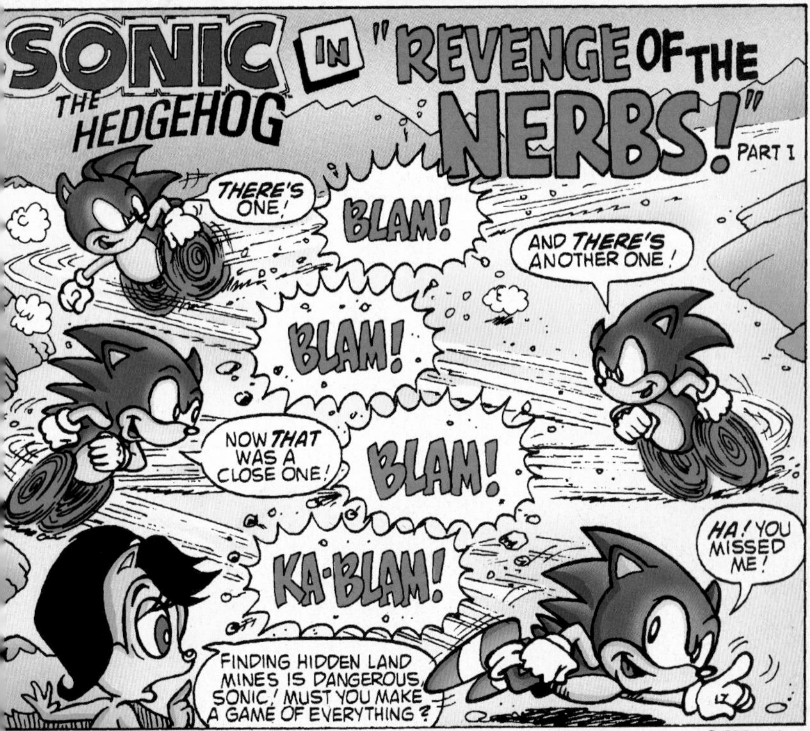
SONIC THE HEDGEHOG IN "REVENGE OF THE NERBS!" PART I
THERE'S ONE!
BLAM!
AND THERE'S ANOTHER ONE!
BLAM!
NOW THAT WAS A CLOSE ONE!
BLAM!
HA! YOU MISSED ME!
KA-BLAM!
FINDING HIDDEN LAND MINES IS DANGEROUS, SONIC! MUST YOU MAKE A GAME OF EVERYTHING?

SCRIPT: ANGELO DECESARE • PENCILS: DAVE MANAK • INKING: ART MAWHINNEY • LETTERS: BILL YOSHIDA • COLORS & PRODUCTION: BARRY GROSSMAN • EDITORS: VICTOR GORELICK AND PAUL CASTIGLIA • EDITOR-IN CHIEF: RICHARD GOLDWATER

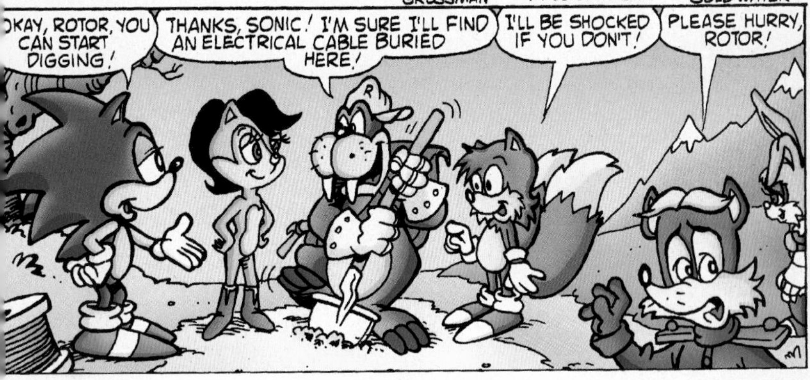
OKAY, ROTOR, YOU CAN START DIGGING!
THANKS, SONIC! I'M SURE I'LL FIND AN ELECTRICAL CABLE BURIED HERE!
I'LL BE SHOCKED IF YOU DON'T!
PLEASE HURRY, ROTOR!

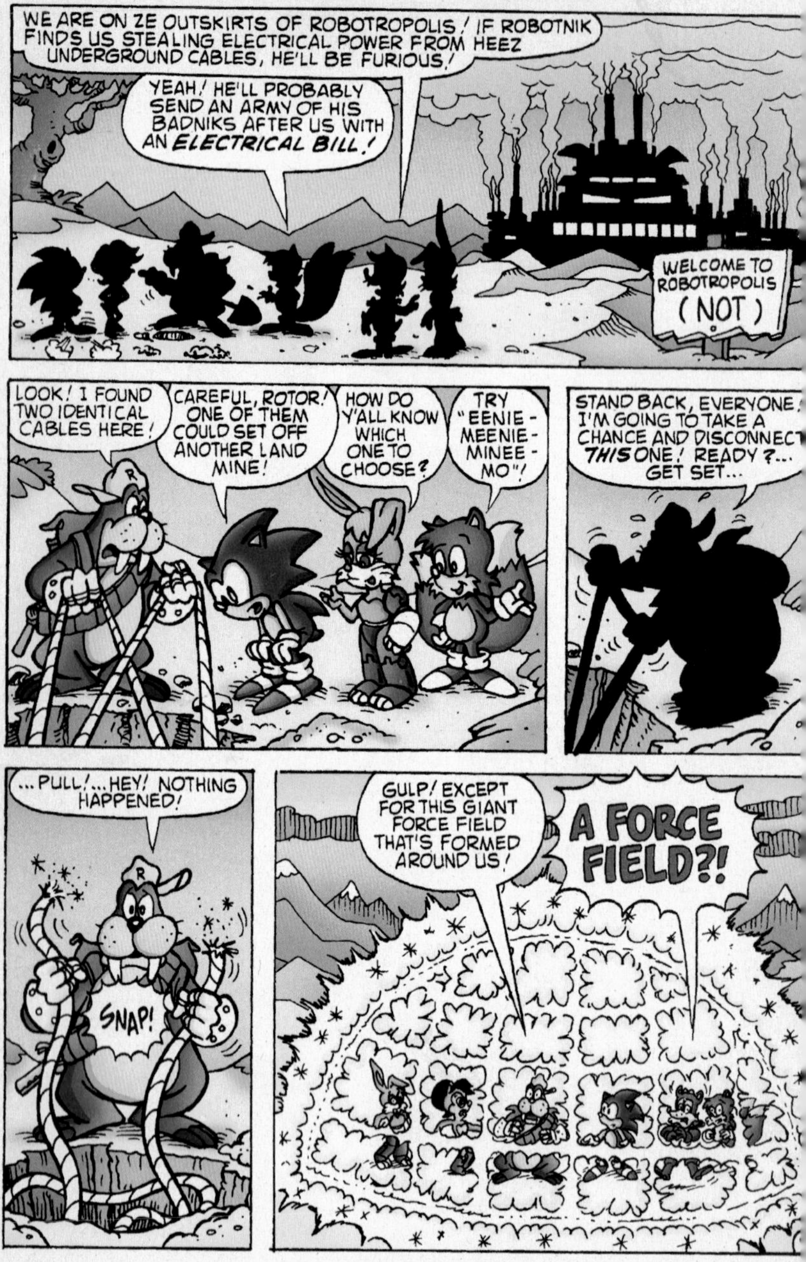
WE ARE ON ZE OUTSKIRTS OF ROBOTROPOLIS! IF ROBOTNIK FINDS US STEALING ELECTRICAL POWER FROM HEEZ UNDERGROUND CABLES, HE'LL BE FURIOUS!
YEAH! HE'LL PROBABLY SEND AN ARMY OF HIS BADNIKS AFTER US WITH AN ELECTRICAL BILL!
WELCOME TO ROBOTROPOLIS (NOT)
LOOK! I FOUND TWO IDENTICAL CABLES HERE!
CAREFUL, ROTOR! ONE OF THEM COULD SET OFF ANOTHER LAND MINE!
HOW DO Y'ALL KNOW WHICH ONE TO CHOOSE?
TRY "EENIE-MEENIE-MINEE-MO"!
STAND BACK, EVERYONE! I'M GOING TO TAKE A CHANCE AND DISCONNECT THIS ONE! READY?... GET SET...
...PULL!...HEY! NOTHING HAPPENED!
SNAP!
GULP! EXCEPT FOR THIS GIANT FORCE FIELD THAT'S FORMED AROUND US!
A FORCE FIELD?!

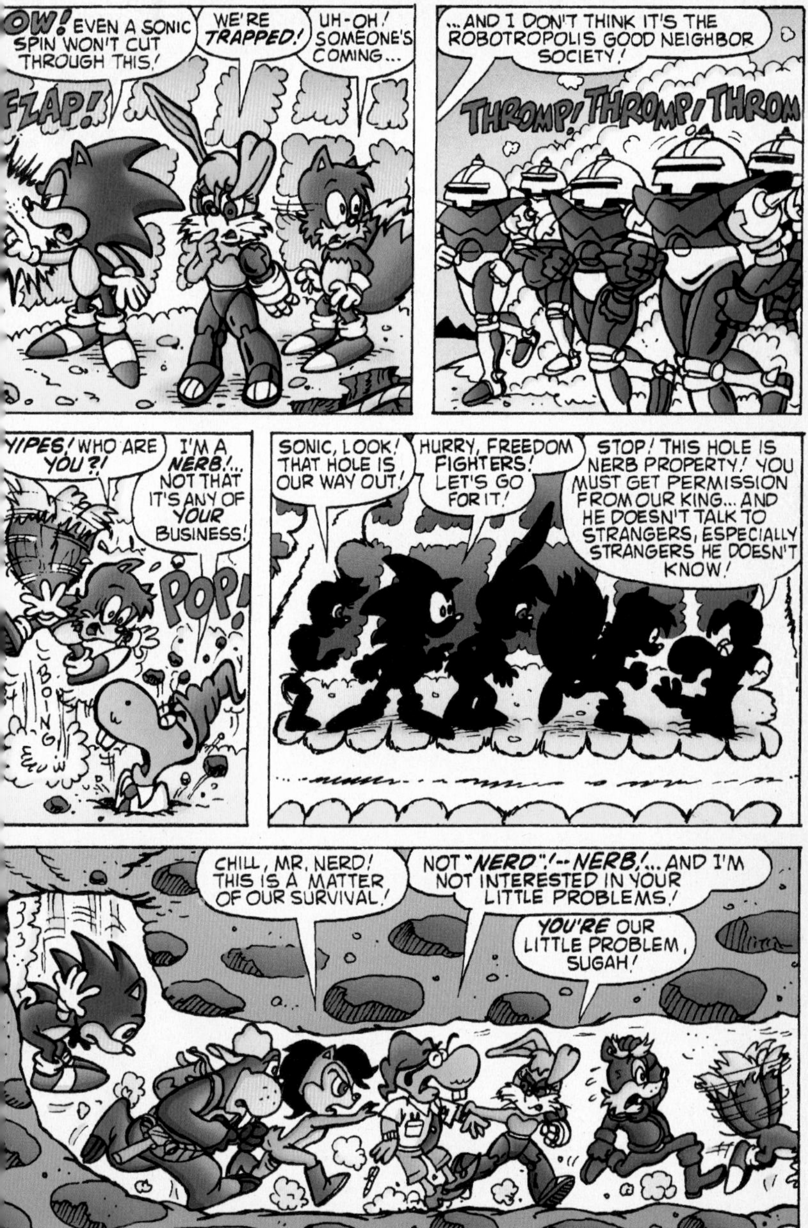
OW! EVEN A SONIC SPIN WON'T CUT THROUGH THIS!
FZAP!
WE'RE TRAPPED!
UH-OH! SOMEONE'S COMING...
...AND I DON'T THINK IT'S THE ROBOTROPOLIS GOOD NEIGHBOR SOCIETY!
THROMP! THROMP! THROM
YIPES! WHO ARE YOU?!
I'M A NERB!... NOT THAT IT'S ANY OF YOUR BUSINESS!
POP
BOING
SONIC, LOOK! THAT HOLE IS OUR WAY OUT!
HURRY, FREEDOM FIGHTERS! LET'S GO FOR IT!
STOP! THIS HOLE IS NERB PROPERTY! YOU MUST GET PERMISSION FROM OUR KING... AND HE DOESN'T TALK TO STRANGERS, ESPECIALLY STRANGERS HE DOESN'T KNOW!
CHILL, MR. NERD! THIS IS A MATTER OF OUR SURVIVAL!
NOT "NERD"!--NERB!... AND I'M NOT INTERESTED IN YOUR LITTLE PROBLEMS!
YOU'RE OUR LITTLE PROBLEM, SUGAH!
3

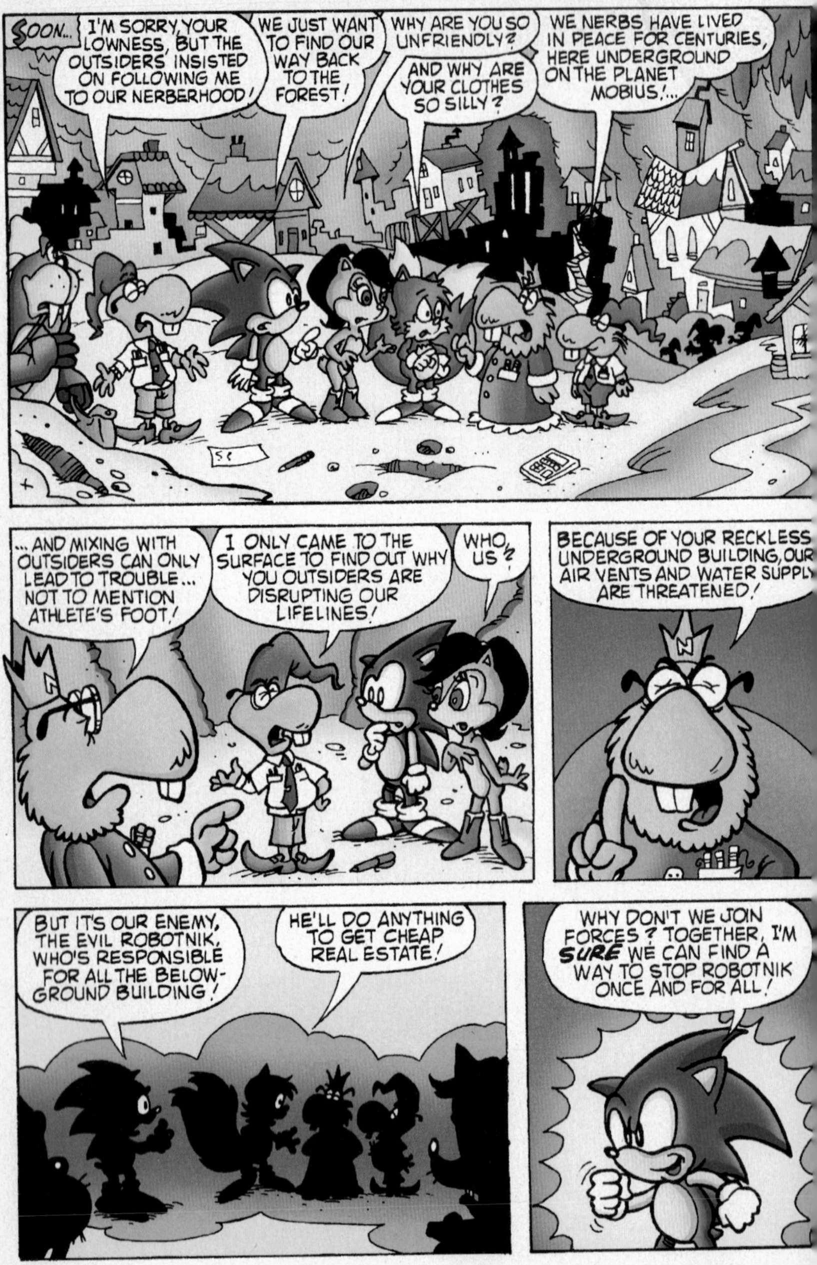
SOON...
I'M SORRY, YOUR LOWNESS, BUT THE OUTSIDERS INSISTED ON FOLLOWING ME TO OUR NERBERHOOD!
WE JUST WANT TO FIND OUR WAY BACK TO THE FOREST!
WHY ARE YOU SO UNFRIENDLY?
AND WHY ARE YOUR CLOTHES SO SILLY?
WE NERBS HAVE LIVED IN PEACE FOR CENTURIES, HERE UNDERGROUND ON THE PLANET MOBIUS!...
...AND MIXING WITH OUTSIDERS CAN ONLY LEAD TO TROUBLE... NOT TO MENTION ATHLETE'S FOOT!
I ONLY CAME TO THE SURFACE TO FIND OUT WHY YOU OUTSIDERS ARE DISRUPTING OUR LIFELINES!
WHO, US?
BECAUSE OF YOUR RECKLESS UNDERGROUND BUILDING, OUR AIR VENTS AND WATER SUPPLY ARE THREATENED!
BUT IT'S OUR ENEMY, THE EVIL ROBOTNIK, WHO'S RESPONSIBLE FOR ALL THE BELOW-GROUND BUILDING!
HE'LL DO ANYTHING TO GET CHEAP REAL ESTATE!
WHY DON'T WE JOIN FORCES? TOGETHER, I'M SURE WE CAN FIND A WAY TO STOP ROBOTNIK ONCE AND FOR ALL!

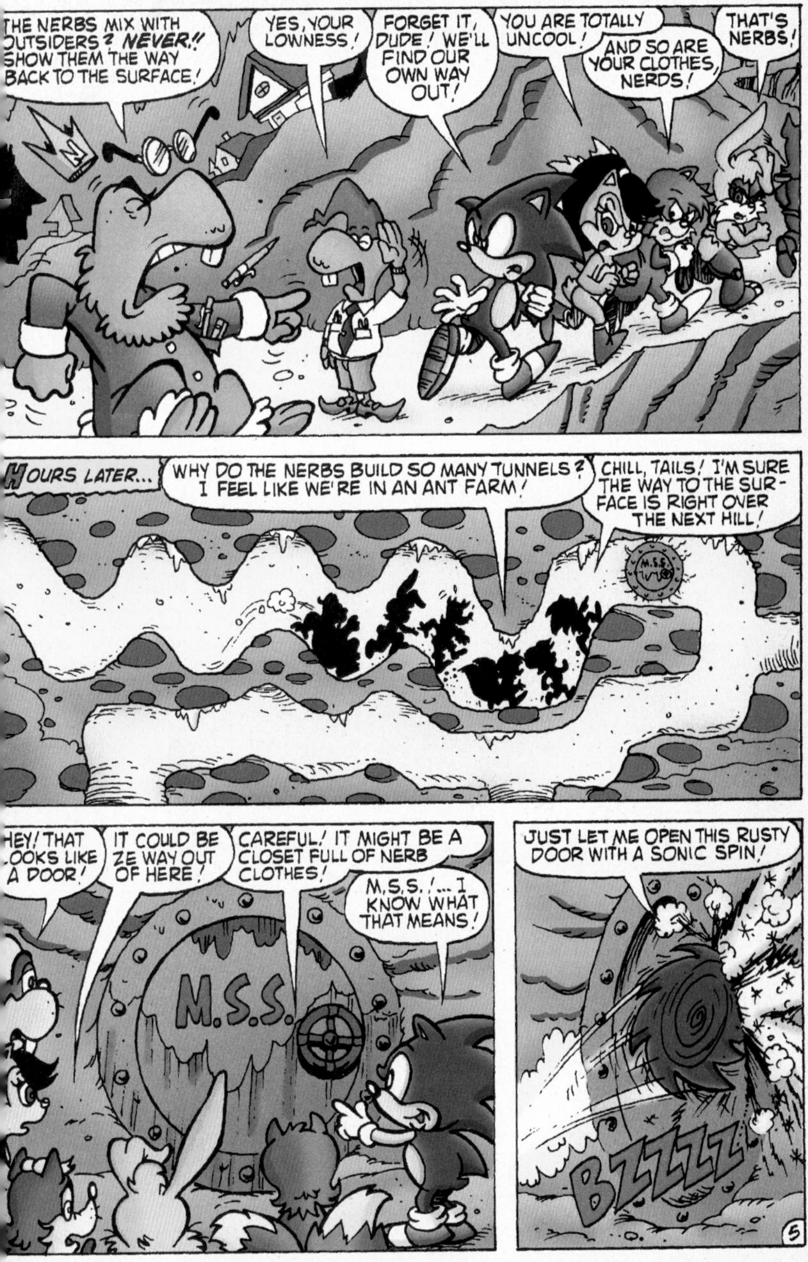
THE NERBS MIX WITH OUTSIDERS? NEVER!! SHOW THEM THE WAY BACK TO THE SURFACE!
YES, YOUR LOWNESS!
FORGET IT, DUDE! WE'LL FIND OUR OWN WAY OUT!
YOU ARE TOTALLY UNCOOL!
AND SO ARE YOUR CLOTHES, NERDS!
THAT'S NERBS!
HOURS LATER...
WHY DO THE NERBS BUILD SO MANY TUNNELS? I FEEL LIKE WE'RE IN AN ANT FARM!
CHILL, TAILS! I'M SURE THE WAY TO THE SURFACE IS RIGHT OVER THE NEXT HILL!
M.S.S.
HEY! THAT LOOKS LIKE A DOOR!
IT COULD BE ZE WAY OUT OF HERE!
CAREFUL! IT MIGHT BE A CLOSET FULL OF NERB CLOTHES!
M.S.S.!... I KNOW WHAT THAT MEANS!
M.S.S.
JUST LET ME OPEN THIS RUSTY DOOR WITH A SONIC SPIN!
BZZZZZ

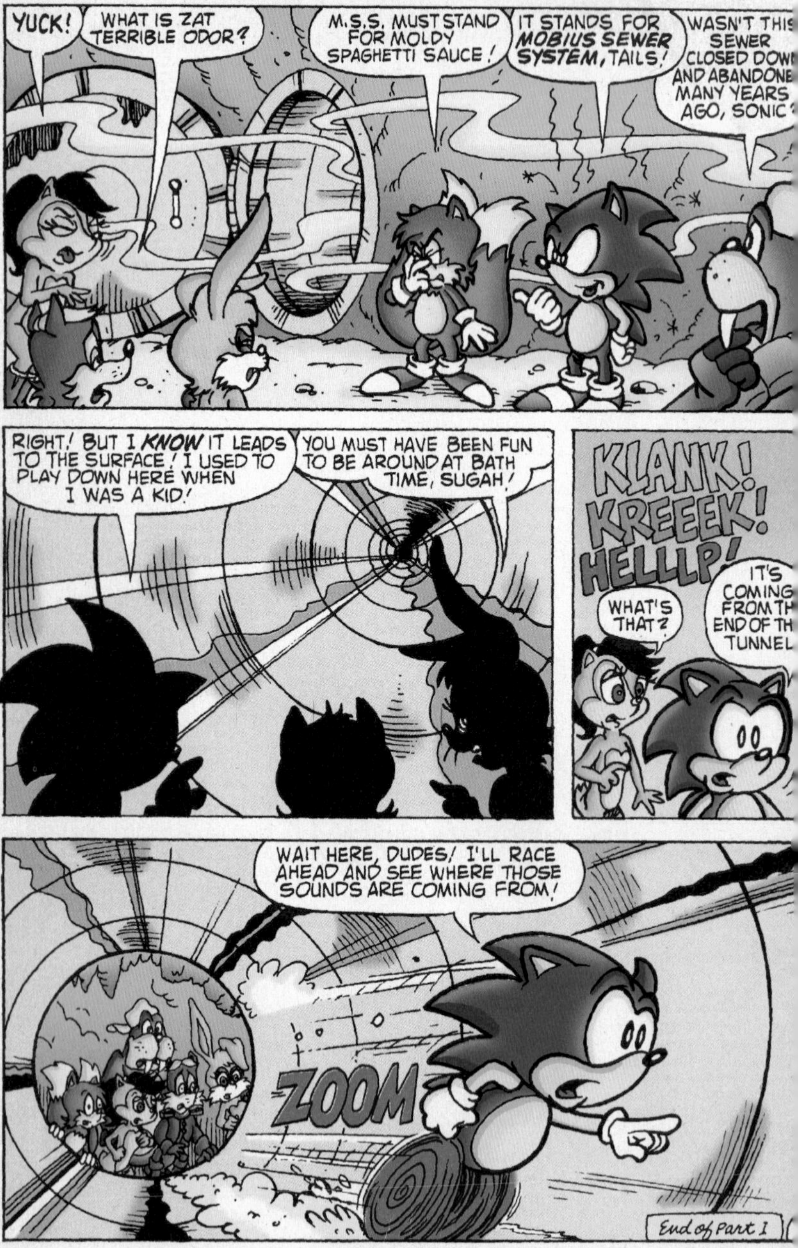

YUCK!
WHAT IS ZAT TERRIBLE ODOR?
M.S.S. MUST STAND FOR MOLDY SPAGHETTI SAUCE!
IT STANDS FOR *MOBIUS SEWER SYSTEM*, TAILS!
WASN'T THIS SEWER CLOSED DOWN AND ABANDONED MANY YEARS AGO, SONIC?
RIGHT! BUT I *KNOW* IT LEADS TO THE SURFACE! I USED TO PLAY DOWN HERE WHEN I WAS A KID!
YOU MUST HAVE BEEN FUN TO BE AROUND AT BATH TIME, SUGAH!
KLANK! KREEEK! HELLLP!
WHAT'S THAT?
IT'S COMING FROM TH END OF TH TUNNEL
WAIT HERE, DUDES! I'LL RACE AHEAD AND SEE WHERE THOSE SOUNDS ARE COMING FROM!
ZOOM
End of Part I

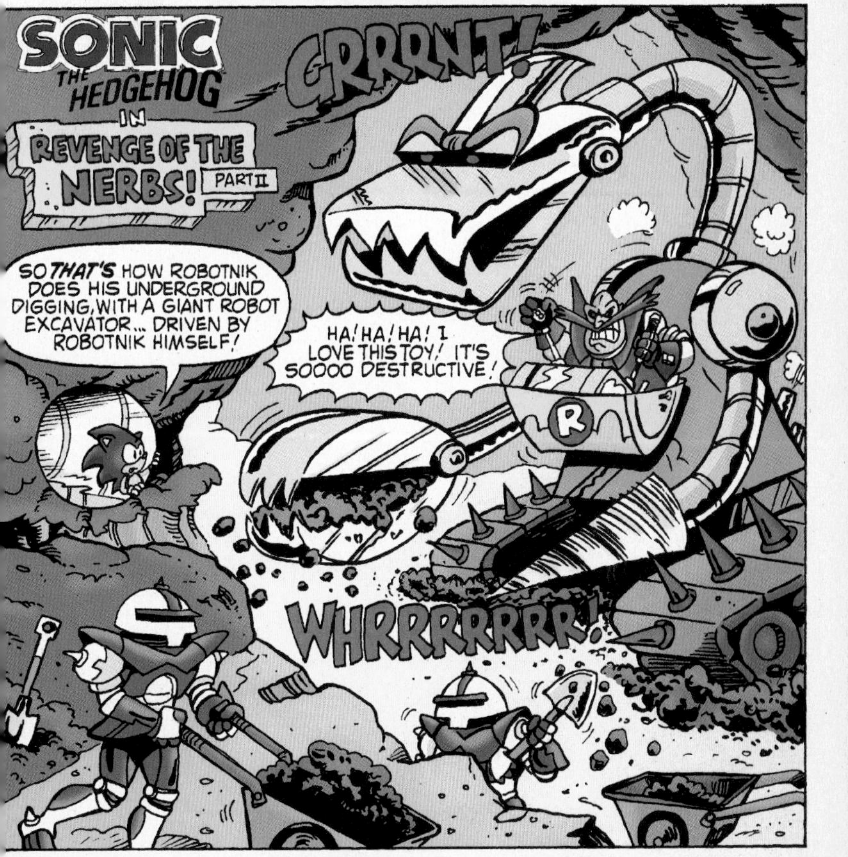
SONIC THE HEDGEHOG IN
REVENGE OF THE NERBS! PART II
GRRRNT!
SO THAT'S HOW ROBOTNIK DOES HIS UNDERGROUND DIGGING, WITH A GIANT ROBOT EXCAVATOR... DRIVEN BY ROBOTNIK HIMSELF!
HA! HA! HA! I LOVE THIS TOY! IT'S SOOOO DESTRUCTIVE!
WHRRRRRRR!

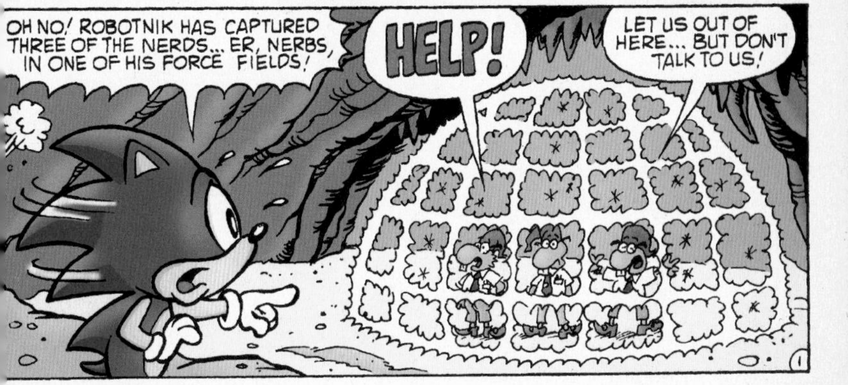
OH NO! ROBOTNIK HAS CAPTURED THREE OF THE NERDS... ER, NERBS, IN ONE OF HIS FORCE FIELDS!
HELP!
LET US OUT OF HERE... BUT DON'T TALK TO US!

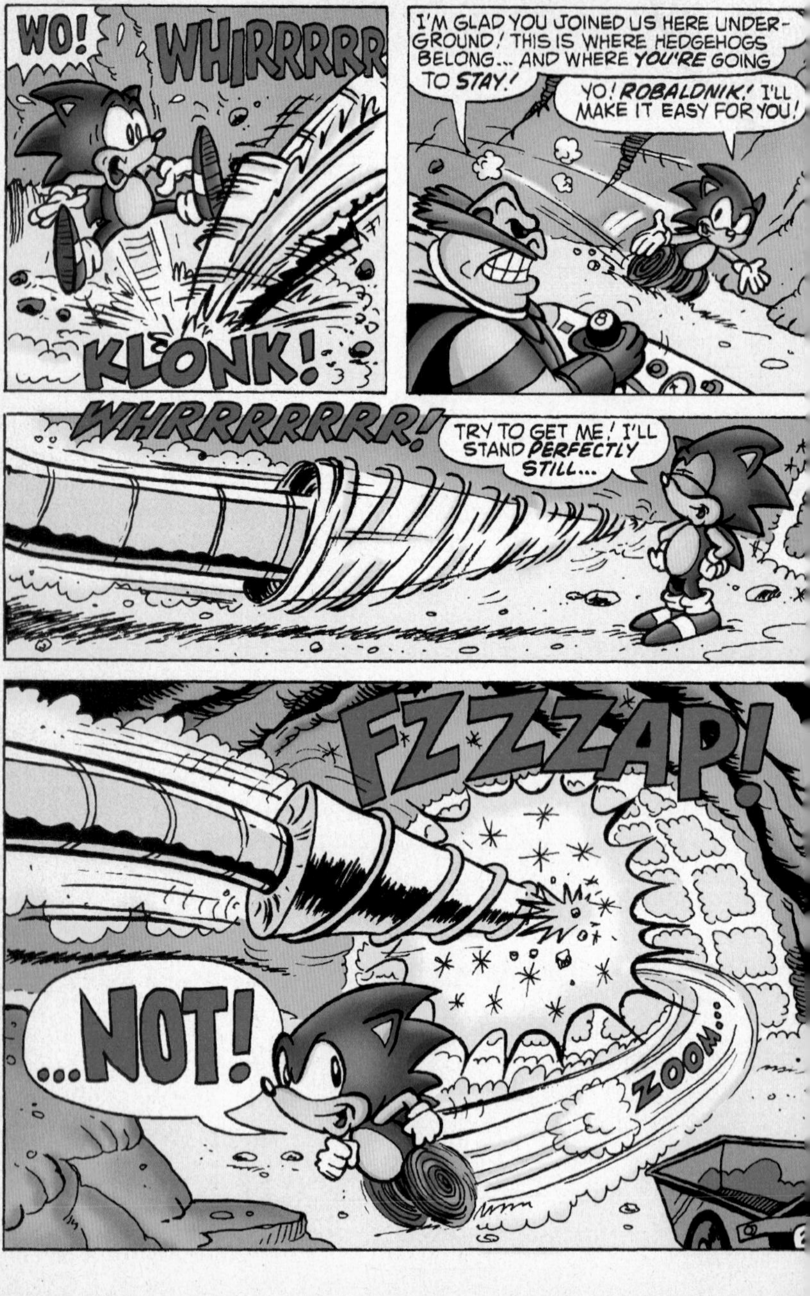
WO!
WHIRRRRR
KLONK!
I'M GLAD YOU JOINED US HERE UNDERGROUND! THIS IS WHERE HEDGEHOGS BELONG... AND WHERE YOU'RE GOING TO STAY!
YO! ROBALDNIK! I'LL MAKE IT EASY FOR YOU!
WHRRRRRRRR!
TRY TO GET ME! I'LL STAND PERFECTLY STILL...
FZZZAP!
...NOT!
ZOOM...

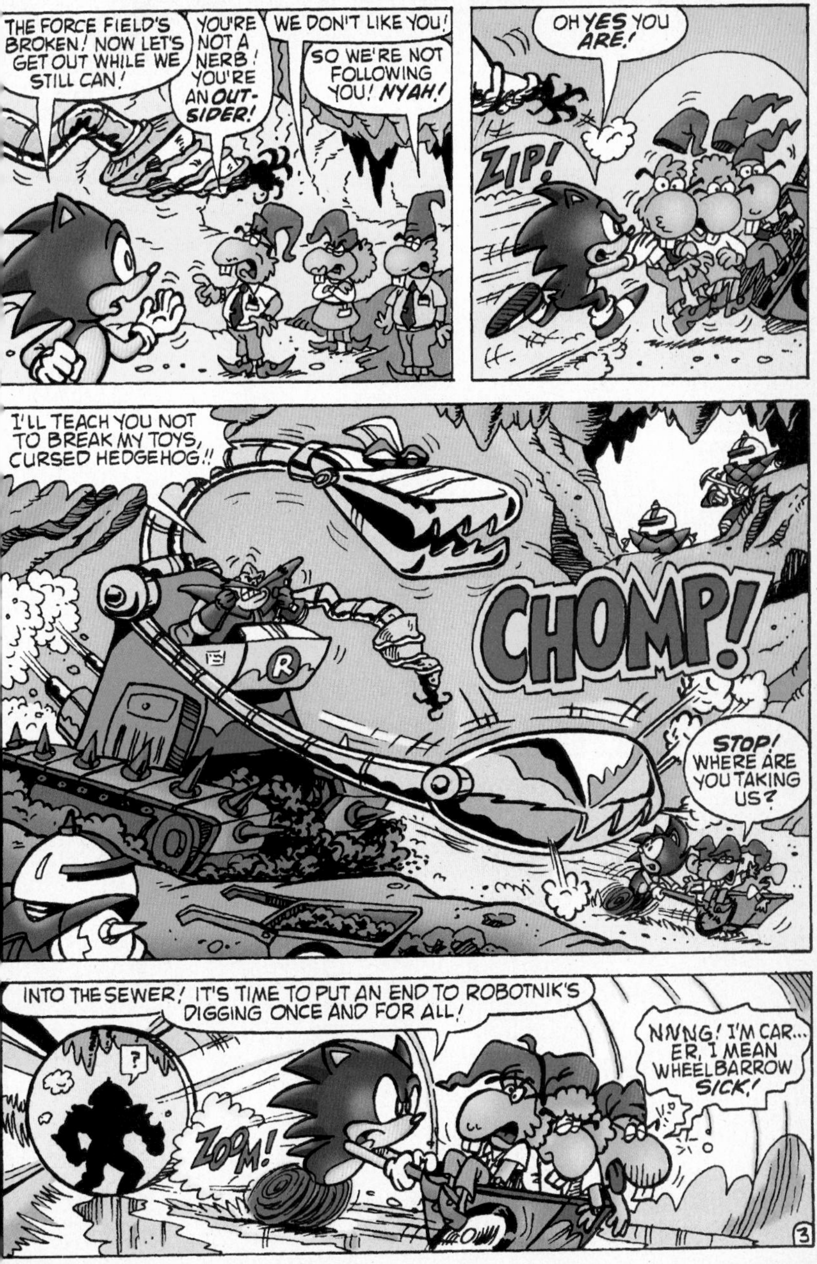
THE FORCE FIELD'S BROKEN! NOW LET'S GET OUT WHILE WE STILL CAN!
YOU'RE NOT A NERB! YOU'RE AN OUTSIDER!
WE DON'T LIKE YOU!
SO WE'RE NOT FOLLOWING YOU! NYAH!
OH YES YOU ARE!
ZIP!
I'LL TEACH YOU NOT TO BREAK MY TOYS, CURSED HEDGEHOG!!
CHOMP!
STOP! WHERE ARE YOU TAKING US?
INTO THE SEWER! IT'S TIME TO PUT AN END TO ROBOTNIK'S DIGGING ONCE AND FOR ALL!
?
ZOOM!
NNNG! I'M CAR... ER, I MEAN WHEELBARROW SICK!
3

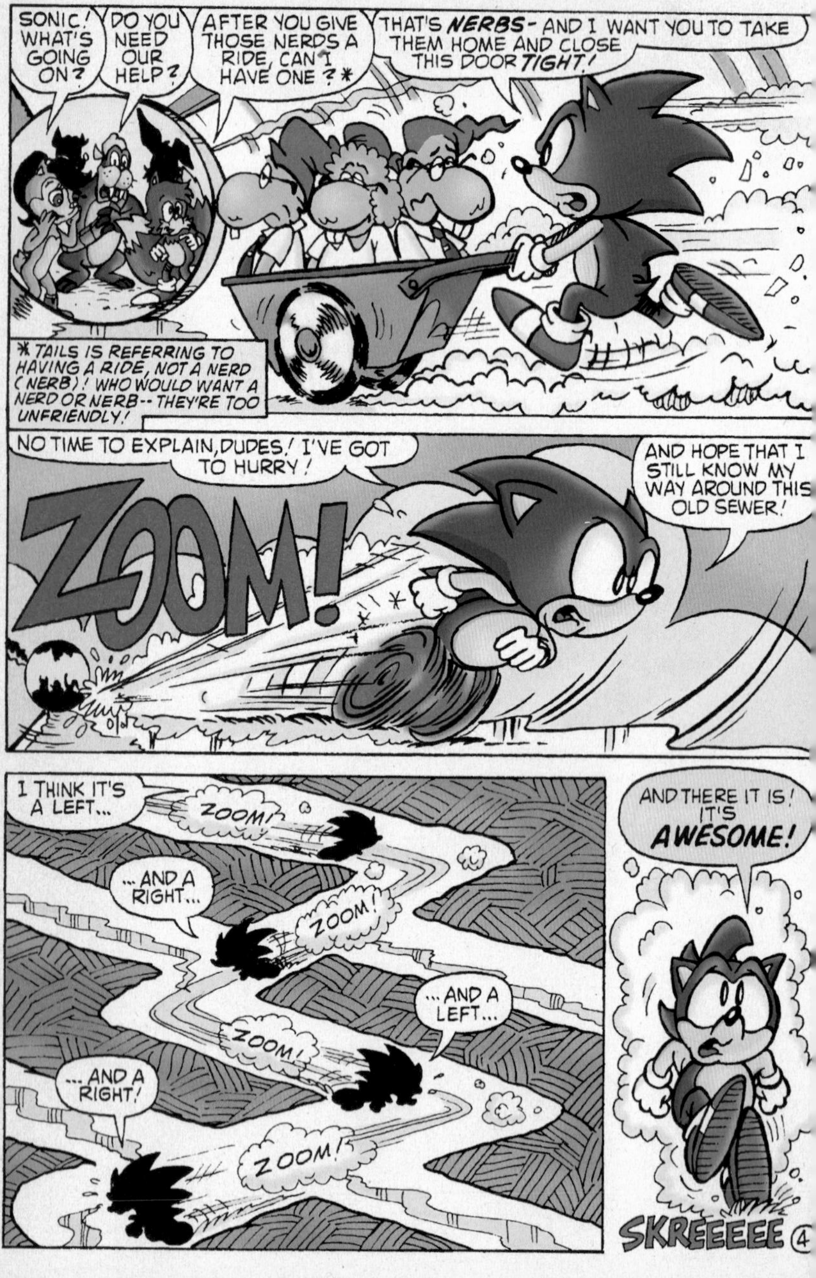
SONIC! WHAT'S GOING ON?
DO YOU NEED OUR HELP?
AFTER YOU GIVE THOSE NERDS A RIDE, CAN I HAVE ONE?*
THAT'S NERBS- AND I WANT YOU TO TAKE THEM HOME AND CLOSE THIS DOOR TIGHT!
*TAILS IS REFERRING TO HAVING A RIDE, NOT A NERD (NERB)! WHO WOULD WANT A NERD OR NERB-- THEY'RE TOO UNFRIENDLY!
NO TIME TO EXPLAIN, DUDES! I'VE GOT TO HURRY!
AND HOPE THAT I STILL KNOW MY WAY AROUND THIS OLD SEWER!
ZOOM!
I THINK IT'S A LEFT...
ZOOM!
...AND A RIGHT...
ZOOM!
...AND A LEFT...
ZOOM!
...AND A RIGHT!
ZOOM!
AND THERE IT IS! IT'S AWESOME!
SKREEEEEE

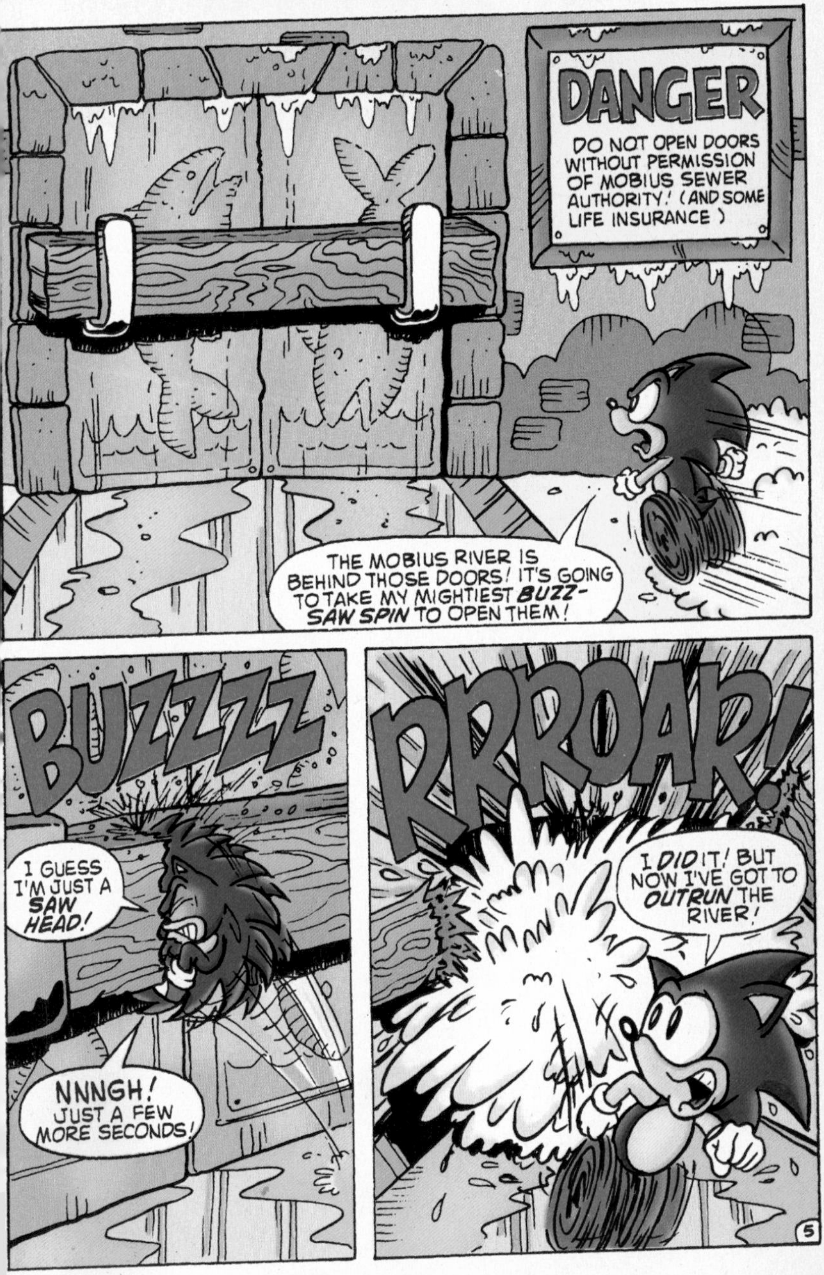
DANGER
DO NOT OPEN DOORS WITHOUT PERMISSION OF MOBIUS SEWER AUTHORITY! (AND SOME LIFE INSURANCE)
THE MOBIUS RIVER IS BEHIND THOSE DOORS! IT'S GOING TO TAKE MY MIGHTIEST BUZZ-SAW SPIN TO OPEN THEM!
BUZZZZ
I GUESS I'M JUST A SAW HEAD!
NNNGH! JUST A FEW MORE SECONDS!
RRROAR!
I DID IT! BUT NOW I'VE GOT TO OUTRUN THE RIVER!
5

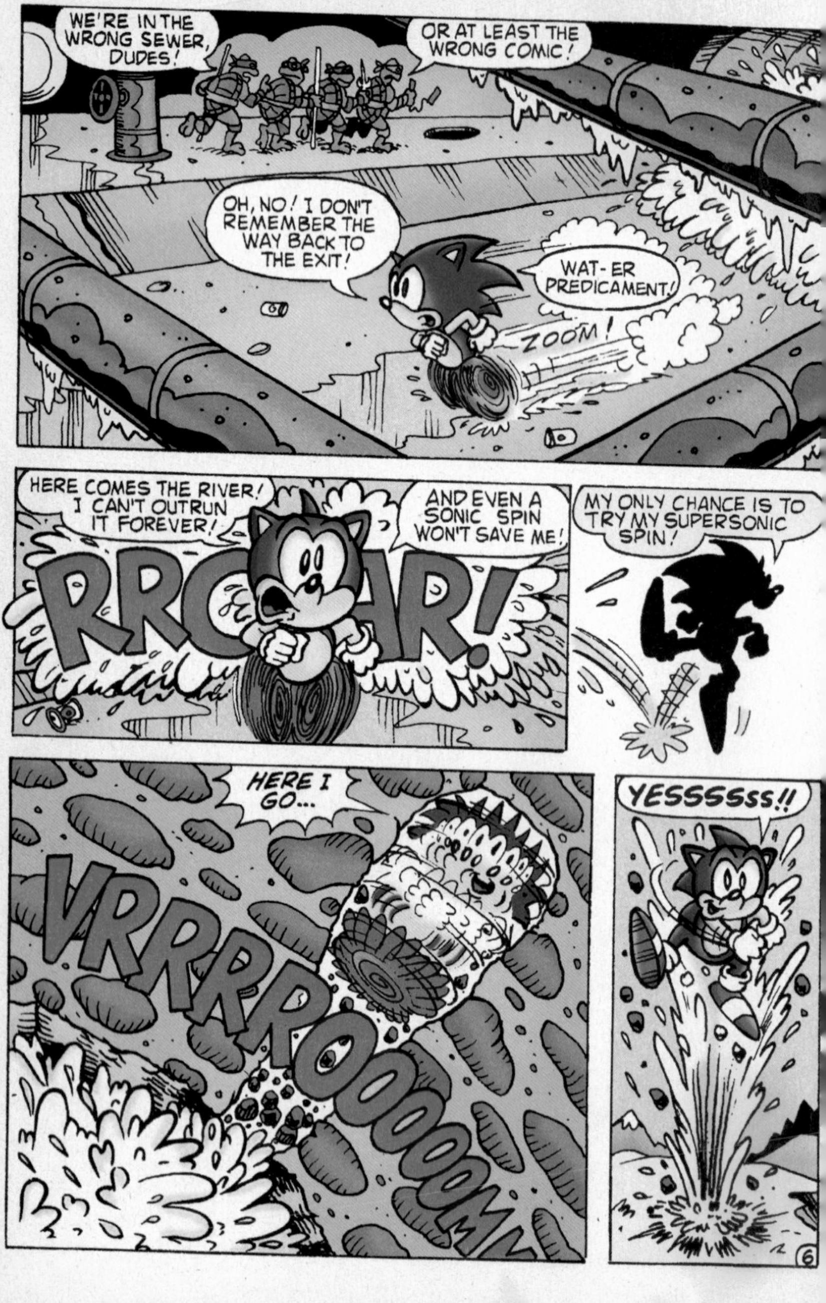
WE'RE IN THE WRONG SEWER, DUDES!
OR AT LEAST THE WRONG COMIC!
OH, NO! I DON'T REMEMBER THE WAY BACK TO THE EXIT!
WAT-ER PREDICAMENT!
ZOOM!
HERE COMES THE RIVER! I CAN'T OUTRUN IT FOREVER!
AND EVEN A SONIC SPIN WON'T SAVE ME!
MY ONLY CHANCE IS TO TRY MY SUPERSONIC SPIN!
HERE I GO...
VRRRROOOOOOM!
YESSSSSS!!

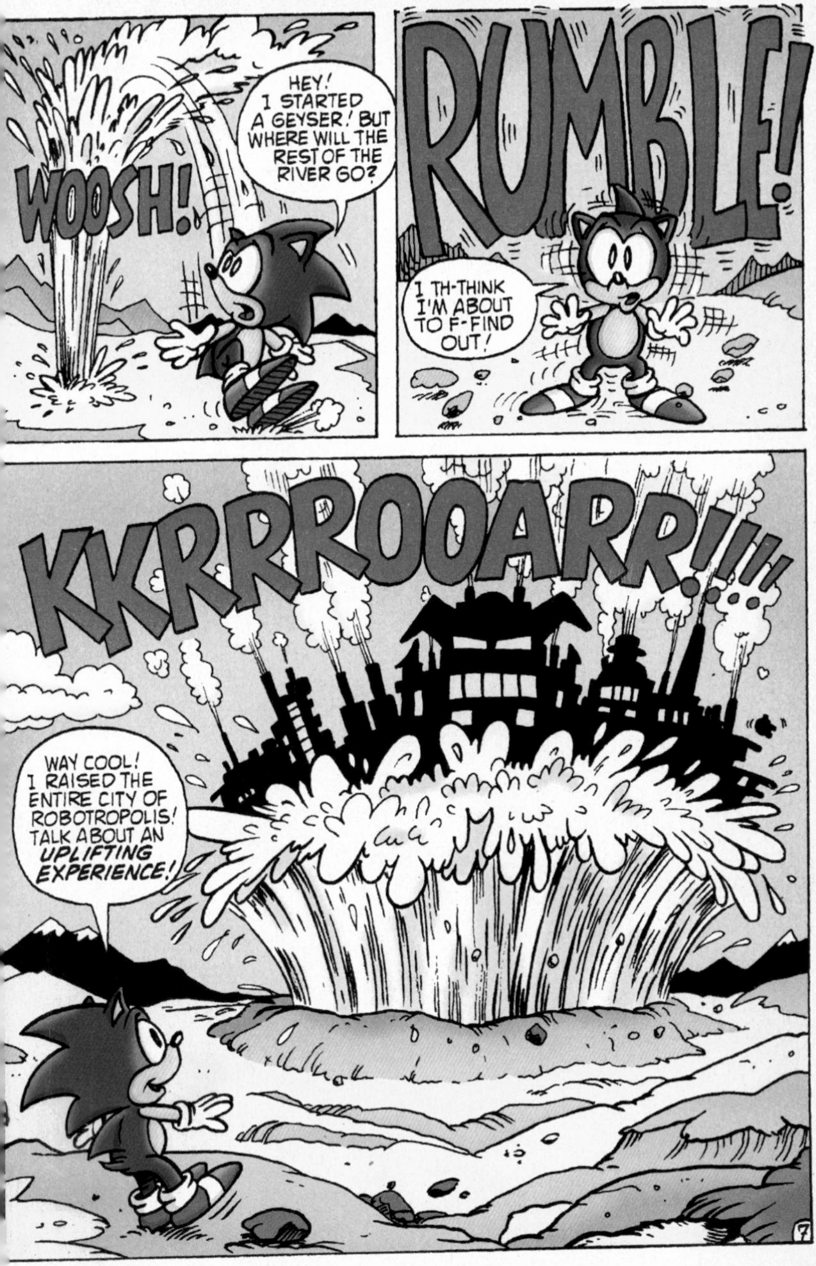
WOOSH!
HEY! I STARTED A GEYSER! BUT WHERE WILL THE REST OF THE RIVER GO?
RUMBLE!
I TH-THINK I'M ABOUT TO F-FIND OUT!
KKRRROOARR!!!!
WAY COOL! I RAISED THE ENTIRE CITY OF ROBOTROPOLIS! TALK ABOUT AN *UPLIFTING EXPERIENCE!*

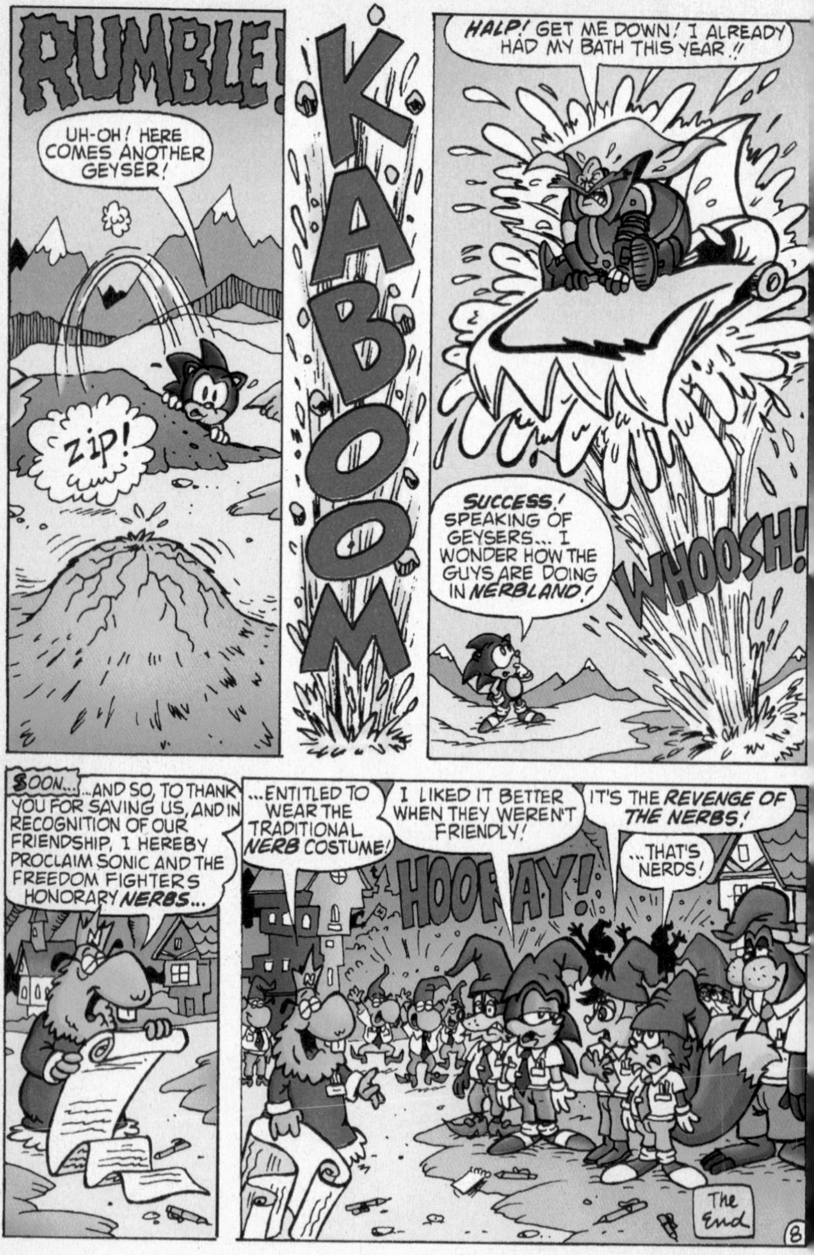
RUMBLE!
UH-OH! HERE COMES ANOTHER GEYSER!
zip!
KABOOM
HALP! GET ME DOWN! I ALREADY HAD MY BATH THIS YEAR!!
SUCCESS! SPEAKING OF GEYSERS... I WONDER HOW THE GUYS ARE DOING IN NERBLAND!
WHOOSH!
SOON...
...AND SO, TO THANK YOU FOR SAVING US, AND IN RECOGNITION OF OUR FRIENDSHIP, I HEREBY PROCLAIM SONIC AND THE FREEDOM FIGHTERS HONORARY NERBS...
...ENTITLED TO WEAR THE TRADITIONAL NERB COSTUME!
I LIKED IT BETTER WHEN THEY WEREN'T FRIENDLY!
IT'S THE REVENGE OF THE NERBS!
...THAT'S NERDS!
HOORAY!
The End
8

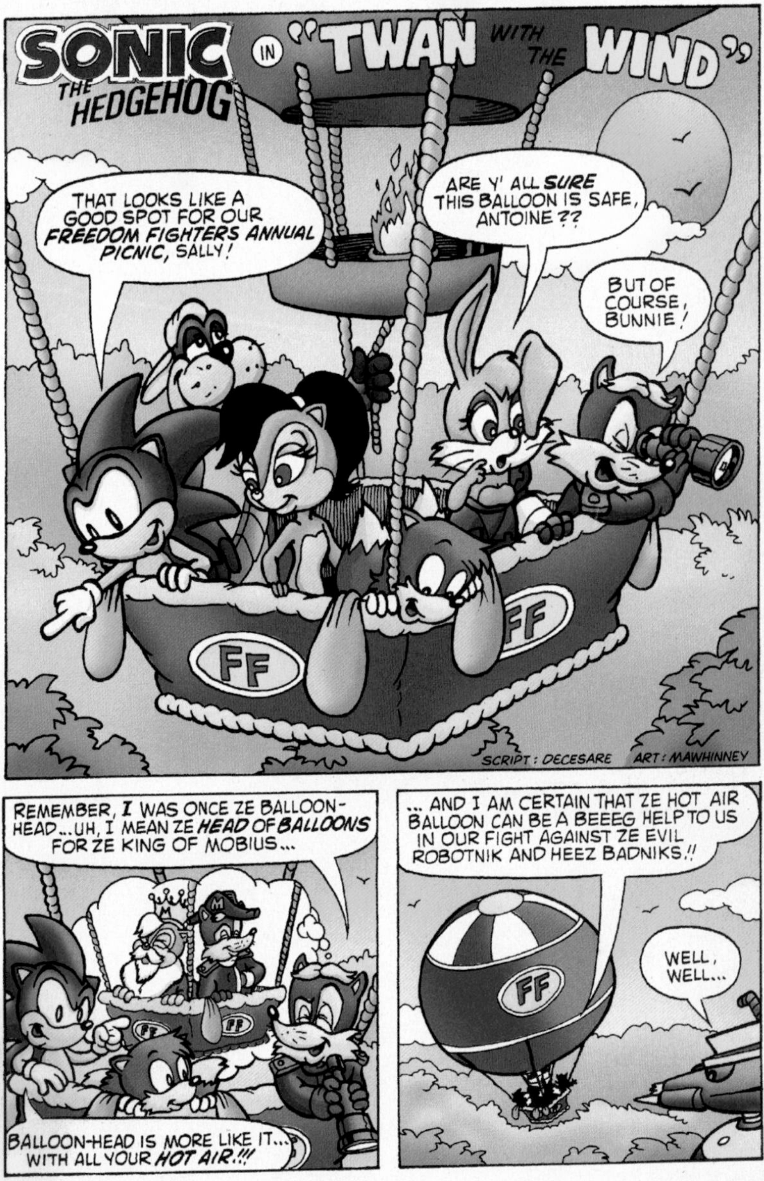
SONIC THE HEDGEHOG
IN "TWAN WITH THE WIND"
THAT LOOKS LIKE A GOOD SPOT FOR OUR FREEDOM FIGHTERS ANNUAL PICNIC, SALLY!
ARE Y' ALL SURE THIS BALLOON IS SAFE, ANTOINE??
BUT OF COURSE, BUNNIE!
SCRIPT: DECESARE ART: MAWHINNEY
REMEMBER, I WAS ONCE ZE BALLOON-HEAD...UH, I MEAN ZE HEAD OF BALLOONS FOR ZE KING OF MOBIUS...
BALLOON-HEAD IS MORE LIKE IT... WITH ALL YOUR HOT AIR.!!!
... AND I AM CERTAIN THAT ZE HOT AIR BALLOON CAN BE A BEEEG HELP TO US IN OUR FIGHT AGAINST ZE EVIL ROBOTNIK AND HEEZ BADNIKS.!!
WELL, WELL...

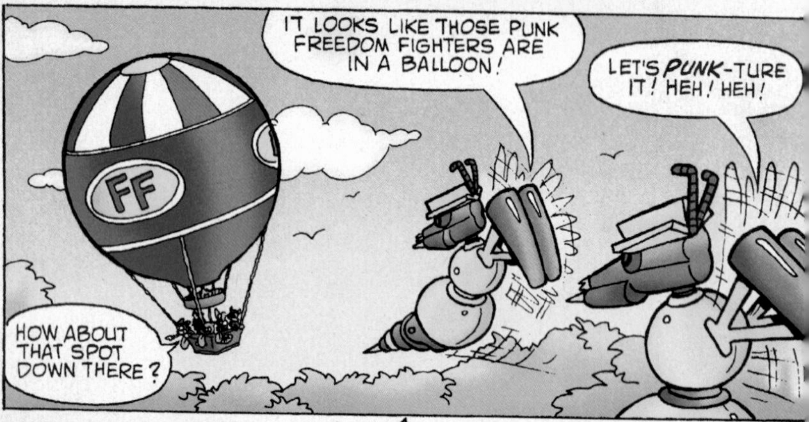
IT LOOKS LIKE THOSE PUNK FREEDOM FIGHTERS ARE IN A BALLOON!
LET'S PUNK-TURE IT! HEH! HEH!
HOW ABOUT THAT SPOT DOWN THERE?
FF

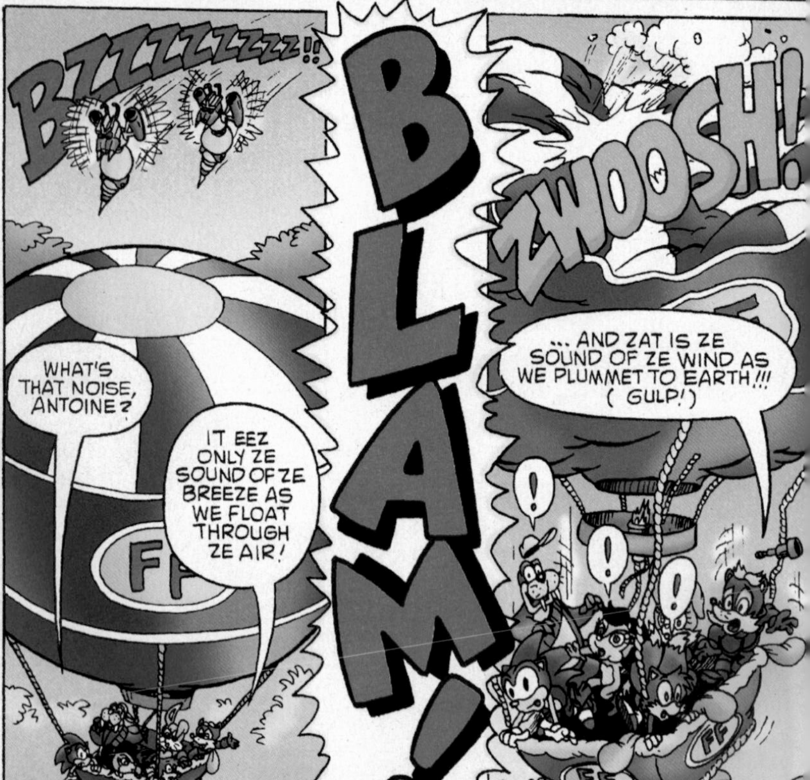
BZZZZZZZZZ!!
WHAT'S THAT NOISE, ANTOINE?
IT EEZ ONLY ZE SOUND OF ZE BREEZE AS WE FLOAT THROUGH ZE AIR!
FF
BLAM!
ZWOOSH!
...AND ZAT IS ZE SOUND OF ZE WIND AS WE PLUMMET TO EARTH!!! (GULP!)
!
!
!
FF

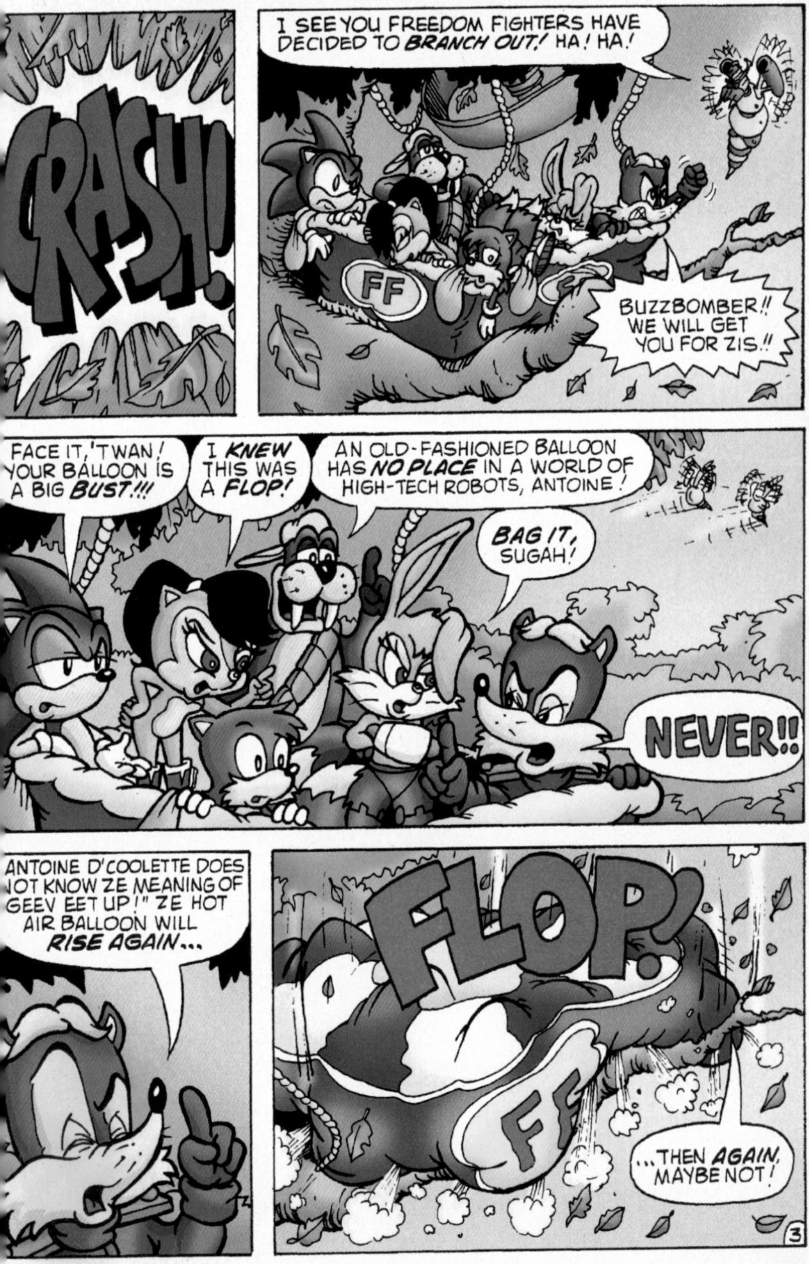
CRASH!
I SEE YOU FREEDOM FIGHTERS HAVE DECIDED TO BRANCH OUT! HA! HA!
BUZZBOMBER!! WE WILL GET YOU FOR ZIS!!
FACE IT, 'TWAN! YOUR BALLOON IS A BIG BUST!!!
I KNEW THIS WAS A FLOP!
AN OLD-FASHIONED BALLOON HAS NO PLACE IN A WORLD OF HIGH-TECH ROBOTS, ANTOINE!
BAG IT, SUGAH!
NEVER!!
ANTOINE D'COOLETTE DOES NOT KNOW ZE MEANING OF GEEV EET UP!" ZE HOT AIR BALLOON WILL RISE AGAIN...
FLOP!
...THEN AGAIN, MAYBE NOT!
3

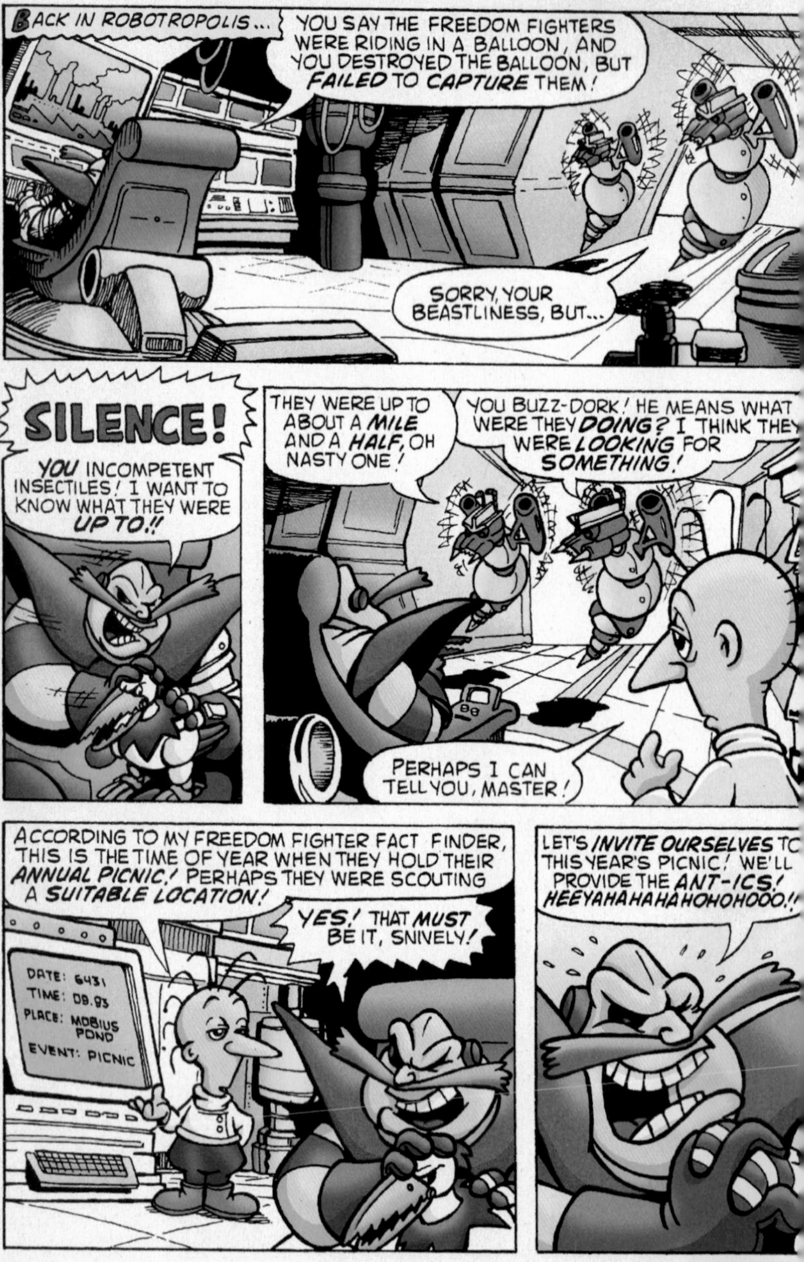
BACK IN ROBOTROPOLIS...
YOU SAY THE FREEDOM FIGHTERS WERE RIDING IN A BALLOON, AND YOU DESTROYED THE BALLOON, BUT FAILED TO CAPTURE THEM!
SORRY, YOUR BEASTLINESS, BUT...
SILENCE!
YOU INCOMPETENT INSECTILES! I WANT TO KNOW WHAT THEY WERE UP TO!!
THEY WERE UP TO ABOUT A MILE AND A HALF, OH NASTY ONE!
YOU BUZZ-DORK! HE MEANS WHAT WERE THEY DOING? I THINK THEY WERE LOOKING FOR SOMETHING!
PERHAPS I CAN TELL YOU, MASTER!
ACCORDING TO MY FREEDOM FIGHTER FACT FINDER, THIS IS THE TIME OF YEAR WHEN THEY HOLD THEIR ANNUAL PICNIC! PERHAPS THEY WERE SCOUTING A SUITABLE LOCATION!
DATE: 6431
TIME: 09.93
PLACE: MOBIUS POND
EVENT: PICNIC
YES! THAT MUST BE IT, SNIVELY!
LET'S INVITE OURSELVES TO THIS YEAR'S PICNIC! WE'LL PROVIDE THE ANT-ICS! HEEYAHAHAHAHOHOHOOO!!

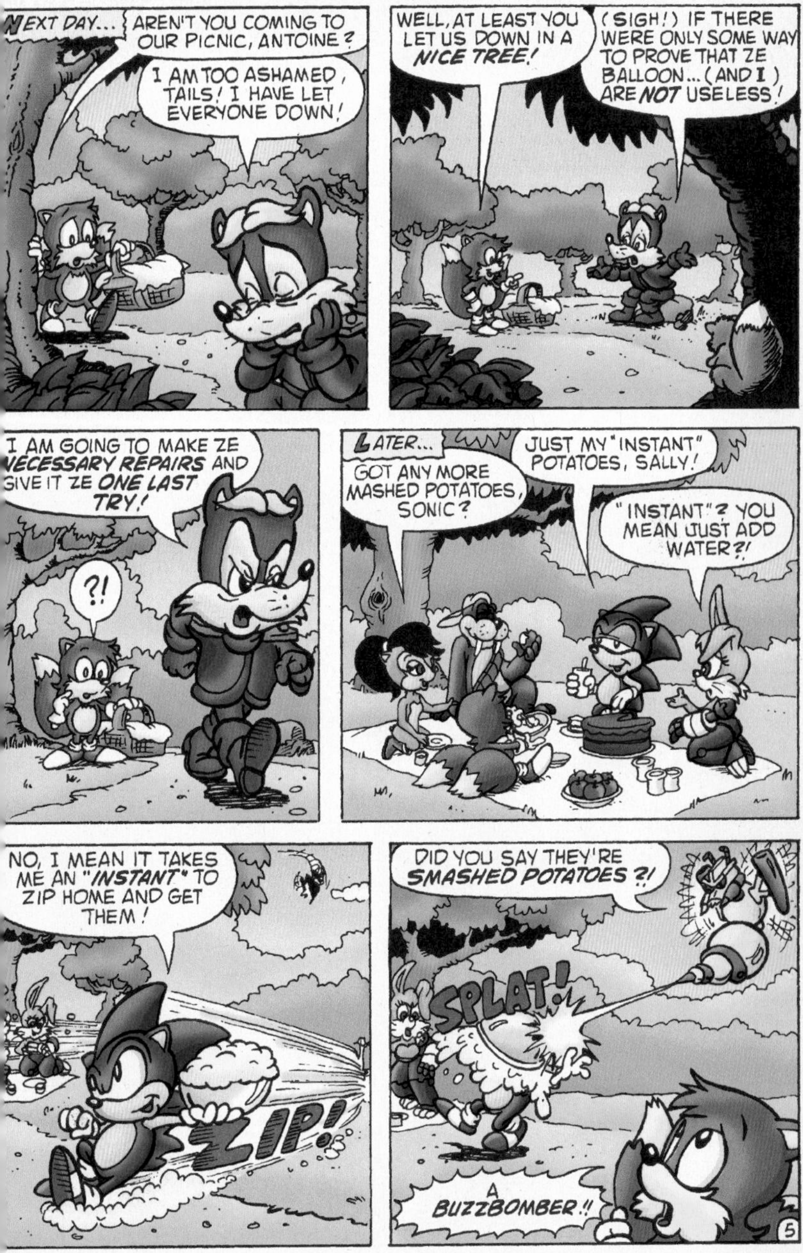
NEXT DAY...
AREN'T YOU COMING TO OUR PICNIC, ANTOINE?
I AM TOO ASHAMED, TAILS! I HAVE LET EVERYONE DOWN!
WELL, AT LEAST YOU LET US DOWN IN A NICE TREE!
(SIGH!) IF THERE WERE ONLY SOME WAY TO PROVE THAT ZE BALLOON... (AND I) ARE NOT USELESS!
I AM GOING TO MAKE ZE NECESSARY REPAIRS AND GIVE IT ZE ONE LAST TRY!
?!
LATER...
GOT ANY MORE MASHED POTATOES, SONIC?
JUST MY "INSTANT" POTATOES, SALLY!
"INSTANT"? YOU MEAN JUST ADD WATER?!
NO, I MEAN IT TAKES ME AN "INSTANT" TO ZIP HOME AND GET THEM!
ZIP!
DID YOU SAY THEY'RE SMASHED POTATOES?!
SPLAT!
A BUZZBOMBER!!

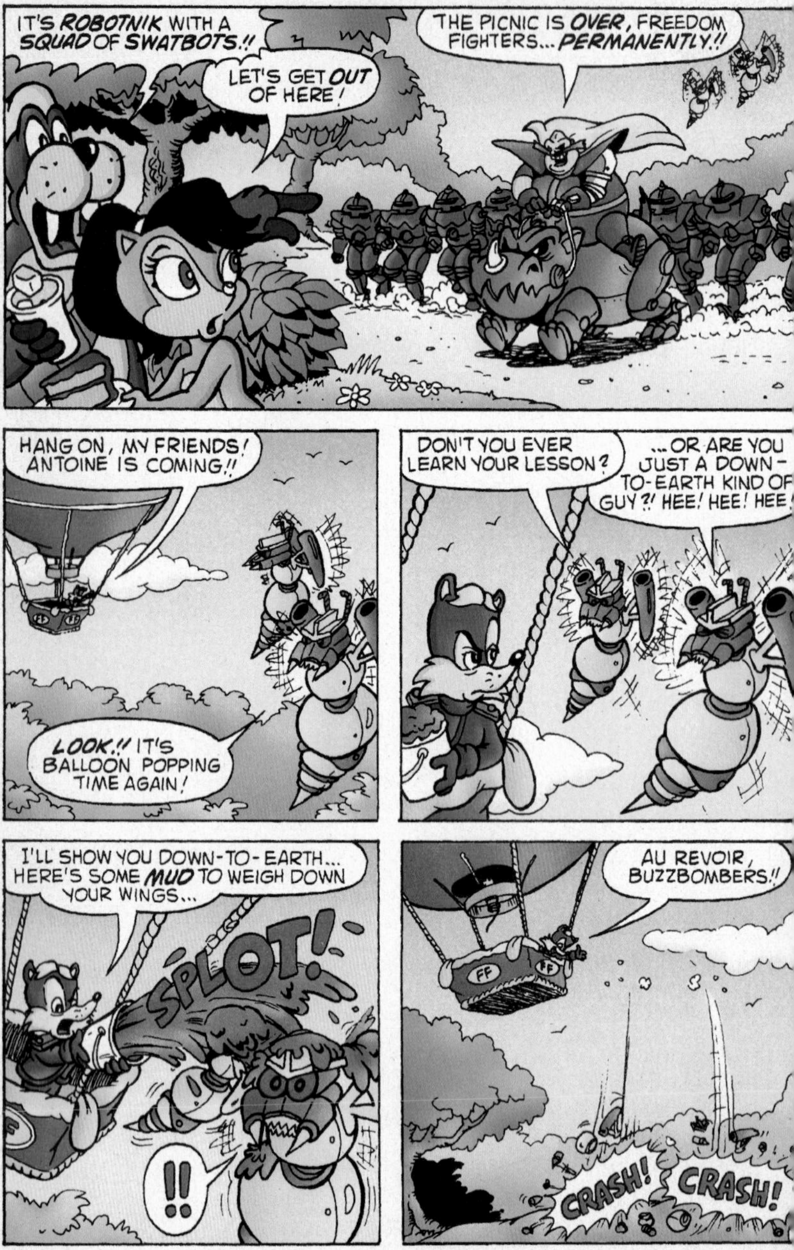

IT'S ROBOTNIK WITH A SQUAD OF SWATBOTS.!!
LET'S GET OUT OF HERE!
THE PICNIC IS OVER, FREEDOM FIGHTERS... PERMANENTLY.!!
HANG ON, MY FRIENDS! ANTOINE IS COMING!!
LOOK.!! IT'S BALLOON POPPING TIME AGAIN!
DON'T YOU EVER LEARN YOUR LESSON?
...OR ARE YOU JUST A DOWN-TO-EARTH KIND OF GUY?! HEE! HEE! HEE!
I'LL SHOW YOU DOWN-TO-EARTH... HERE'S SOME MUD TO WEIGH DOWN YOUR WINGS...
SPLOT!
!!
AU REVOIR, BUZZBOMBERS!!
CRASH!
CRASH!

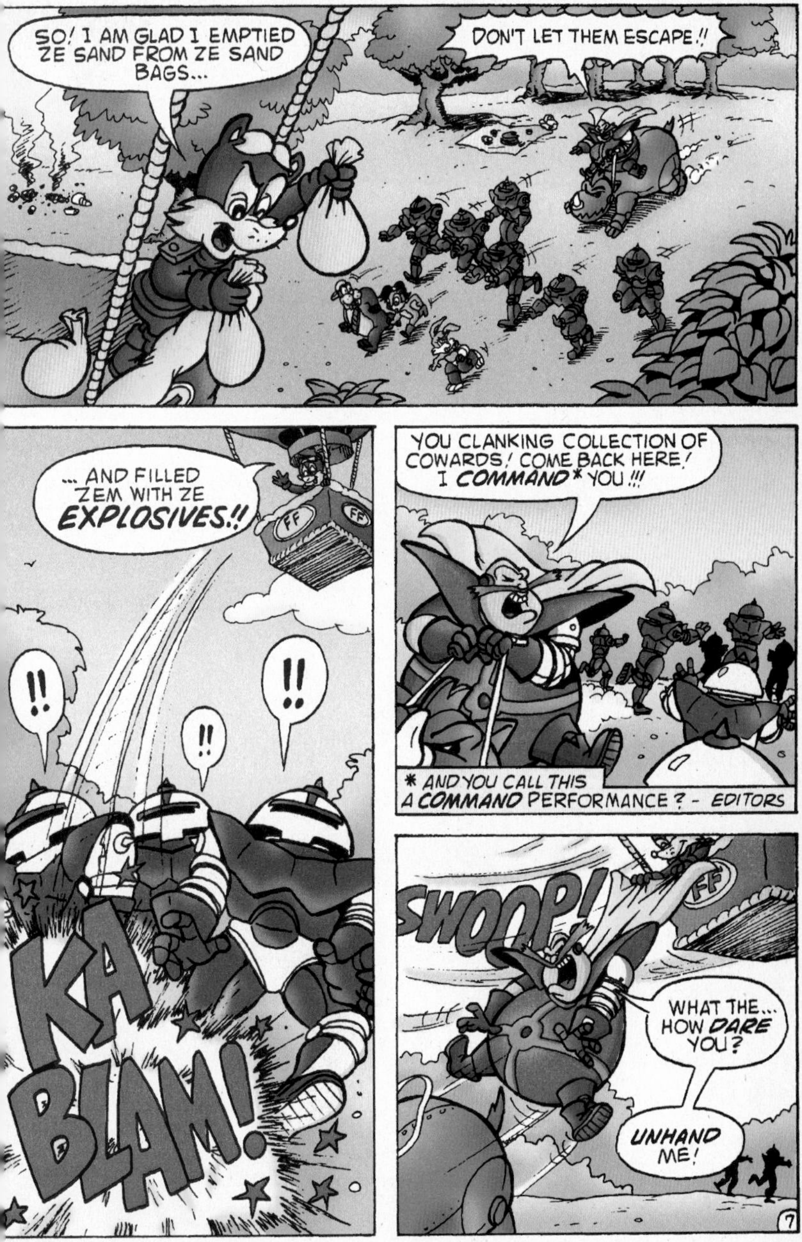
SO! I AM GLAD I EMPTIED ZE SAND FROM ZE SAND BAGS...
DON'T LET THEM ESCAPE!!
... AND FILLED ZEM WITH ZE EXPLOSIVES!!
!!
!!
!!
KA BLAM!
YOU CLANKING COLLECTION OF COWARDS! COME BACK HERE! I COMMAND* YOU!!!
* AND YOU CALL THIS A COMMAND PERFORMANCE? - EDITORS
SWOOP!
WHAT THE... HOW DARE YOU?
UNHAND ME!
7

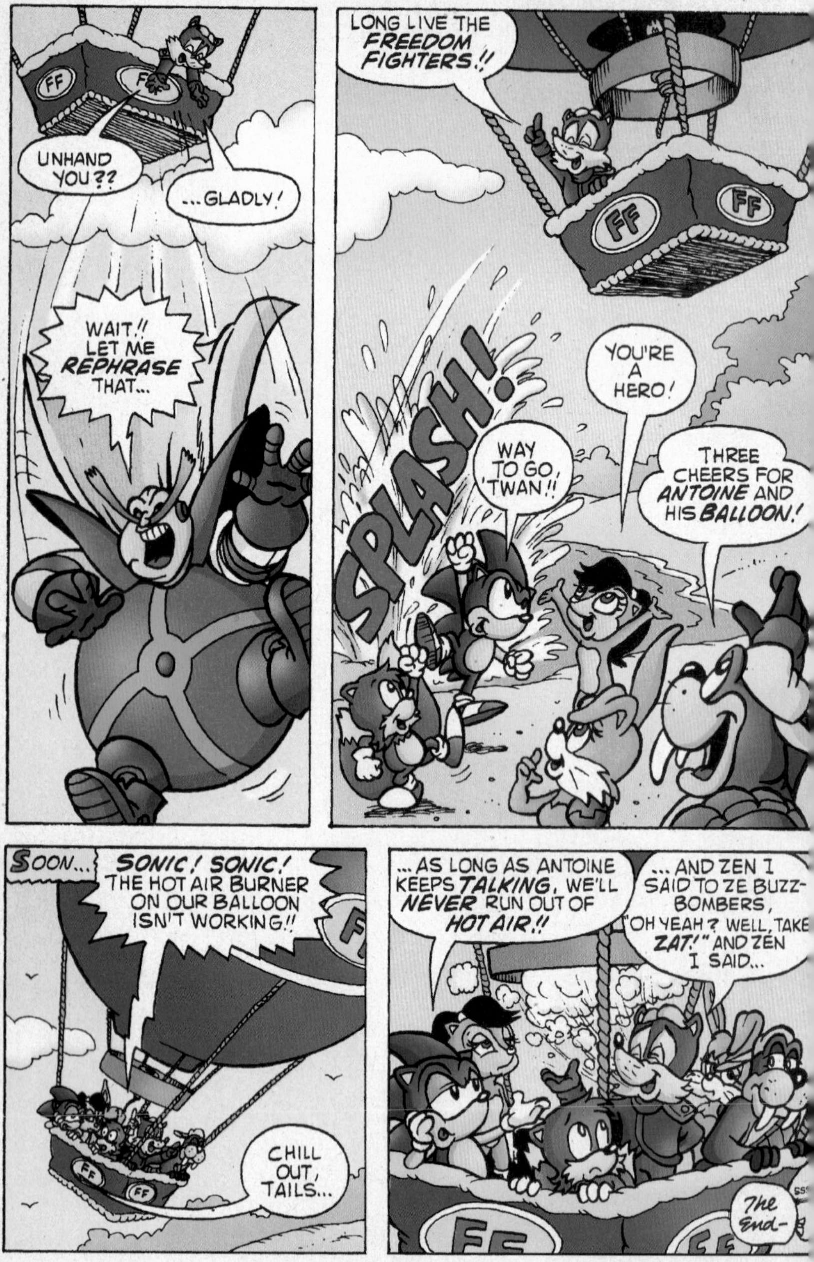
UNHAND YOU??
...GLADLY!
WAIT!! LET ME REPHRASE THAT...
LONG LIVE THE FREEDOM FIGHTERS!!
SPLASH!
YOU'RE A HERO!
WAY TO GO, 'TWAN!!
THREE CHEERS FOR ANTOINE AND HIS BALLOON!
SOON...
SONIC! SONIC! THE HOT AIR BURNER ON OUR BALLOON ISN'T WORKING!!
CHILL OUT, TAILS...
...AS LONG AS ANTOINE KEEPS TALKING, WE'LL NEVER RUN OUT OF HOT AIR!!
...AND ZEN I SAID TO ZE BUZZ-BOMBERS, "OH YEAH? WELL, TAKE ZAT!" AND ZEN I SAID...
The End-

Archie
DVENTURE
SERIES
O.11
UNE
US $1.25
CAN $1.50
TAILS GOES UNDERCOVER
SONIC
THE HEDGEHOG™
I'VE GOT YOU AT LAST!
ROBOTNIK, INC.
"WE LOVE TO POLLUTE AND IT SHOWS"
TNT
I'M NOT JUST A CUT-UP...I'M A CUT-OUT!
MANAK/D'AGOSTINO

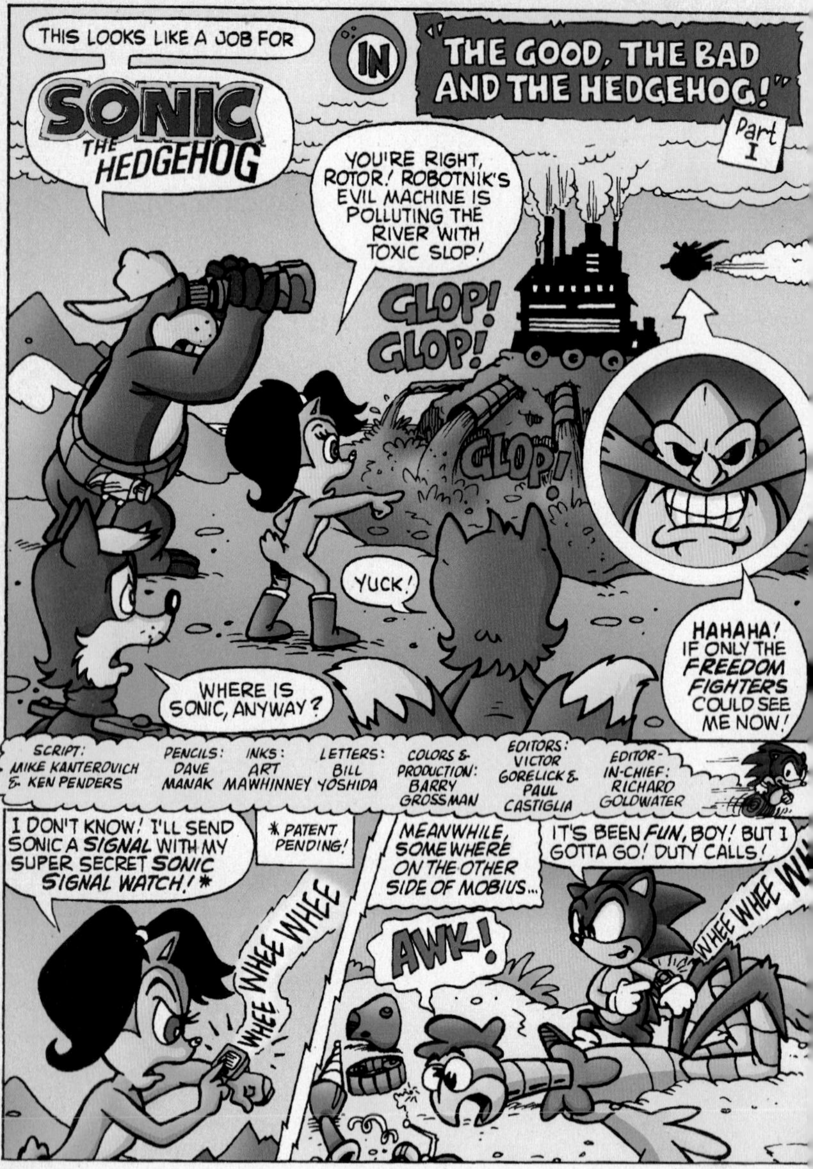
THIS LOOKS LIKE A JOB FOR
SONIC THE HEDGEHOG
IN
"THE GOOD, THE BAD AND THE HEDGEHOG!"
Part I
YOU'RE RIGHT, ROTOR! ROBOTNIK'S EVIL MACHINE IS POLLUTING THE RIVER WITH TOXIC SLOP!
GLOP! GLOP!
GLOP!
YUCK!
HAHAHA! IF ONLY THE FREEDOM FIGHTERS COULD SEE ME NOW!
WHERE IS SONIC, ANYWAY?
SCRIPT: MIKE KANTEROVICH & KEN PENDERS
PENCILS: DAVE MANAK
INKS: ART MAWHINNEY
LETTERS: BILL YOSHIDA
COLORS & PRODUCTION: BARRY GROSSMAN
EDITORS: VICTOR GORELICK & PAUL CASTIGLIA
EDITOR-IN-CHIEF: RICHARD GOLDWATER
I DON'T KNOW! I'LL SEND SONIC A SIGNAL WITH MY SUPER SECRET SONIC SIGNAL WATCH! *
* PATENT PENDING!
WHEE WHEE WHEE
MEANWHILE, SOMEWHERE ON THE OTHER SIDE OF MOBIUS...
IT'S BEEN FUN, BOY! BUT I GOTTA GO! DUTY CALLS!
AWK!
WHEE WHEE

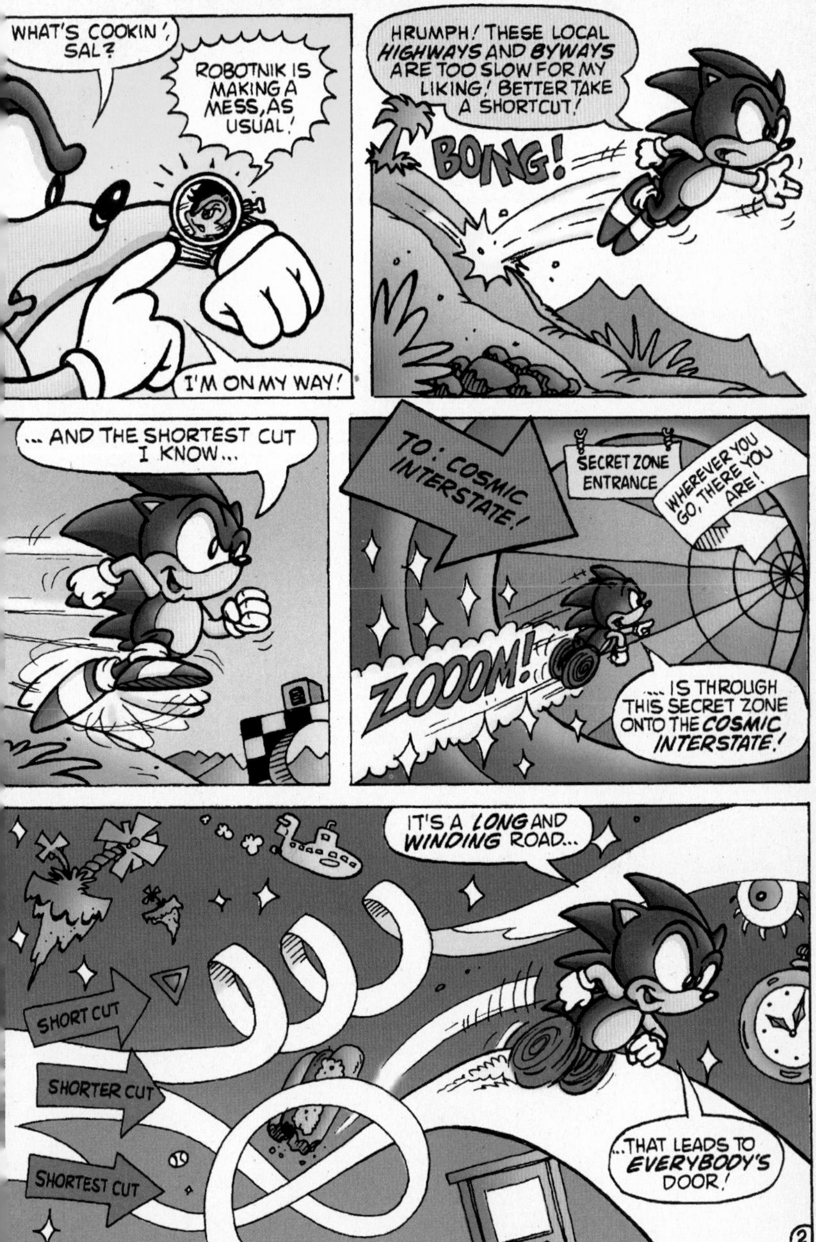
WHAT'S COOKIN', SAL?
ROBOTNIK IS MAKING A MESS, AS USUAL!
I'M ON MY WAY!
HRUMPH! THESE LOCAL *HIGHWAYS* AND *BYWAYS* ARE TOO SLOW FOR MY LIKING! BETTER TAKE A SHORTCUT!
BOING!
... AND THE SHORTEST CUT I KNOW...
TO: COSMIC INTERSTATE!
SECRET ZONE ENTRANCE
WHEREVER YOU GO, THERE YOU ARE!
ZOOOM!
... IS THROUGH THIS SECRET ZONE ONTO THE *COSMIC INTERSTATE!*
IT'S A *LONG* AND *WINDING* ROAD...
SHORT CUT
SHORTER CUT
SHORTEST CUT
...THAT LEADS TO *EVERYBODY'S* DOOR!
2

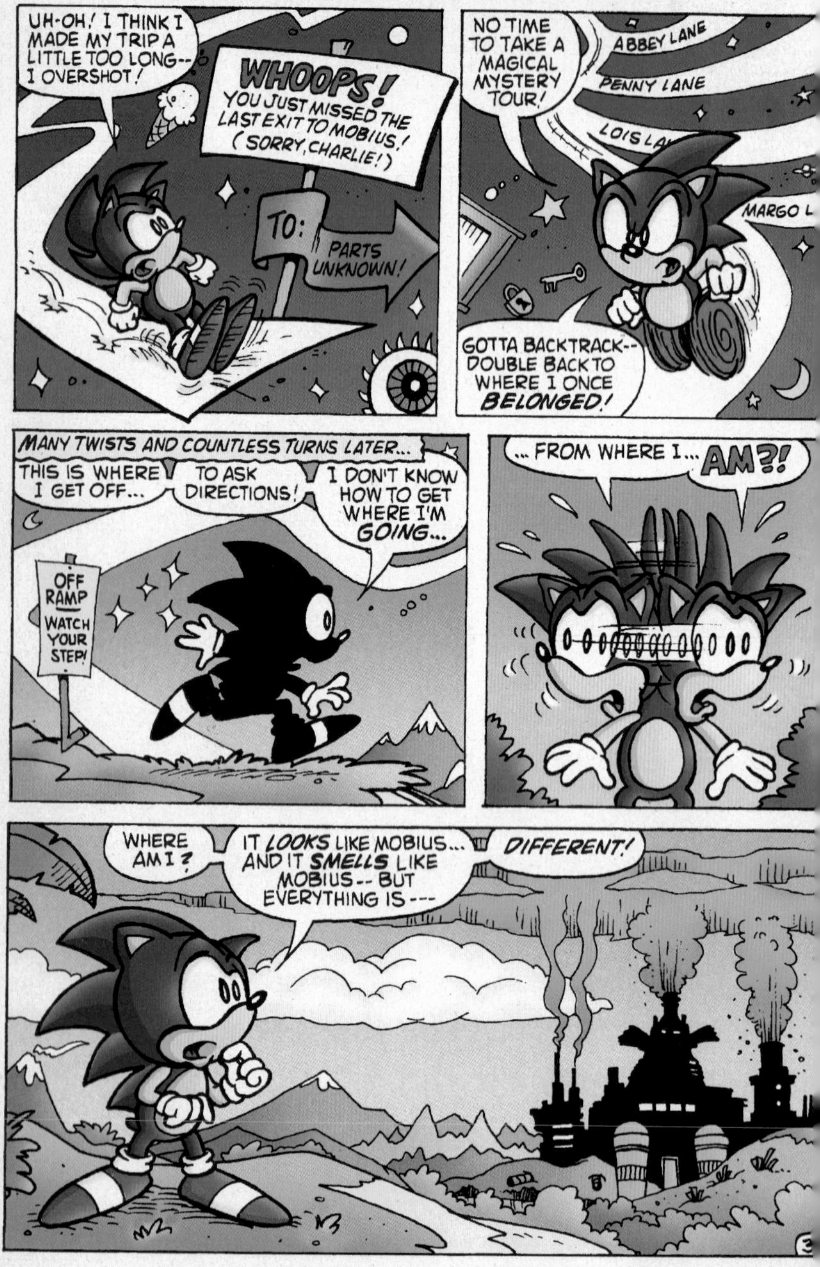
UH-OH! I THINK I MADE MY TRIP A LITTLE TOO LONG-- I OVERSHOT!
WHOOPS! YOU JUST MISSED THE LAST EXIT TO MOBIUS! (SORRY, CHARLIE!)
TO: PARTS UNKNOWN!
NO TIME TO TAKE A MAGICAL MYSTERY TOUR!
ABBEY LANE
PENNY LANE
GOTTA BACKTRACK-- DOUBLE BACK TO WHERE I ONCE BELONGED!
MANY TWISTS AND COUNTLESS TURNS LATER...
THIS IS WHERE I GET OFF...
TO ASK DIRECTIONS!
I DON'T KNOW HOW TO GET WHERE I'M GOING...
OFF RAMP
WATCH YOUR STEP!
... FROM WHERE I... AM?!
WHERE AM I?
IT LOOKS LIKE MOBIUS... AND IT SMELLS LIKE MOBIUS -- BUT EVERYTHING IS ---
DIFFERENT!

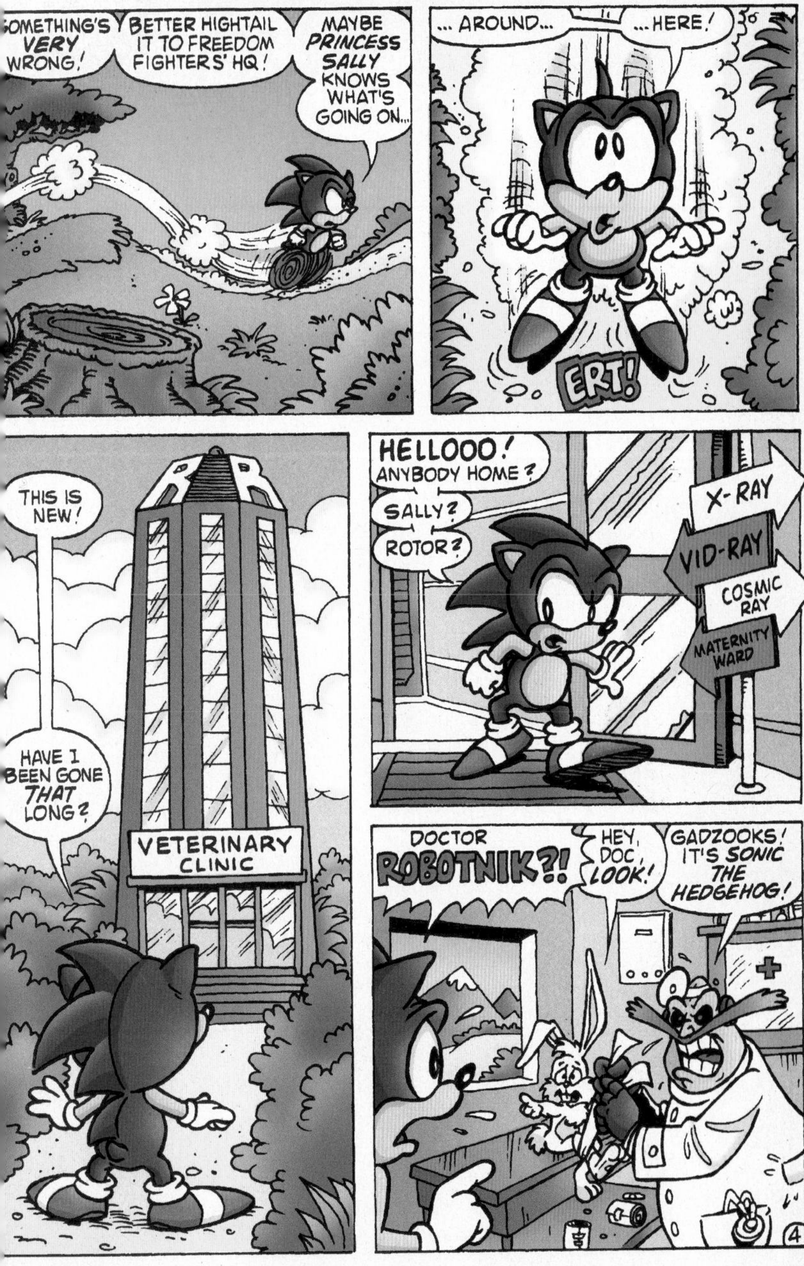

SOMETHING'S VERY WRONG!
BETTER HIGHTAIL IT TO FREEDOM FIGHTERS' HQ!
MAYBE PRINCESS SALLY KNOWS WHAT'S GOING ON...
... AROUND...
...HERE!
ERT!
THIS IS NEW!
HAVE I BEEN GONE THAT LONG?
VETERINARY CLINIC
HELLOOO! ANYBODY HOME?
SALLY?
ROTOR?
X-RAY
VID-RAY
COSMIC RAY
MATERNITY WARD
DOCTOR ROBOTNIK?!
HEY, DOC, LOOK!
GADZOOKS! IT'S SONIC THE HEDGEHOG!
4

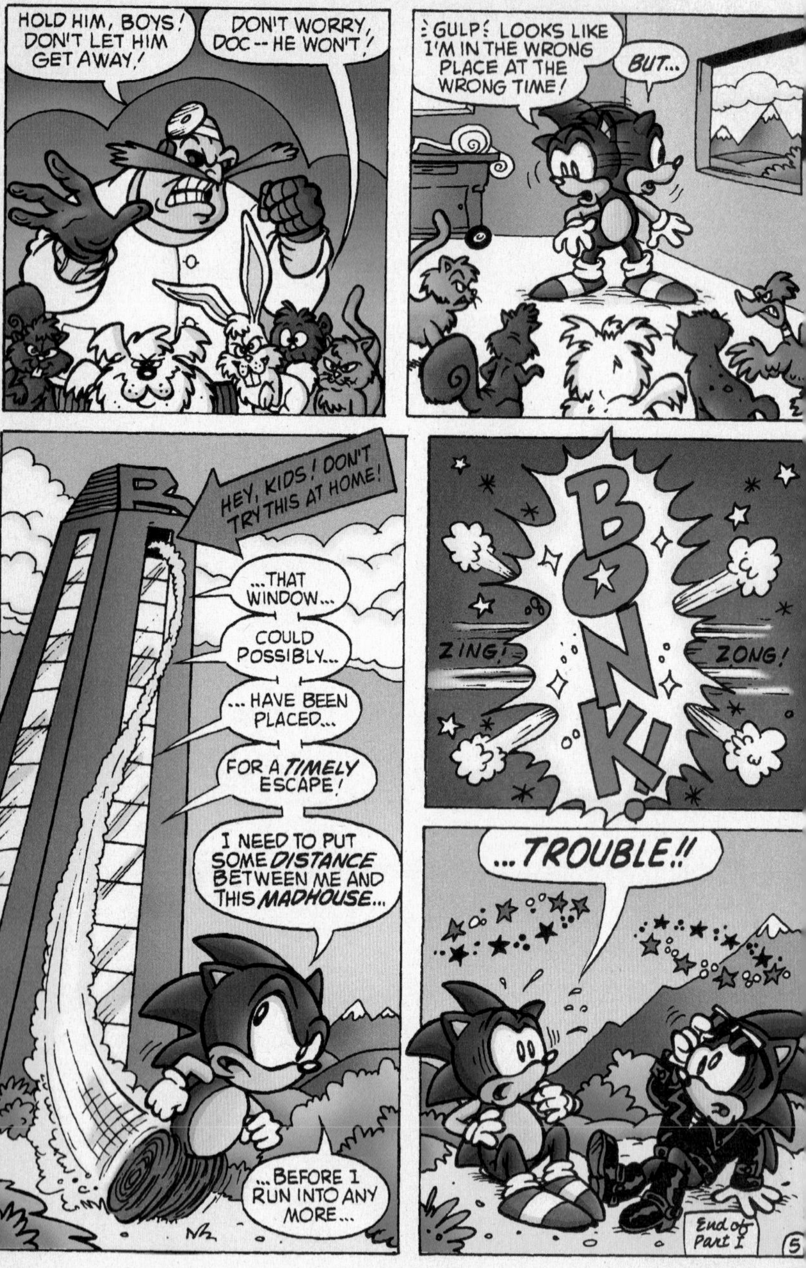
HOLD HIM, BOYS! DON'T LET HIM GET AWAY!
DON'T WORRY, DOC -- HE WON'T!
GULP! LOOKS LIKE I'M IN THE WRONG PLACE AT THE WRONG TIME!
BUT...
HEY, KIDS! DON'T TRY THIS AT HOME!
...THAT WINDOW...
COULD POSSIBLY...
... HAVE BEEN PLACED...
FOR A TIMELY ESCAPE!
I NEED TO PUT SOME DISTANCE BETWEEN ME AND THIS MADHOUSE...
...BEFORE I RUN INTO ANY MORE...
BONK!
ZING!
ZONG!
...TROUBLE!!
End of Part I

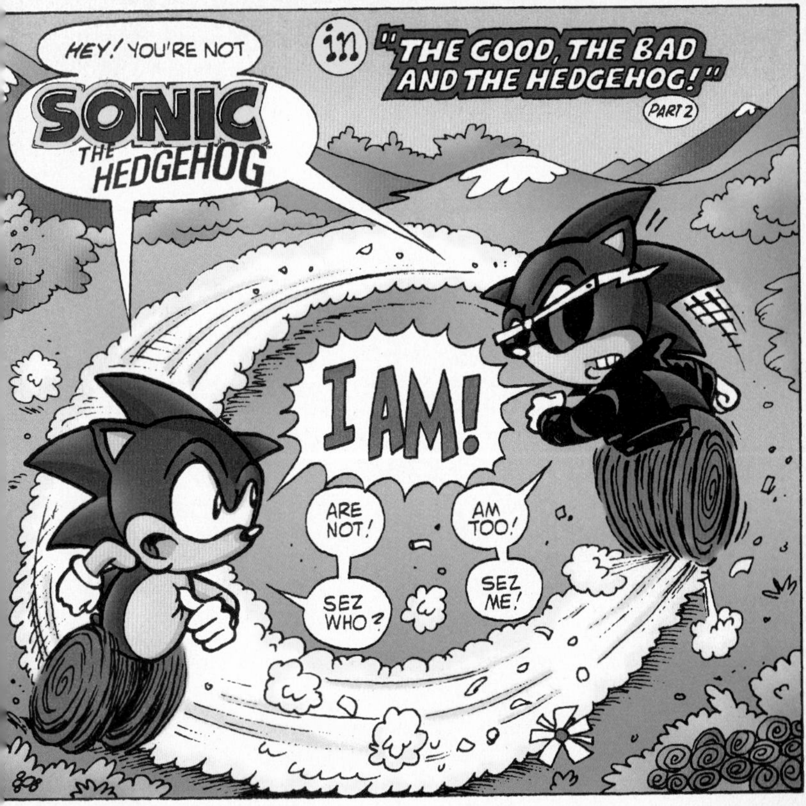
HEY! YOU'RE NOT
SONIC THE HEDGEHOG
in "THE GOOD, THE BAD AND THE HEDGEHOG!"
PART 2
I AM!
ARE NOT!
AM TOO!
SEZ WHO?
SEZ ME!

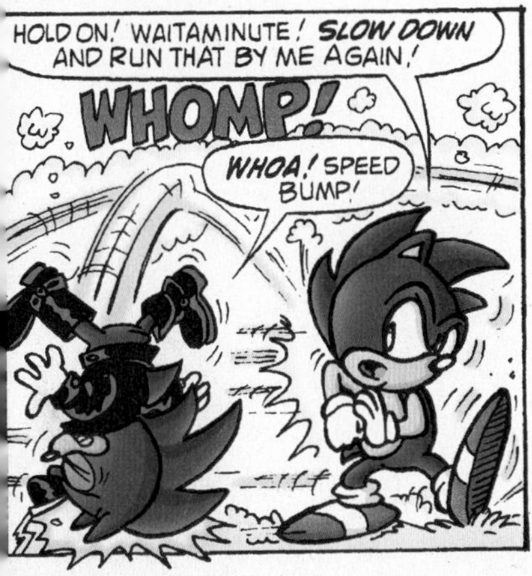
HOLD ON! WAITAMINUTE! SLOW DOWN AND RUN THAT BY ME AGAIN!
WHOMP!
WHOA! SPEED BUMP!

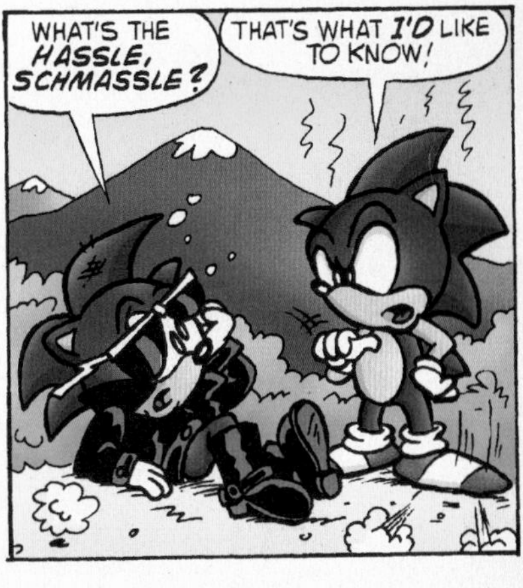
WHAT'S THE HASSLE, SCHMASSLE?
THAT'S WHAT I'D LIKE TO KNOW!

ONE WRONG TURN ON THE *COSMIC INTERSTATE,* AND SUDDENLY I'M BESIDE MYSELF!

COSMIC INTERSTATE?

I THINK I KNOW THE *DEAL,* SCHLEMIEL!

WAIT HERE!

WHOOSH!

I'LL DRAW YOU A *PICTURE!*

BUT IT *AIN'T* GONNA BE A VERY *PRETTY* ONE!

ZIP!

YOU CAN GET *ANYWHERE* FROM THE COSMIC INTERSTATE!

BUT IF YOU CROS THIS IMAGINAR LINE...

EVERY-

HERE

THERE

WHERE

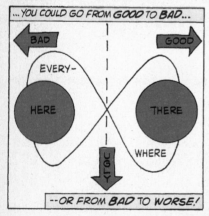

...YOU COULD GO FROM *GOOD* TO *BAD*...

BAD

GOOD

EVERY-

HERE

THERE

WHERE

UGLY

--OR FROM *BAD* TO *WORSE!*

COMPRENDE?

NO! I'M ALL *TURNED AROUND!*

EXACTLY! THAT'S MY POINT!

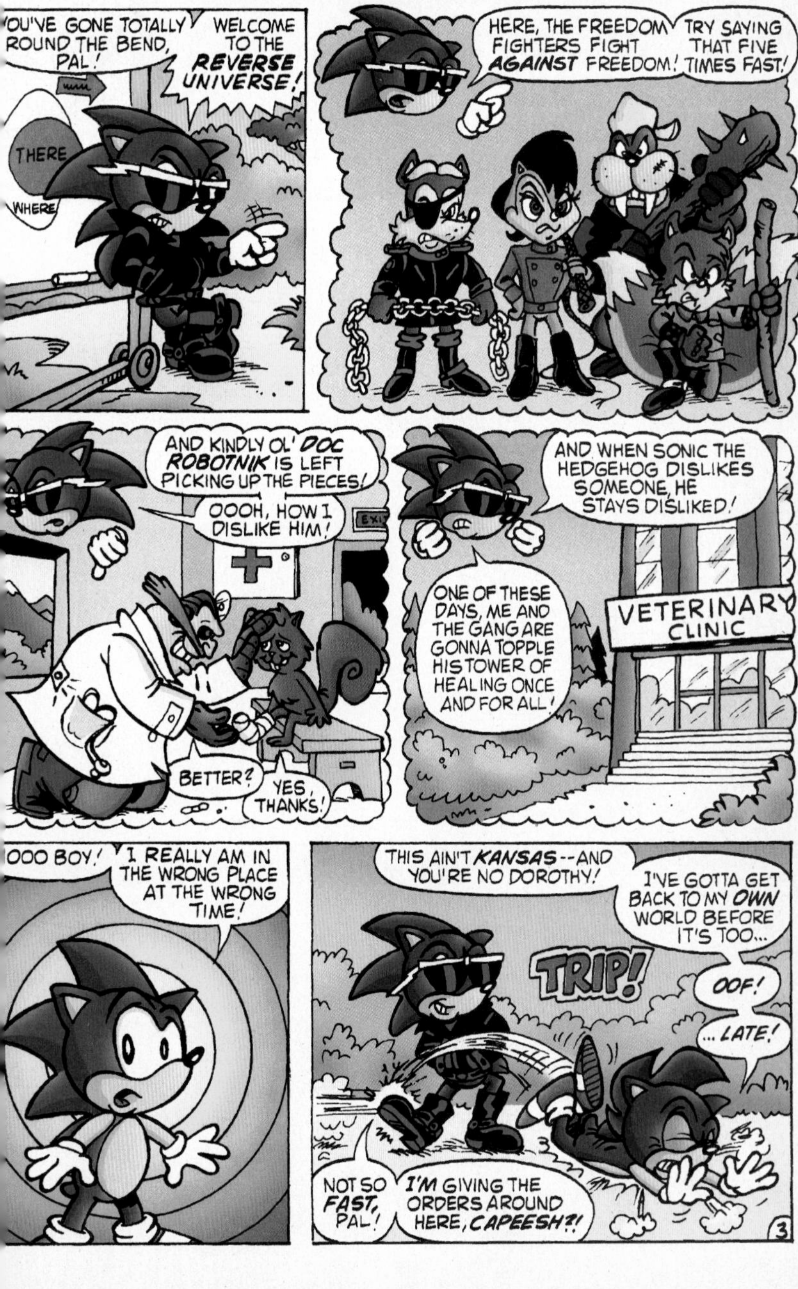

YOU'VE GONE TOTALLY ROUND THE BEND, PAL!
WELCOME TO THE REVERSE UNIVERSE!
THERE
WHERE
HERE, THE FREEDOM FIGHTERS FIGHT AGAINST FREEDOM!
TRY SAYING THAT FIVE TIMES FAST!
AND KINDLY OL' DOC ROBOTNIK IS LEFT PICKING UP THE PIECES!
OOOH, HOW I DISLIKE HIM!
BETTER?
YES, THANKS!
AND WHEN SONIC THE HEDGEHOG DISLIKES SOMEONE, HE STAYS DISLIKED!
ONE OF THESE DAYS, ME AND THE GANG ARE GONNA TOPPLE HIS TOWER OF HEALING ONCE AND FOR ALL!
VETERINARY CLINIC
OOO BOY!
I REALLY AM IN THE WRONG PLACE AT THE WRONG TIME!
THIS AIN'T KANSAS--AND YOU'RE NO DOROTHY!
I'VE GOTTA GET BACK TO MY OWN WORLD BEFORE IT'S TOO...
TRIP!
OOF!
...LATE!
NOT SO FAST, PAL!
I'M GIVING THE ORDERS AROUND HERE, CAPEESH?!

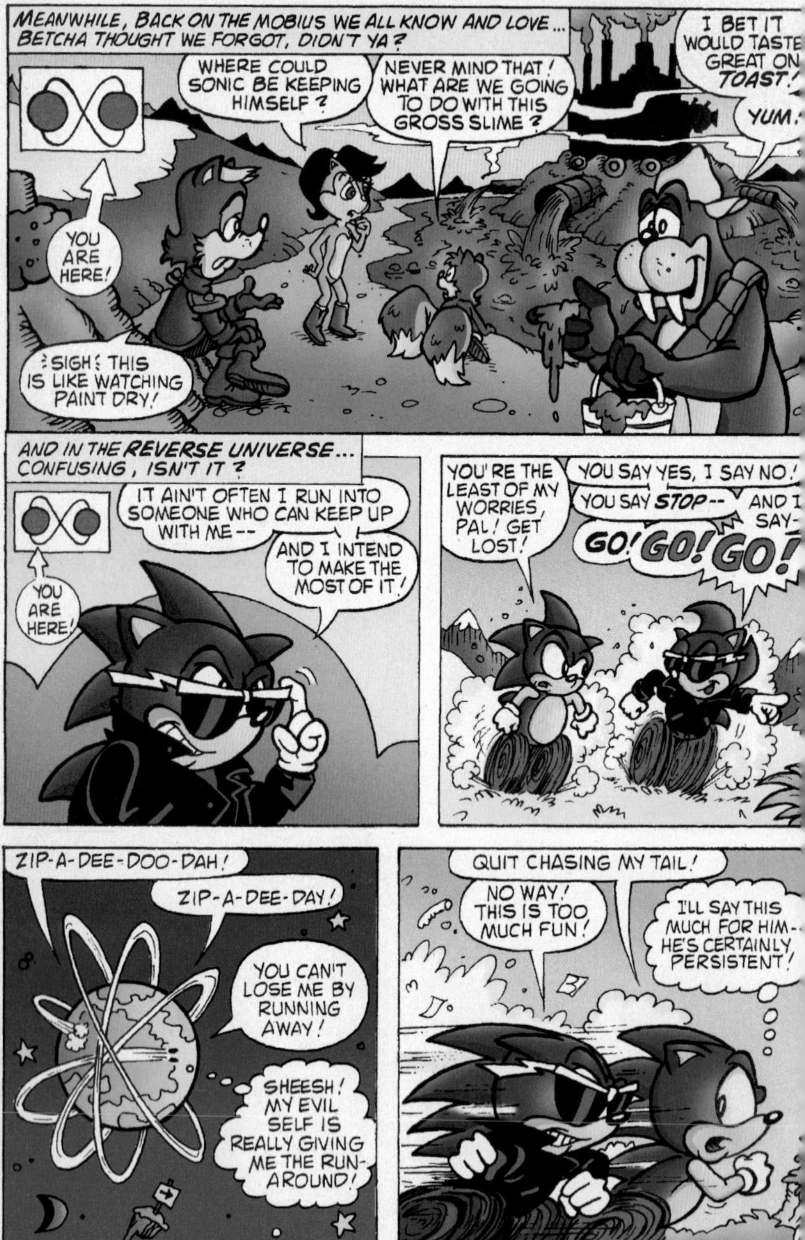
MEANWHILE, BACK ON THE MOBIUS WE ALL KNOW AND LOVE... BETCHA THOUGHT WE FORGOT, DIDN'T YA?
YOU ARE HERE!
WHERE COULD SONIC BE KEEPING HIMSELF?
NEVER MIND THAT! WHAT ARE WE GOING TO DO WITH THIS GROSS SLIME?
I BET IT WOULD TASTE GREAT ON TOAST!
YUM!
SIGH THIS IS LIKE WATCHING PAINT DRY!
AND IN THE REVERSE UNIVERSE... CONFUSING, ISN'T IT?
YOU ARE HERE!
IT AIN'T OFTEN I RUN INTO SOMEONE WHO CAN KEEP UP WITH ME--
AND I INTEND TO MAKE THE MOST OF IT!
YOU'RE THE LEAST OF MY WORRIES, PAL! GET LOST!
YOU SAY YES, I SAY NO!
YOU SAY STOP--
AND I SAY-
GO! GO! GO!
ZIP-A-DEE-DOO-DAH!
ZIP-A-DEE-DAY!
YOU CAN'T LOSE ME BY RUNNING AWAY!
SHEESH! MY EVIL SELF IS REALLY GIVING ME THE RUN-AROUND!
QUIT CHASING MY TAIL!
NO WAY! THIS IS TOO MUCH FUN!
I'LL SAY THIS MUCH FOR HIM--HE'S CERTAINLY PERSISTENT!

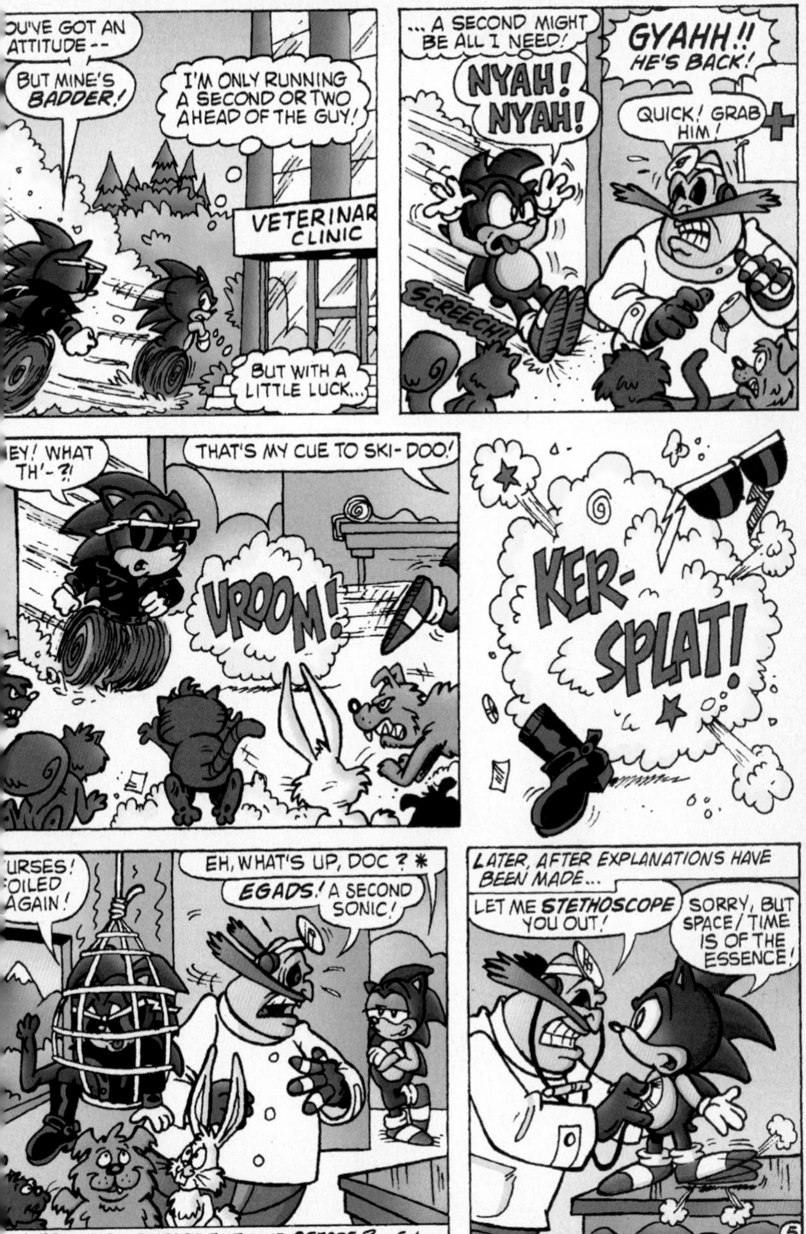
OU'VE GOT AN ATTITUDE --
BUT MINE'S BADDER!
I'M ONLY RUNNING A SECOND OR TWO AHEAD OF THE GUY!
VETERINAR CLINIC
BUT WITH A LITTLE LUCK...
... A SECOND MIGHT BE ALL I NEED!
NYAH! NYAH!
SCREECH!!
GYAHH!! HE'S BACK!
QUICK! GRAB HIM!
EY! WHAT TH'-?!
THAT'S MY CUE TO SKI-DOO!
VROOM!
KER-SPLAT!
URSES! OILED AGAIN!
EH, WHAT'S UP, DOC? *
EGADS! A SECOND SONIC!
* WHERE HAVE WE HEARD THAT LINE BEFORE? - Ed.
LATER, AFTER EXPLANATIONS HAVE BEEN MADE...
LET ME STETHOSCOPE YOU OUT!
SORRY, BUT SPACE/TIME IS OF THE ESSENCE!
5

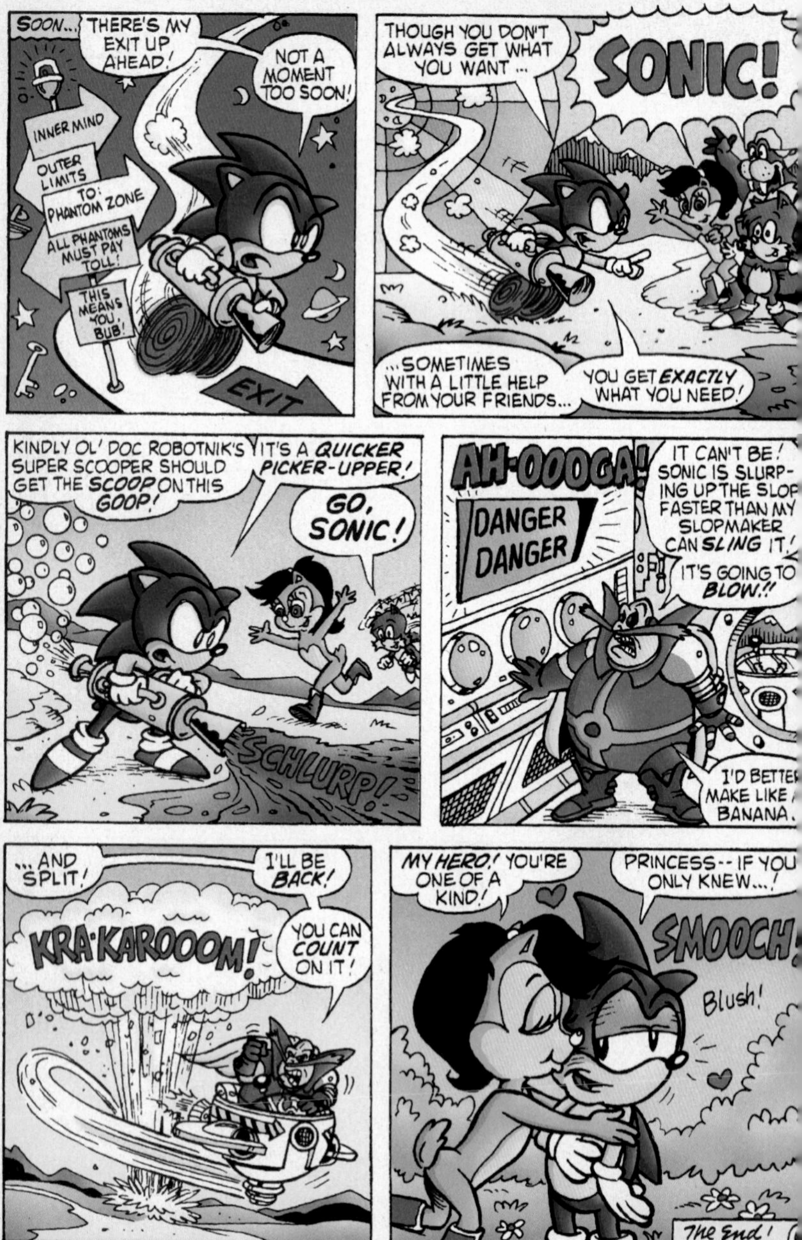

SOON...
THERE'S MY EXIT UP AHEAD!
NOT A MOMENT TOO SOON!
INNER MIND
OUTER LIMITS
TO: PHANTOM ZONE
ALL PHANTOMS MUST PAY TOLL!
THIS MEANS YOU, BUB!
EXIT
THOUGH YOU DON'T ALWAYS GET WHAT YOU WANT ...
SONIC!
...SOMETIMES WITH A LITTLE HELP FROM YOUR FRIENDS...
YOU GET EXACTLY WHAT YOU NEED!
KINDLY OL' DOC ROBOTNIK'S SUPER SCOOPER SHOULD GET THE SCOOP ON THIS GOOP!
IT'S A QUICKER PICKER-UPPER!
GO, SONIC!
SCHLURP!
AH-OOOGA!
DANGER DANGER
IT CAN'T BE! SONIC IS SLURPING UP THE SLOP FASTER THAN MY SLOPMAKER CAN SLING IT!
IT'S GOING TO BLOW!!
I'D BETTER MAKE LIKE A BANANA.
...AND SPLIT!
I'LL BE BACK!
KRA-KAROOOM!
YOU CAN COUNT ON IT!
MY HERO! YOU'RE ONE OF A KIND!
PRINCESS-- IF YOU ONLY KNEW...!
SMOOCH!
Blush!
The End!

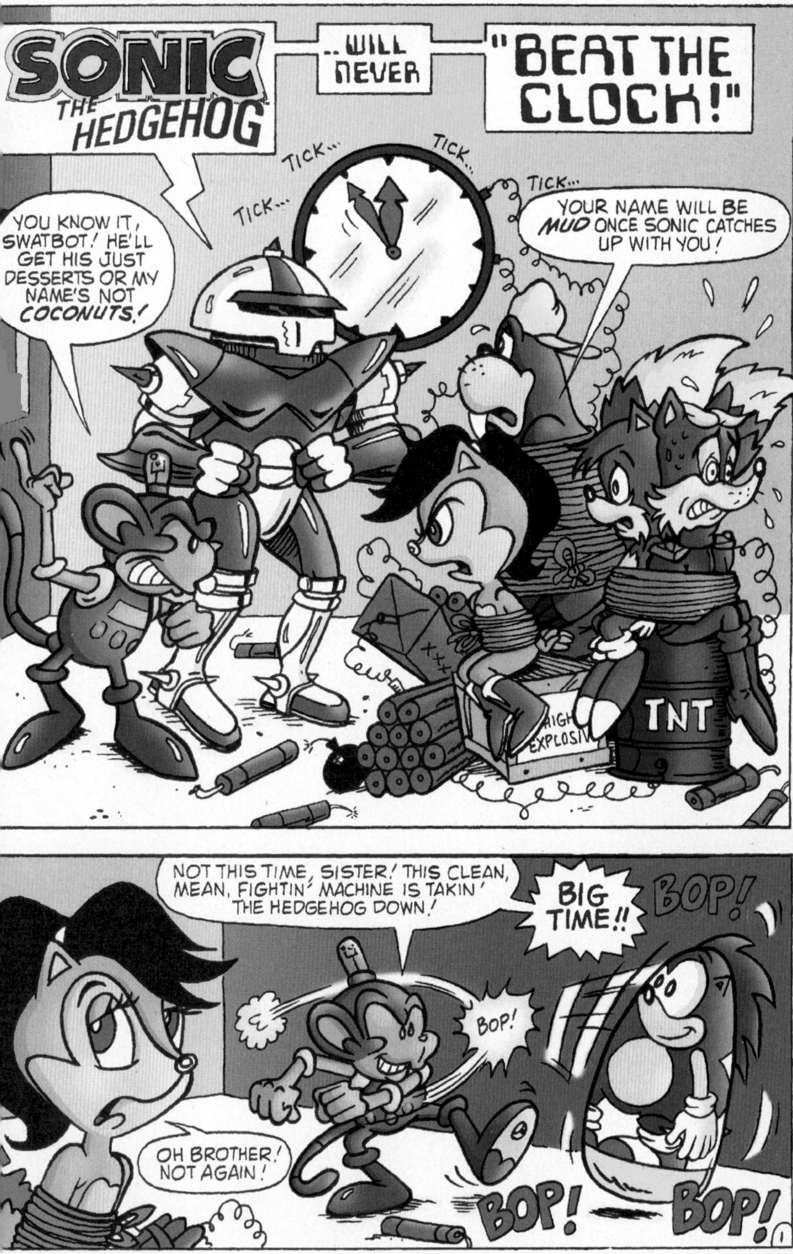
SONIC THE HEDGEHOG
...WILL NEVER
"BEAT THE CLOCK!"
TICK... TICK... TICK... TICK...
YOU KNOW IT, SWATBOT! HE'LL GET HIS JUST DESSERTS OR MY NAME'S NOT COCONUTS!
YOUR NAME WILL BE MUD ONCE SONIC CATCHES UP WITH YOU!
TNT
HIGH EXPLOSIV
NOT THIS TIME, SISTER! THIS CLEAN, MEAN, FIGHTIN' MACHINE IS TAKIN' THE HEDGEHOG DOWN!
BIG TIME!!
BOP!
BOP!
OH BROTHER! NOT AGAIN!
BOP!
BOP!

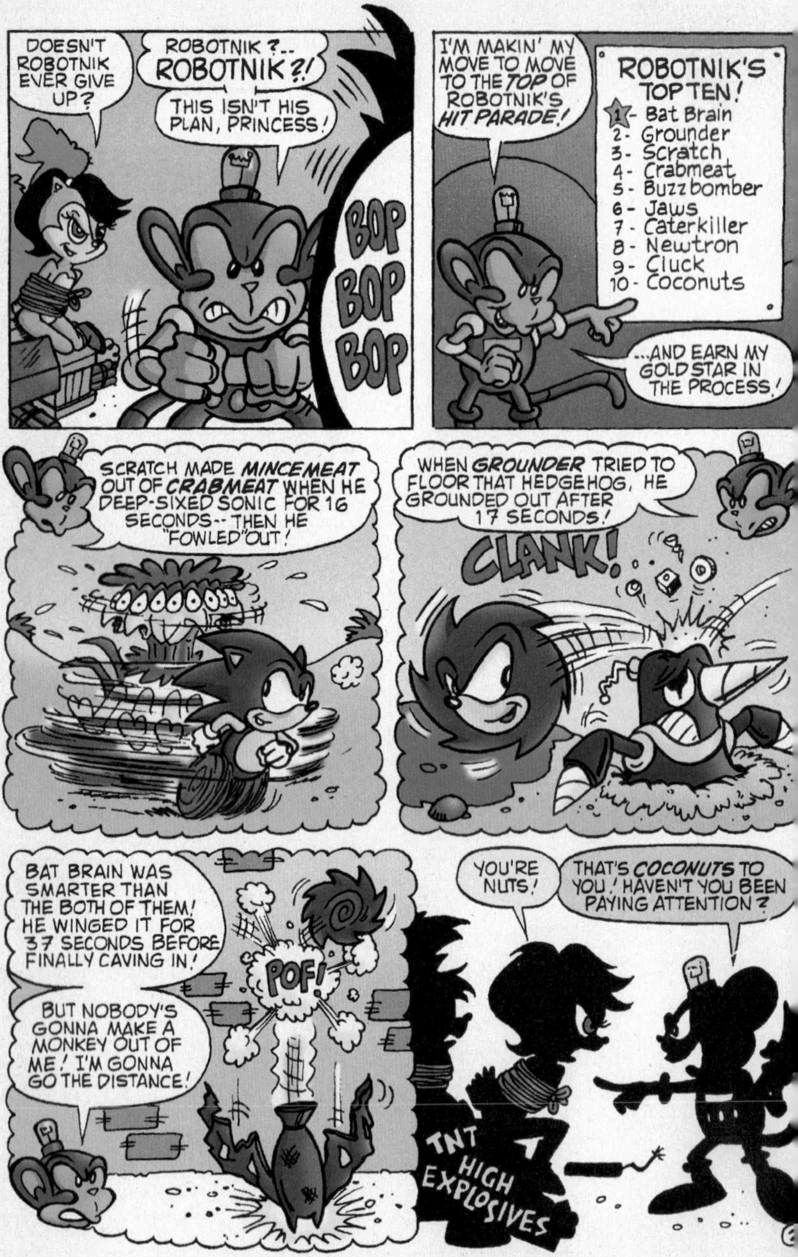
DOESN'T ROBOTNIK EVER GIVE UP?
ROBOTNIK ?.. ROBOTNIK ?!
THIS ISN'T HIS PLAN, PRINCESS!
BOP BOP BOP
I'M MAKIN' MY MOVE TO MOVE TO THE TOP OF ROBOTNIK'S HIT PARADE!
ROBOTNIK'S TOP TEN!
1 - Bat Brain
2 - Grounder
3 - Scratch
4 - Crabmeat
5 - Buzzbomber
6 - Jaws
7 - Caterkiller
8 - Newtron
9 - Cluck
10 - Coconuts
...AND EARN MY GOLD STAR IN THE PROCESS!
SCRATCH MADE MINCEMEAT OUT OF CRABMEAT WHEN HE DEEP-SIXED SONIC FOR 16 SECONDS-- THEN HE "FOWLED" OUT!
WHEN GROUNDER TRIED TO FLOOR THAT HEDGEHOG, HE GROUNDED OUT AFTER 17 SECONDS!
CLANK!
BAT BRAIN WAS SMARTER THAN THE BOTH OF THEM! HE WINGED IT FOR 37 SECONDS BEFORE FINALLY CAVING IN!
BUT NOBODY'S GONNA MAKE A MONKEY OUT OF ME! I'M GONNA GO THE DISTANCE!
POF!
YOU'RE NUTS!
THAT'S COCONUTS TO YOU! HAVEN'T YOU BEEN PAYING ATTENTION?
TNT HIGH EXPLOSIVES

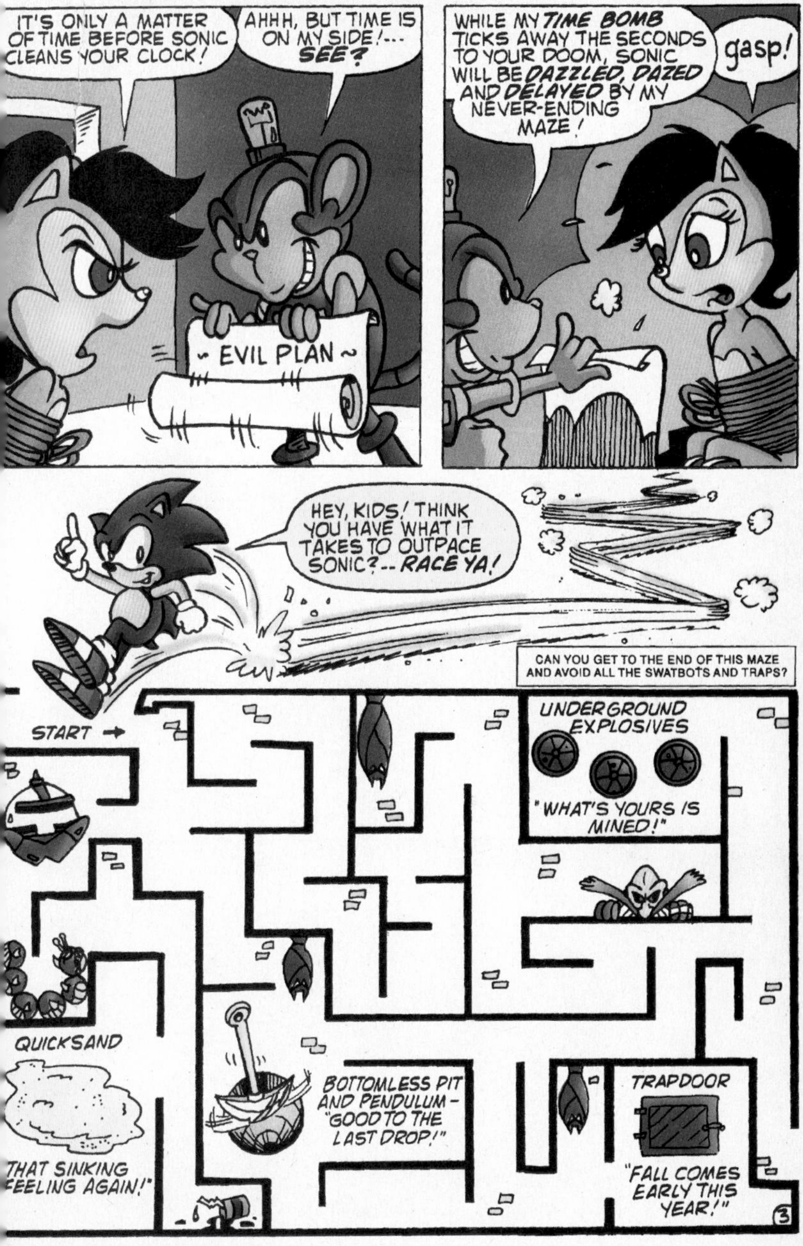
IT'S ONLY A MATTER OF TIME BEFORE SONIC CLEANS YOUR CLOCK!
AHHH, BUT TIME IS ON MY SIDE!-- SEE?
EVIL PLAN
WHILE MY TIME BOMB TICKS AWAY THE SECONDS TO YOUR DOOM, SONIC WILL BE DAZZLED, DAZED AND DELAYED BY MY NEVER-ENDING MAZE!
gasp!
HEY, KIDS! THINK YOU HAVE WHAT IT TAKES TO OUTPACE SONIC?-- RACE YA!
CAN YOU GET TO THE END OF THIS MAZE AND AVOID ALL THE SWATBOTS AND TRAPS?
START →
UNDERGROUND EXPLOSIVES
"WHAT'S YOURS IS MINED!"
QUICKSAND
THAT SINKING FEELING AGAIN!"
BOTTOMLESS PIT AND PENDULUM - "GOOD TO THE LAST DROP!"
TRAPDOOR
"FALL COMES EARLY THIS YEAR!"

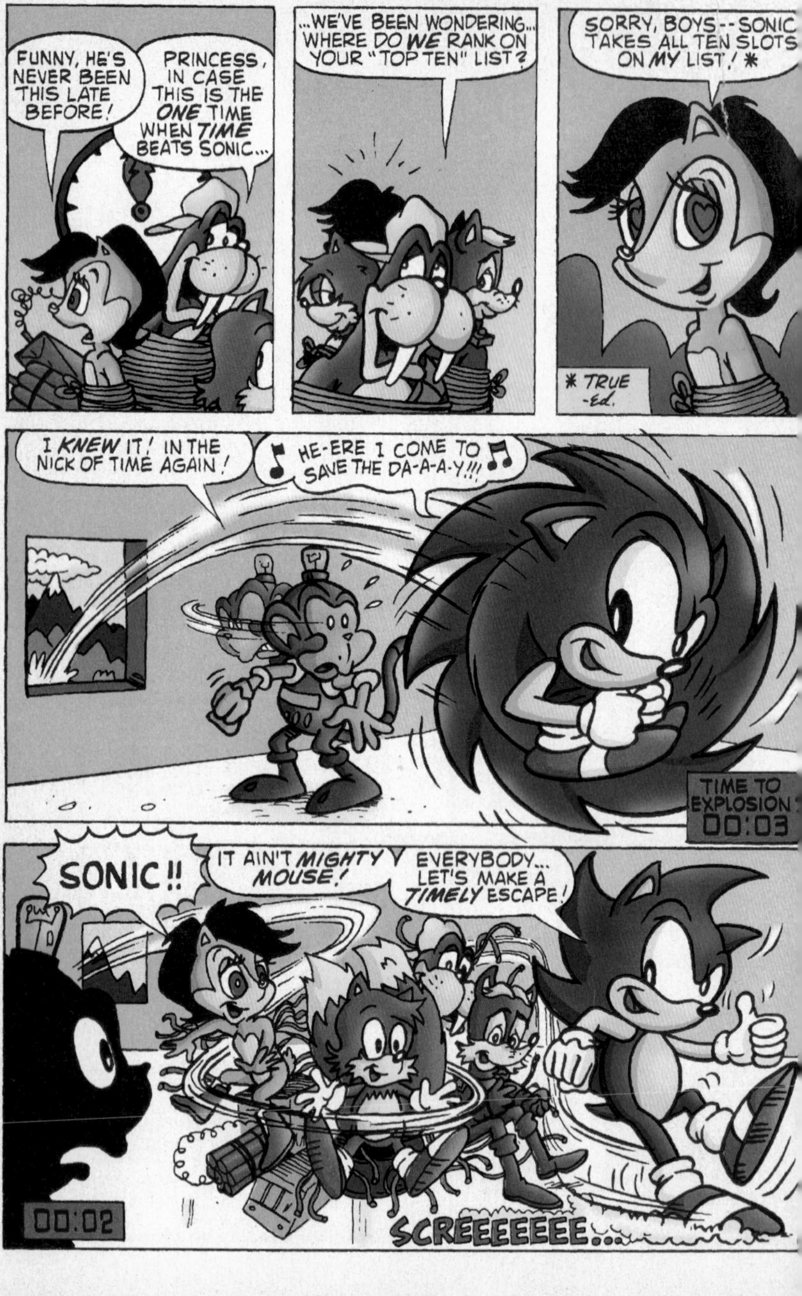
FUNNY, HE'S NEVER BEEN THIS LATE BEFORE!
PRINCESS, IN CASE THIS IS THE ONE TIME WHEN TIME BEATS SONIC...
...WE'VE BEEN WONDERING... WHERE DO WE RANK ON YOUR "TOP TEN" LIST?
SORRY, BOYS--SONIC TAKES ALL TEN SLOTS ON MY LIST! *
* TRUE -Ed.
I KNEW IT! IN THE NICK OF TIME AGAIN!
HE-ERE I COME TO SAVE THE DA-A-A-Y!!!
TIME TO EXPLOSION
00:03
SONIC!!
IT AIN'T MIGHTY MOUSE!
EVERYBODY... LET'S MAKE A TIMELY ESCAPE!
00:02
SCREEEEEEEE...

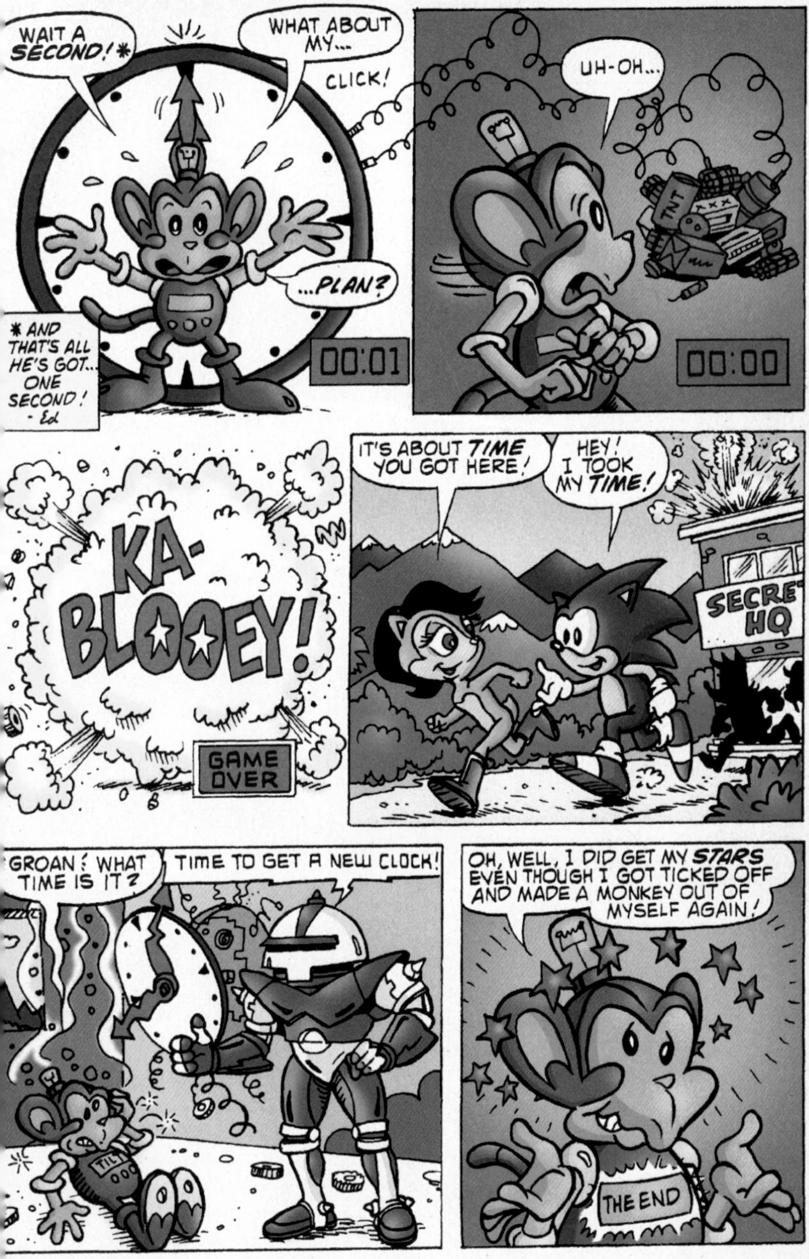
WAIT A SECOND! *
WHAT ABOUT MY...
CLICK!
...PLAN?
* AND THAT'S ALL HE'S GOT... ONE SECOND! - Ed
00:01
UH-OH...
TNT
00:00
KA-BLOOEY!
GAME OVER
IT'S ABOUT TIME YOU GOT HERE!
HEY! I TOOK MY TIME!
SECRE HQ
GROAN! WHAT TIME IS IT?
TIME TO GET A NEW CLOCK!
TILT
OH, WELL, I DID GET MY STARS EVEN THOUGH I GOT TICKED OFF AND MADE A MONKEY OUT OF MYSELF AGAIN!
THE END

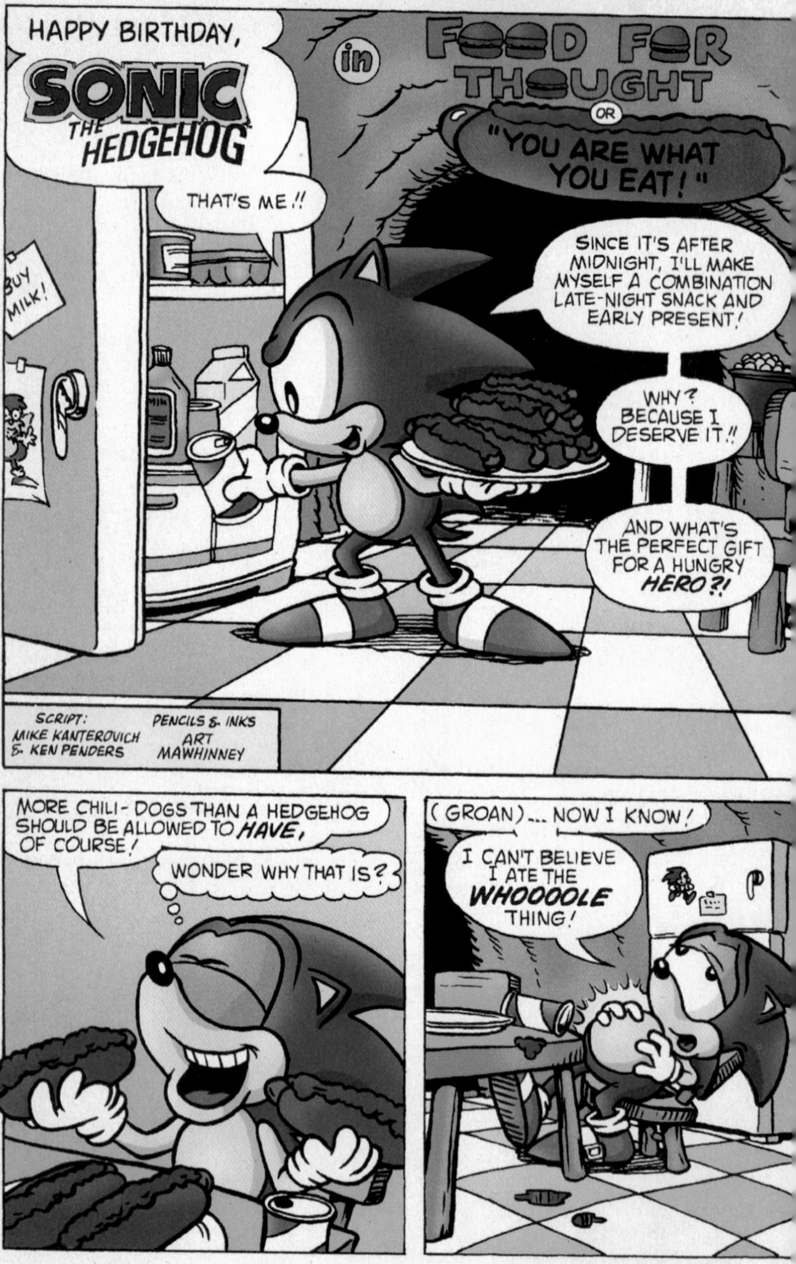
HAPPY BIRTHDAY,
SONIC THE HEDGEHOG
in
FOOD FOR THOUGHT
OR
"YOU ARE WHAT YOU EAT!"
THAT'S ME!!
BUY MILK!
SINCE IT'S AFTER MIDNIGHT, I'LL MAKE MYSELF A COMBINATION LATE-NIGHT SNACK AND EARLY PRESENT!
WHY? BECAUSE I DESERVE IT!!
AND WHAT'S THE PERFECT GIFT FOR A HUNGRY HERO?!
SCRIPT: MIKE KANTEROVICH & KEN PENDERS
PENCILS & INKS ART MAWHINNEY
MORE CHILI-DOGS THAN A HEDGEHOG SHOULD BE ALLOWED TO HAVE, OF COURSE!
WONDER WHY THAT IS?
(GROAN)... NOW I KNOW!
I CAN'T BELIEVE I ATE THE WHOOOOLE THING!

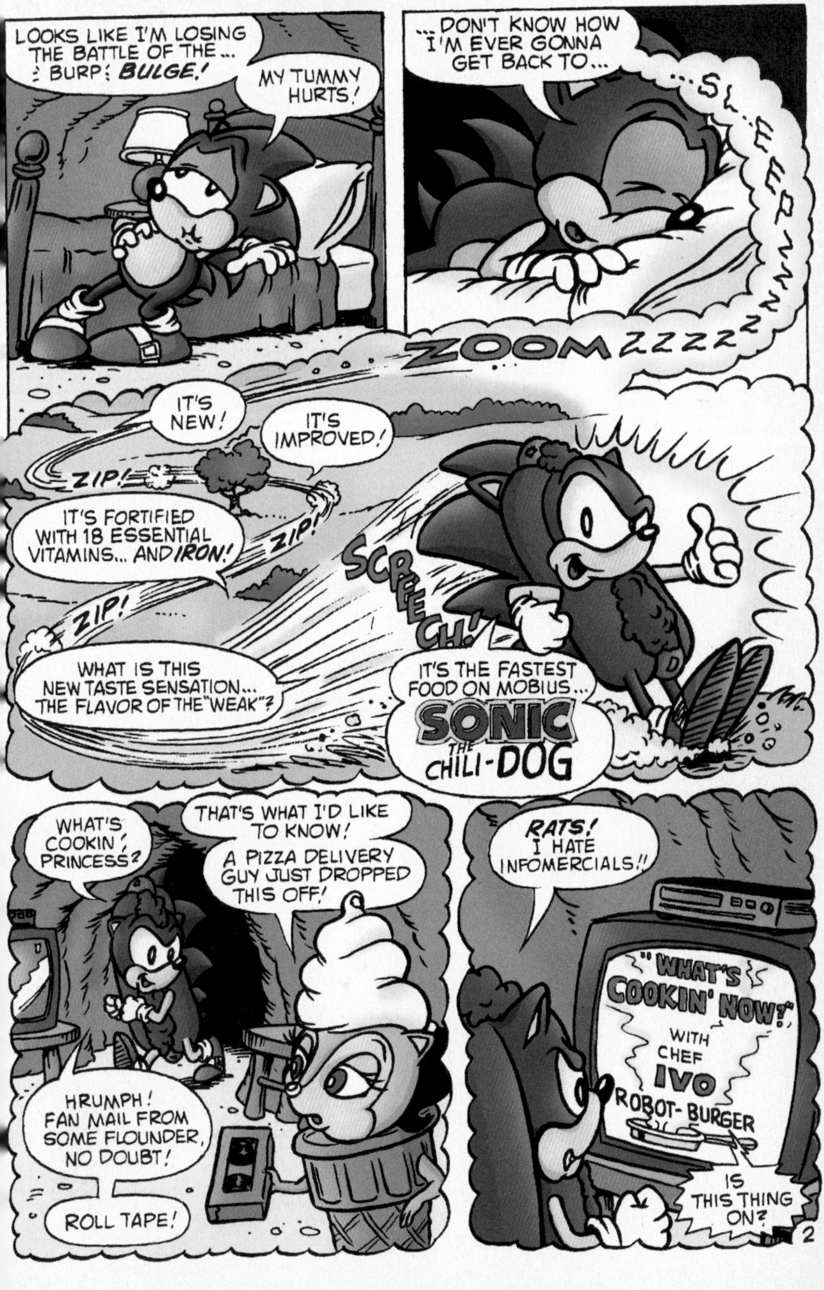
LOOKS LIKE I'M LOSING THE BATTLE OF THE... ⁝ BURP ⁝ BULGE!
MY TUMMY HURTS!
... DON'T KNOW HOW I'M EVER GONNA GET BACK TO...
...SL...EEPZZZ
ZOOM ZZZZZ
IT'S NEW!
IT'S IMPROVED!
ZIP!
IT'S FORTIFIED WITH 18 ESSENTIAL VITAMINS... AND IRON!
ZIP!
SCREECH!
ZIP!
WHAT IS THIS NEW TASTE SENSATION... THE FLAVOR OF THE "WEAK"?
IT'S THE FASTEST FOOD ON MOBIUS... SONIC THE CHILI-DOG
WHAT'S COOKIN', PRINCESS?
THAT'S WHAT I'D LIKE TO KNOW!
A PIZZA DELIVERY GUY JUST DROPPED THIS OFF!
HRUMPH! FAN MAIL FROM SOME FLOUNDER, NO DOUBT!
ROLL TAPE!
RATS! I HATE INFOMERCIALS!!
"WHAT'S COOKIN' NOW?" WITH CHEF IVO
ROBOT-BURGER
IS THIS THING ON?

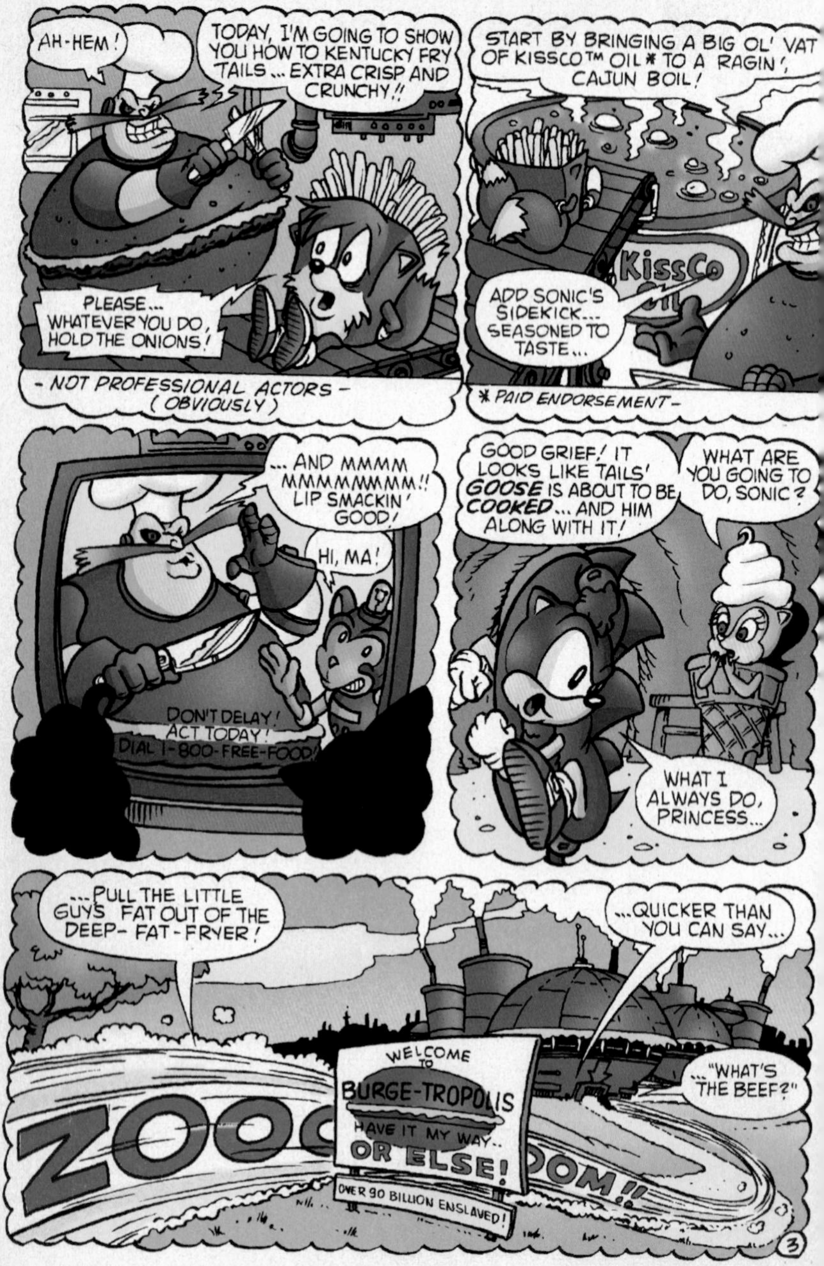
AH-HEM!
TODAY, I'M GOING TO SHOW YOU HOW TO KENTUCKY FRY TAILS... EXTRA CRISP AND CRUNCHY!!
PLEASE... WHATEVER YOU DO, HOLD THE ONIONS!
- NOT PROFESSIONAL ACTORS - (OBVIOUSLY)
START BY BRINGING A BIG OL' VAT OF KISSCO™ OIL * TO A RAGIN', CAJUN BOIL!
KissCo
ADD SONIC'S SIDEKICK... SEASONED TO TASTE...
* PAID ENDORSEMENT -
... AND MMMM MMMMMMMM!! LIP SMACKIN' GOOD!
HI, MA!
DON'T DELAY! ACT TODAY! DIAL 1-800-FREE-FOOD!
GOOD GRIEF! IT LOOKS LIKE TAILS' GOOSE IS ABOUT TO BE COOKED... AND HIM ALONG WITH IT!
WHAT ARE YOU GOING TO DO, SONIC?
WHAT I ALWAYS DO, PRINCESS...
...PULL THE LITTLE GUY'S FAT OUT OF THE DEEP-FAT-FRYER!
...QUICKER THAN YOU CAN SAY...
..."WHAT'S THE BEEF?"
WELCOME TO BURGE-TROPOLIS
HAVE IT MY WAY.. OR ELSE!
OVER 90 BILLION ENSLAVED!
ZOO
OOM!!

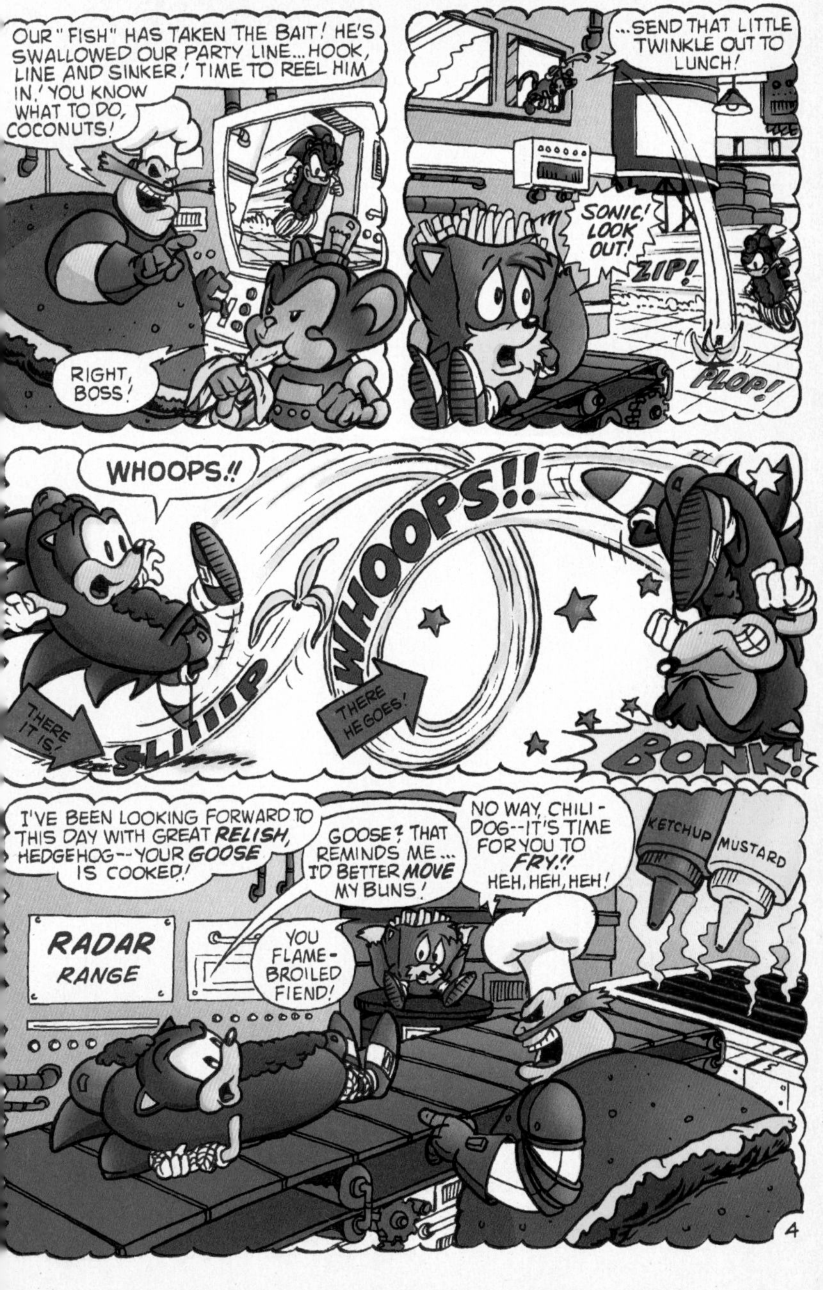
OUR "FISH" HAS TAKEN THE BAIT! HE'S SWALLOWED OUR PARTY LINE... HOOK, LINE AND SINKER! TIME TO REEL HIM IN! YOU KNOW WHAT TO DO, COCONUTS!
RIGHT, BOSS!
...SEND THAT LITTLE TWINKLE OUT TO LUNCH!
SONIC! LOOK OUT!
ZIP!
PLOP!
WHOOPS!!
WHOOPS!!
THERE IT IS!
SLIIIIP
THERE HE GOES!
BONK!
I'VE BEEN LOOKING FORWARD TO THIS DAY WITH GREAT RELISH, HEDGEHOG--YOUR GOOSE IS COOKED!
GOOSE? THAT REMINDS ME... I'D BETTER MOVE MY BUNS!
NO WAY, CHILI-DOG--IT'S TIME FOR YOU TO FRY!! HEH, HEH, HEH!
KETCHUP
MUSTARD
RADAR RANGE
YOU FLAME-BROILED FIEND!

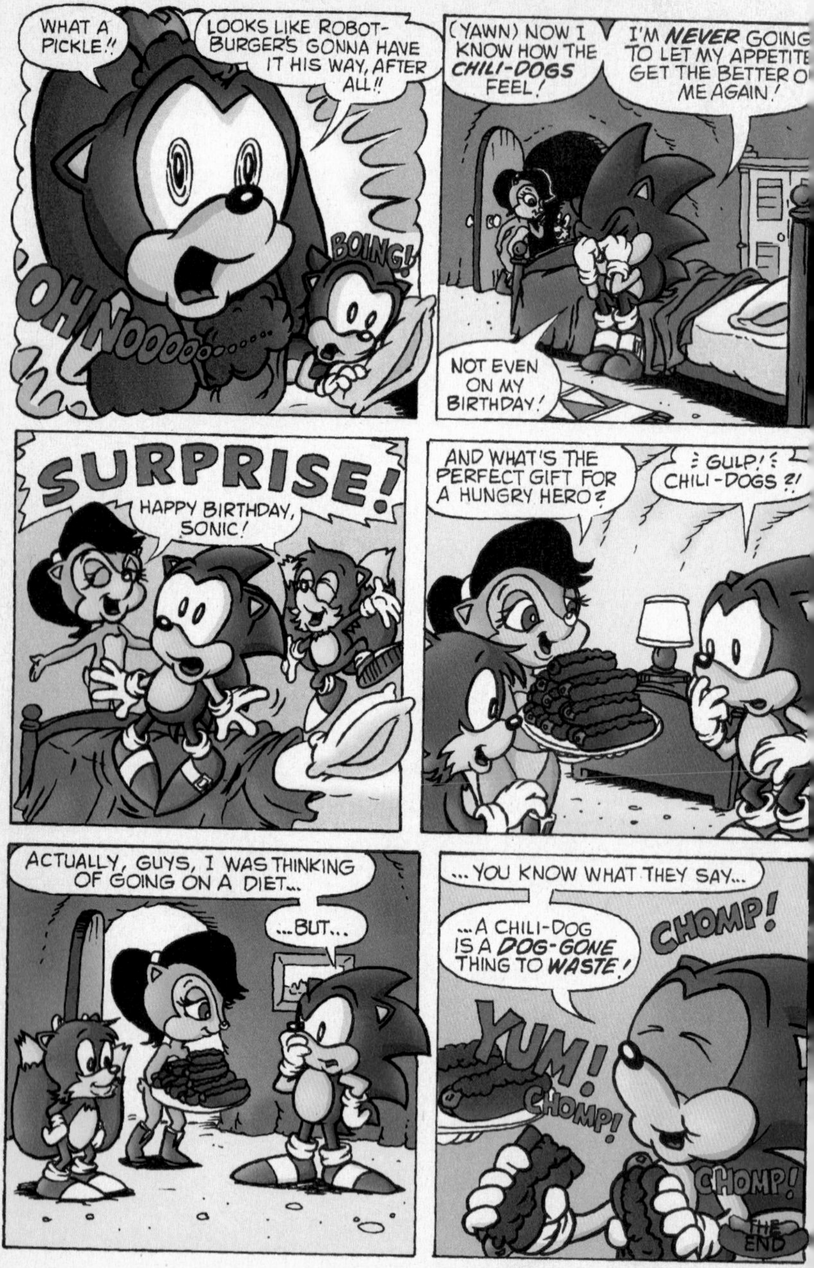
WHAT A PICKLE!!
LOOKS LIKE ROBOT-BURGER'S GONNA HAVE IT HIS WAY, AFTER ALL!!
OH NOOOOoo.......
BOING!
(YAWN) NOW I KNOW HOW THE CHILI-DOGS FEEL!
I'M NEVER GOING TO LET MY APPETITE GET THE BETTER OF ME AGAIN!
NOT EVEN ON MY BIRTHDAY!
SURPRISE!
HAPPY BIRTHDAY, SONIC!
AND WHAT'S THE PERFECT GIFT FOR A HUNGRY HERO?
GULP! CHILI-DOGS ?!
ACTUALLY, GUYS, I WAS THINKING OF GOING ON A DIET...
...BUT...
... YOU KNOW WHAT THEY SAY...
...A CHILI-DOG IS A DOG-GONE THING TO WASTE!
CHOMP!
YUM!
CHOMP!
CHOMP!
THE END

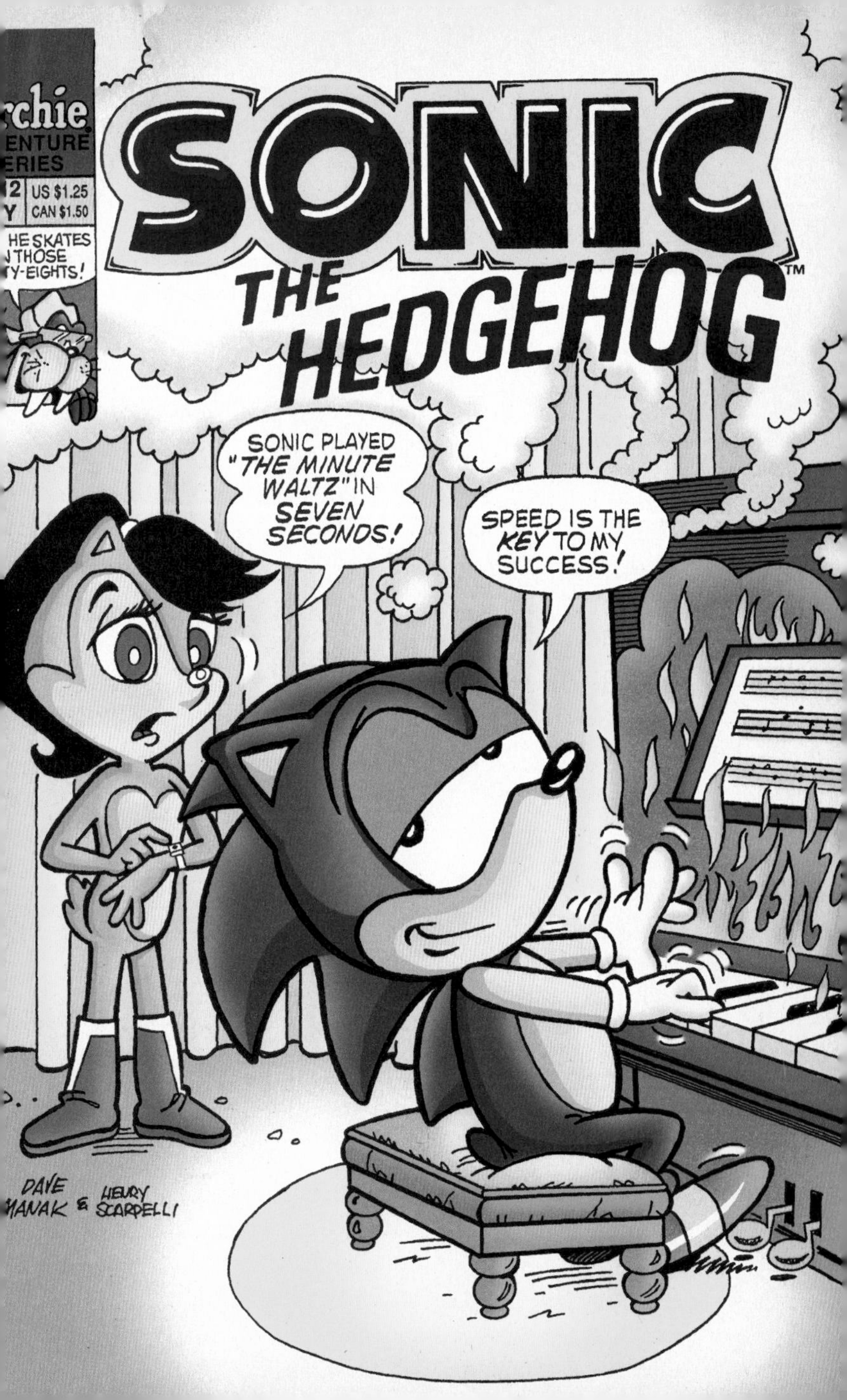

rchie
ENTURE
ERIES
US $1.25
CAN $1.50
HE SKATES
THOSE
TY-EIGHTS!
SONIC
THE HEDGEHOG™
SONIC PLAYED "THE MINUTE WALTZ" IN SEVEN SECONDS!
SPEED IS THE KEY TO MY SUCCESS!
DAVE
MANAK & HENRY SCARPELLI

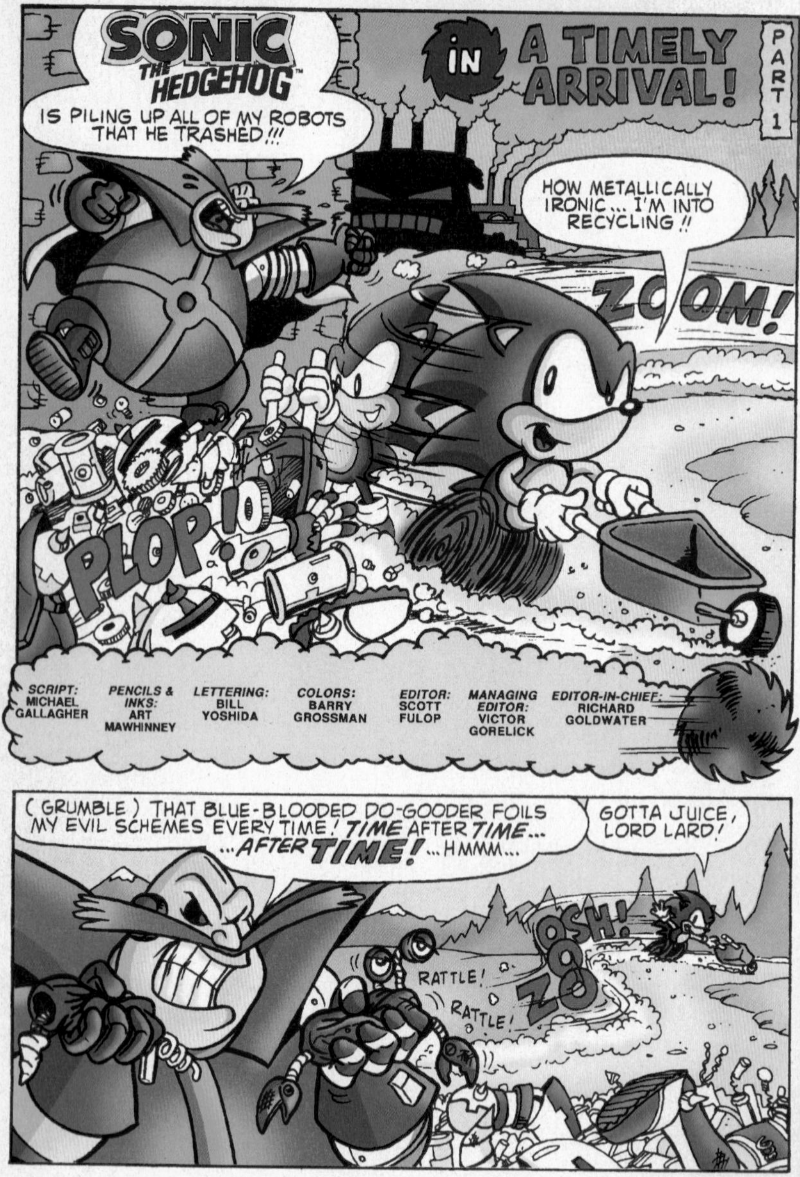
SONIC THE HEDGEHOG™
IS PILING UP ALL OF MY ROBOTS THAT HE TRASHED!!!
IN A TIMELY ARRIVAL!
PART 1
HOW METALLICALLY IRONIC... I'M INTO RECYCLING!!
ZOOM!
PLOP!
SCRIPT: MICHAEL GALLAGHER
PENCILS & INKS: ART MAWHINNEY
LETTERING: BILL YOSHIDA
COLORS: BARRY GROSSMAN
EDITOR: SCOTT FULOP
MANAGING EDITOR: VICTOR GORELICK
EDITOR-IN-CHIEF: RICHARD GOLDWATER
(GRUMBLE) THAT BLUE-BLOODED DO-GOODER FOILS MY EVIL SCHEMES EVERY TIME! TIME AFTER TIME... ...AFTER TIME! ...HMMM...
GOTTA JUICE, LORD LARD!
ZOOSH!
RATTLE! RATTLE!

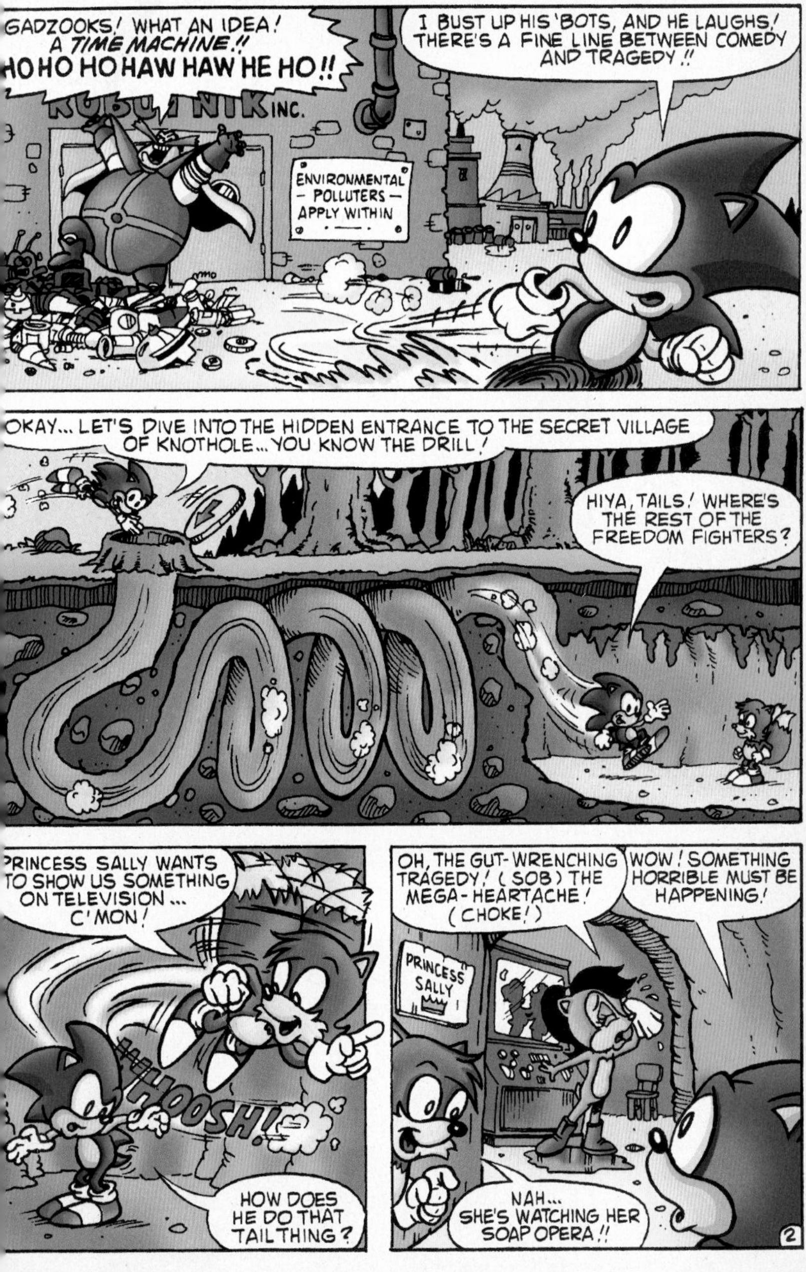
GADZOOKS! WHAT AN IDEA! A TIME MACHINE!! HO HO HO HAW HAW HE HO!!
I BUST UP HIS 'BOTS, AND HE LAUGHS! THERE'S A FINE LINE BETWEEN COMEDY AND TRAGEDY!!
INC.
ENVIRONMENTAL — POLLUTERS — APPLY WITHIN
OKAY... LET'S DIVE INTO THE HIDDEN ENTRANCE TO THE SECRET VILLAGE OF KNOTHOLE... YOU KNOW THE DRILL!
HIYA, TAILS! WHERE'S THE REST OF THE FREEDOM FIGHTERS?
PRINCESS SALLY WANTS TO SHOW US SOMETHING ON TELEVISION ... C'MON!
WHOOSH!
HOW DOES HE DO THAT TAIL THING?
OH, THE GUT-WRENCHING TRAGEDY! (SOB) THE MEGA-HEARTACHE! (CHOKE!)
WOW! SOMETHING HORRIBLE MUST BE HAPPENING!
PRINCESS SALLY
NAH... SHE'S WATCHING HER SOAP OPERA!!

OH, HI, SONIC! I... ...ER...WAS JUST ABOUT TO TURN ON THE NEWS!

SUUUUURE YOU WERE!

RBV* NEWS

HOSTED BY SWATBOT #2176

CLICK!

*ROBOTNIK BELLY-VISION - Ed

GOOD DAY! OUR LUMPY LEADER IVO ROBOTNIK HAS JUST UNVEILED HIS LATEST INVENTION... THE MOBILE MONSTER CHAINSAW!!

INDEED!!

WATCH HOW EASILY IT MOWS DOWN THE GREAT FOREST! IT WOOD CLEAR (Snicker) FIFTY ACRES PER MINUTE!!

BUZZZ WAAAA!

OMIGOSH... DON'T LOOK, KID!!

?

GASP!

AND NOW... THE WEATHER...

I ALREADY KNOW WHAT THE TEMPERATURE IS... MY BOILING POINT!!!

SONIC... WAIT!!

TOO LATE... BIG BLUE IS BRIGHT RED!!

NEEE

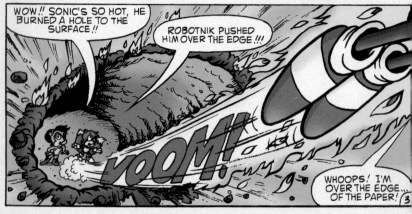

WOW!! SONIC'S SO HOT, HE BURNED A HOLE TO THE SURFACE!!

ROBOTNIK PUSHED HIM OVER THE EDGE!!!

VOOM!

WHOOPS! I'M OVER THE EDGE... OF THE PAPER!

3

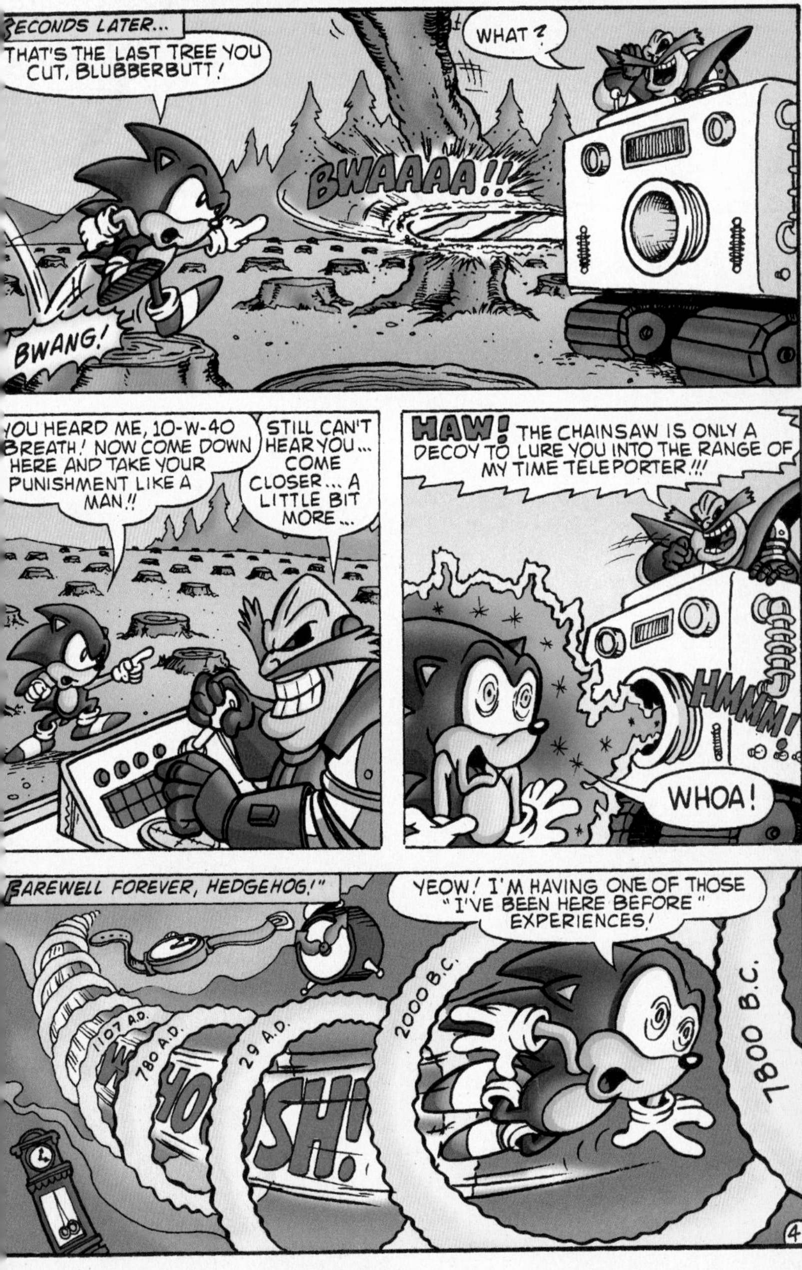
SECONDS LATER...
THAT'S THE LAST TREE YOU CUT, BLUBBERBUTT!
WHAT?
BWAAAA!!
BWANG!
YOU HEARD ME, 10-W-40 BREATH! NOW COME DOWN HERE AND TAKE YOUR PUNISHMENT LIKE A MAN!!
STILL CAN'T HEAR YOU... COME CLOSER... A LITTLE BIT MORE...
HAW! THE CHAINSAW IS ONLY A DECOY TO LURE YOU INTO THE RANGE OF MY TIME TELEPORTER!!!
HMMM!
WHOA!
FAREWELL FOREVER, HEDGEHOG!"
YEOW! I'M HAVING ONE OF THOSE "I'VE BEEN HERE BEFORE" EXPERIENCES!
1107 A.D.
780 A.D.
29 A.D.
2000 B.C.
7800 B.C.
WHOOSH!
4

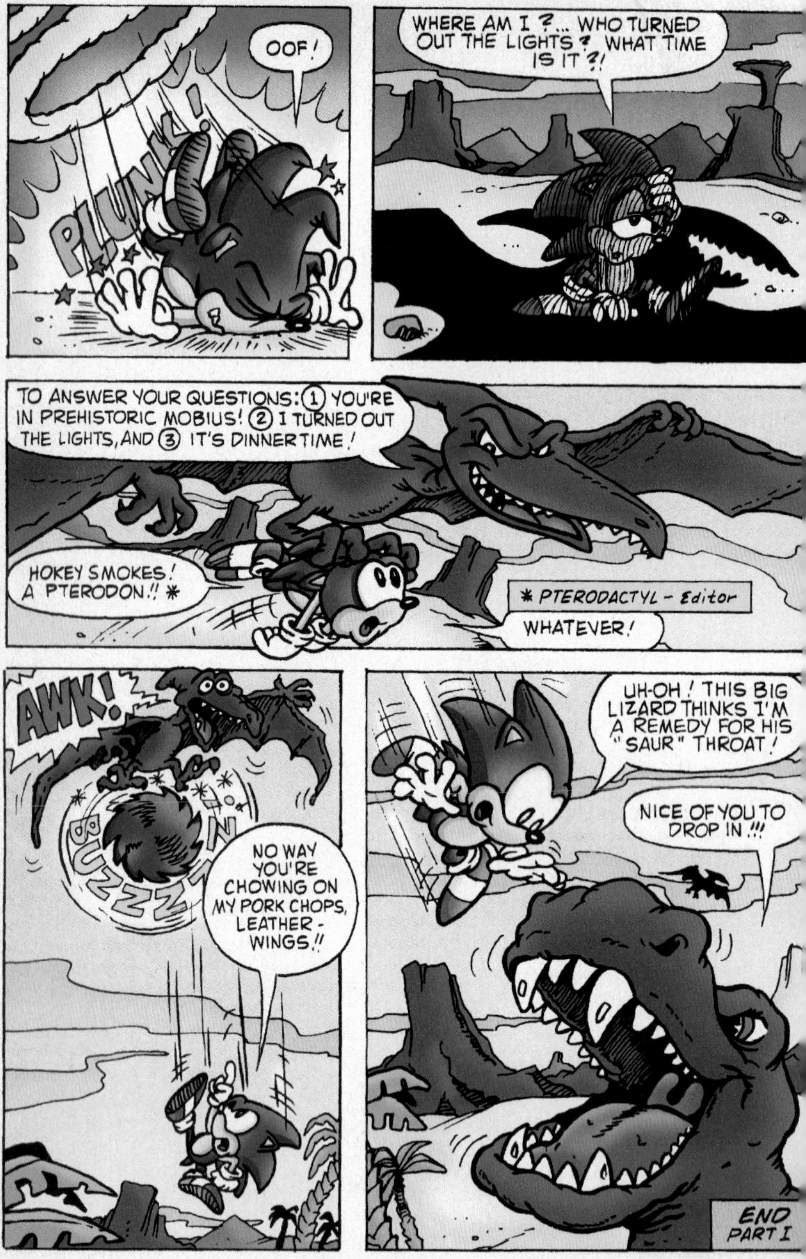
OOF!
PLUNK!
WHERE AM I ?... WHO TURNED OUT THE LIGHTS? WHAT TIME IS IT ?!
TO ANSWER YOUR QUESTIONS: ① YOU'RE IN PREHISTORIC MOBIUS! ② I TURNED OUT THE LIGHTS, AND ③ IT'S DINNERTIME!
HOKEY SMOKES! A PTERODON!! *
* PTERODACTYL - Editor
WHATEVER!
AWK!
BUZZZ
NO WAY YOU'RE CHOWING ON MY PORK CHOPS, LEATHER-WINGS!!
UH-OH! THIS BIG LIZARD THINKS I'M A REMEDY FOR HIS "SAUR" THROAT!
NICE OF YOU TO DROP IN!!!
END PART I

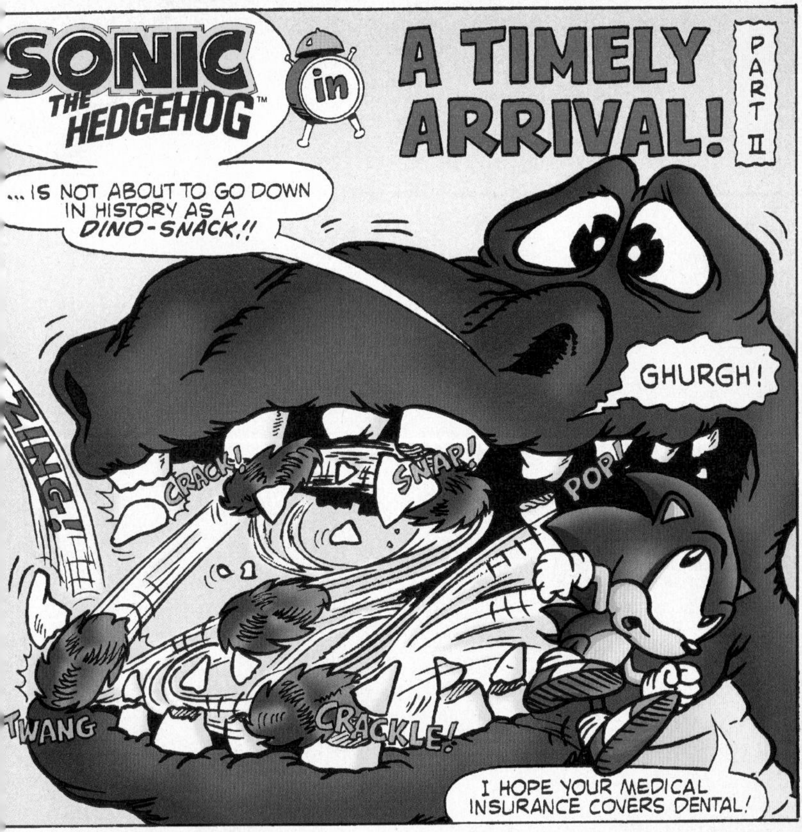
SONIC THE HEDGEHOG™
in
A TIMELY ARRIVAL!
PART II
...IS NOT ABOUT TO GO DOWN IN HISTORY AS A DINO-SNACK!!
GHURGH!
ZING!
CRACK!
SNAP!
POP!
TWANG
CRACKLE!
I HOPE YOUR MEDICAL INSURANCE COVERS DENTAL!

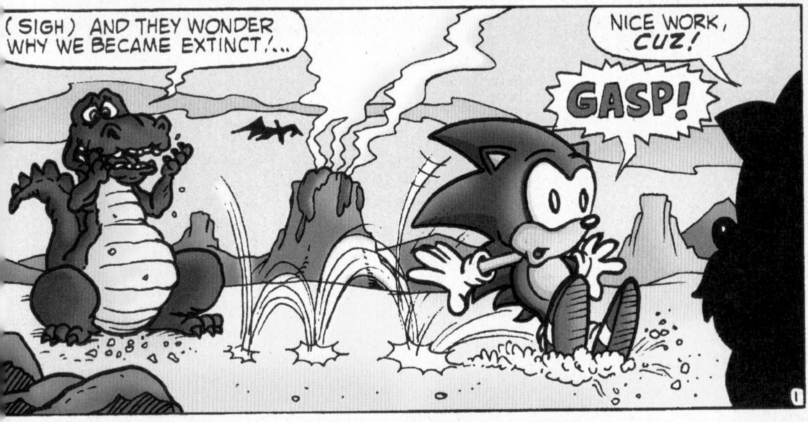
(SIGH) AND THEY WONDER WHY WE BECAME EXTINCT!...
NICE WORK, CUZ!
GASP!

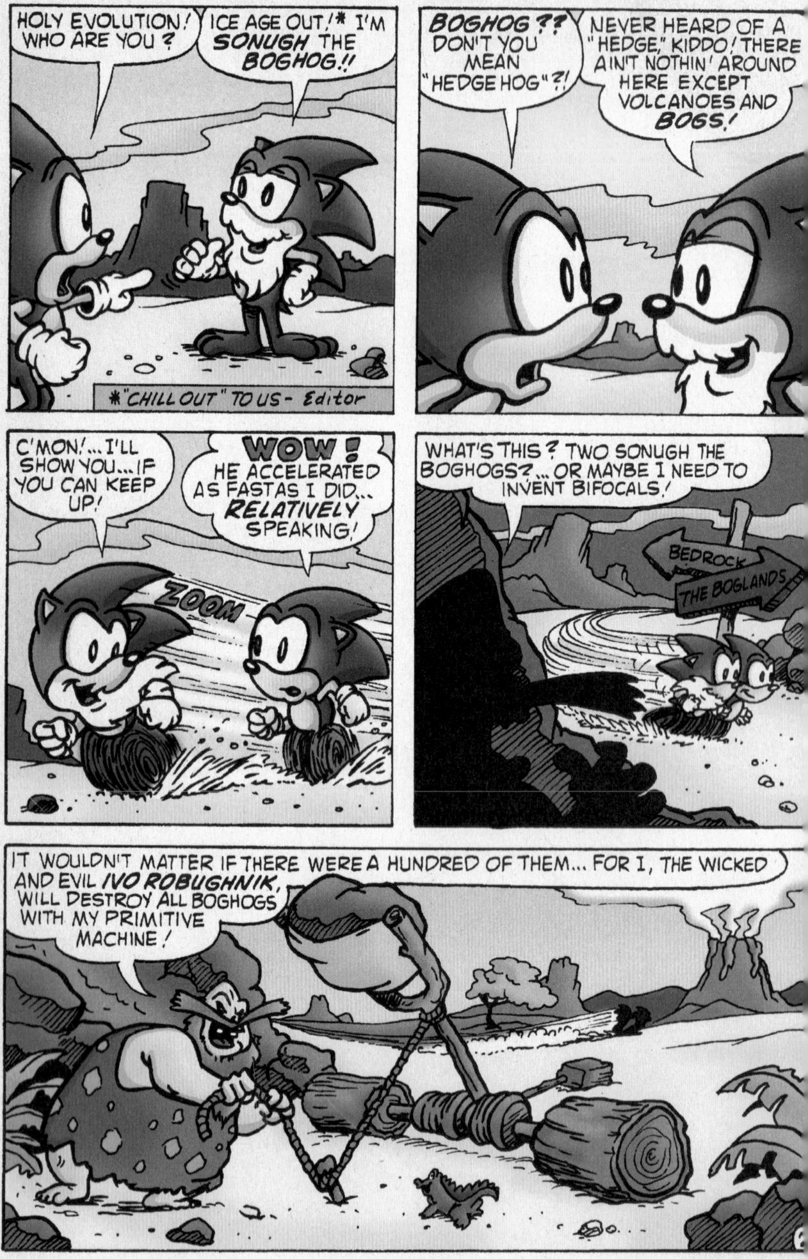
HOLY EVOLUTION! WHO ARE YOU?
ICE AGE OUT!* I'M SONUGH THE BOGHOG!!
*"CHILL OUT" TO US - Editor
BOGHOG?? DON'T YOU MEAN "HEDGE HOG"?!
NEVER HEARD OF A "HEDGE," KIDDO! THERE AIN'T NOTHIN' AROUND HERE EXCEPT VOLCANOES AND BOGS!
C'MON!... I'LL SHOW YOU... IF YOU CAN KEEP UP!
WOW! HE ACCELERATED AS FAST AS I DID... RELATIVELY SPEAKING!
ZOOM
WHAT'S THIS? TWO SONUGH THE BOGHOGS?... OR MAYBE I NEED TO INVENT BIFOCALS!
BEDROCK
THE BOGLANDS
IT WOULDN'T MATTER IF THERE WERE A HUNDRED OF THEM... FOR I, THE WICKED AND EVIL IVO ROBUGHNIK, WILL DESTROY ALL BOGHOGS WITH MY PRIMITIVE MACHINE!

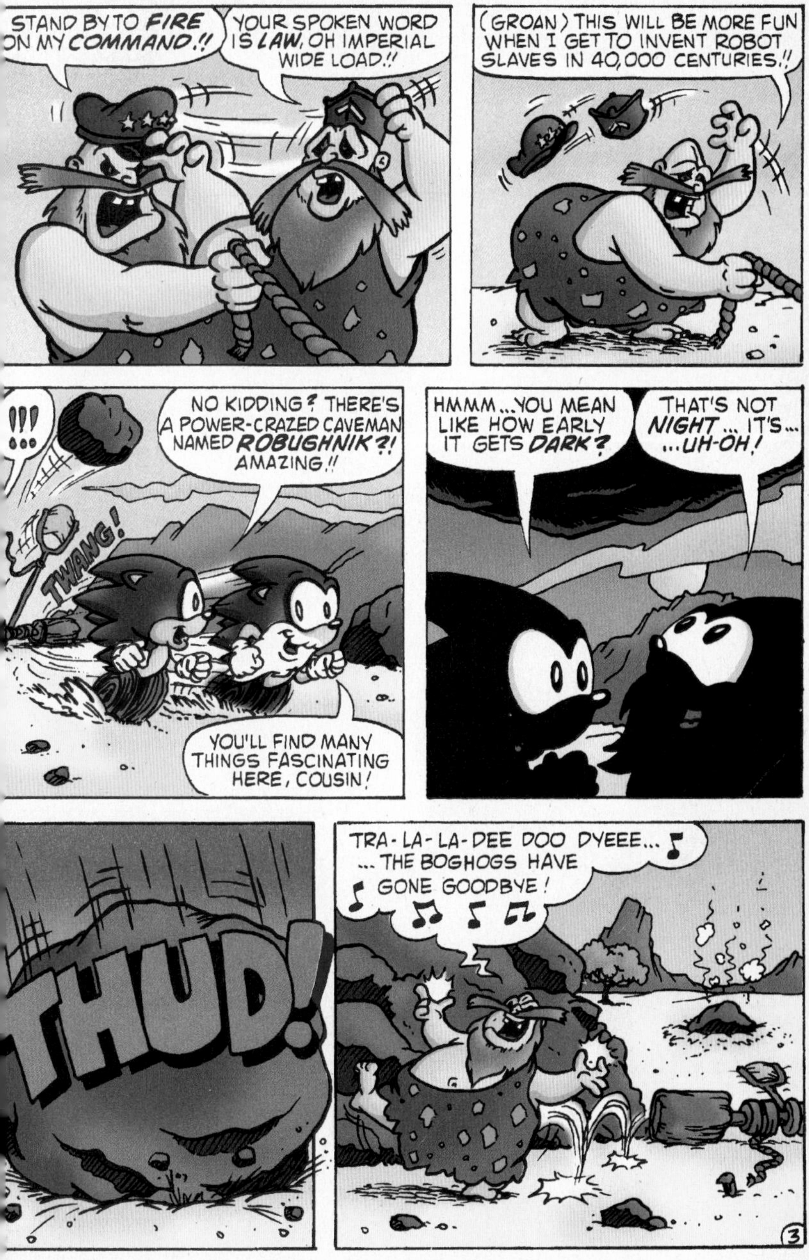
STAND BY TO FIRE ON MY COMMAND.!!
YOUR SPOKEN WORD IS LAW, OH IMPERIAL WIDE LOAD!!
(GROAN) THIS WILL BE MORE FUN WHEN I GET TO INVENT ROBOT SLAVES IN 40,000 CENTURIES!!
!!!
•••
NO KIDDING? THERE'S A POWER-CRAZED CAVEMAN NAMED ROBUGHNIK?! AMAZING!!
TWANG!
YOU'LL FIND MANY THINGS FASCINATING HERE, COUSIN!
HMMM... YOU MEAN LIKE HOW EARLY IT GETS DARK?
THAT'S NOT NIGHT ... IT'S... ...UH-OH!
THUD!
TRA-LA-LA-DEE DOO DYEEE... ... THE BOGHOGS HAVE GONE GOODBYE!
3

AT THAT MOMENT, 400,000 YEARS LATER...

TRA-LA-DEE DO DEE DA... SONIC IS GONE! HOORAY! GOODBYE!!

GASP!

ROBOTNIK! SINGING! DANCING!! SMILING!!!

AHEM.!..HARUMPH.! *CRABMEAT*...YOU WILL *FORGET* EVERYTHING YOU JUST SAW.!!

OH, HOW CAN I ? YOU BROKE YOUR OWN RULES!! IT'S FOREVER ETCHED IN MY MEMORY!!

VERY WELL... LET'S DO IT THE *EASY* WAY...

ARE WE ALL SET OUT THERE, SWAT-BOT?

AFFIRMATIVE, OH OVAL OGRE!

CRUNCH!

I SHALL CUT THE RIBBON AND OPEN THE DISPLAY OF MY TIME MACHINE! WHERE'S THE CROWD?

THEY WENT FOR A KEG OF 10-W-40... HEY!! DID YOU HEAR SOMETHING?

SEE THE INVENTION THAT SQUASHED SONIC

25¢

DANGER-DANGER!!! A SURPRISE ATTACK BY THE FREEDOM FIGHTERS!

EGAD.!.. I *CAN'T* ESCAPE -- MOTHER TOLD ME *NEVER* TO RUN WITH SCISSORS!

FORWARD FOR *SONIC*... AND OUR CAUSE!

FREEDOM FIGHTERS

CHARGE!

4

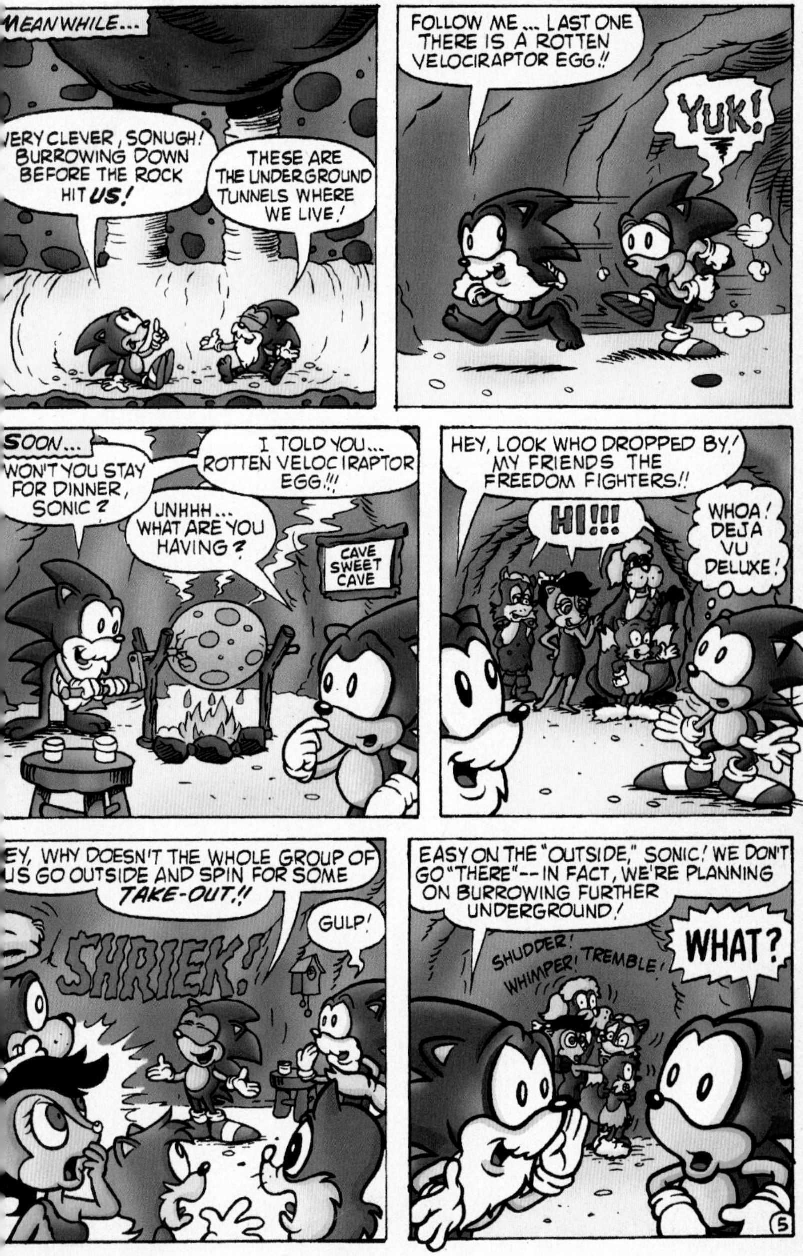
MEANWHILE...
ERY CLEVER, SONUGH! BURROWING DOWN BEFORE THE ROCK HIT US!
THESE ARE THE UNDERGROUND TUNNELS WHERE WE LIVE!
FOLLOW ME... LAST ONE THERE IS A ROTTEN VELOCIRAPTOR EGG!!
YUK!
SOON...
WON'T YOU STAY FOR DINNER, SONIC?
UNHHH... WHAT ARE YOU HAVING?
I TOLD YOU... ROTTEN VELOCIRAPTOR EGG!!!
CAVE SWEET CAVE
HEY, LOOK WHO DROPPED BY! MY FRIENDS THE FREEDOM FIGHTERS!!
HI!!!
WHOA! DEJA VU DELUXE!
EY, WHY DOESN'T THE WHOLE GROUP OF US GO OUTSIDE AND SPIN FOR SOME TAKE-OUT!!
SHRIEK!
GULP!
EASY ON THE "OUTSIDE," SONIC! WE DON'T GO "THERE"-- IN FACT, WE'RE PLANNING ON BURROWING FURTHER UNDERGROUND!
SHUDDER! WHIMPER! TREMBLE!
WHAT?

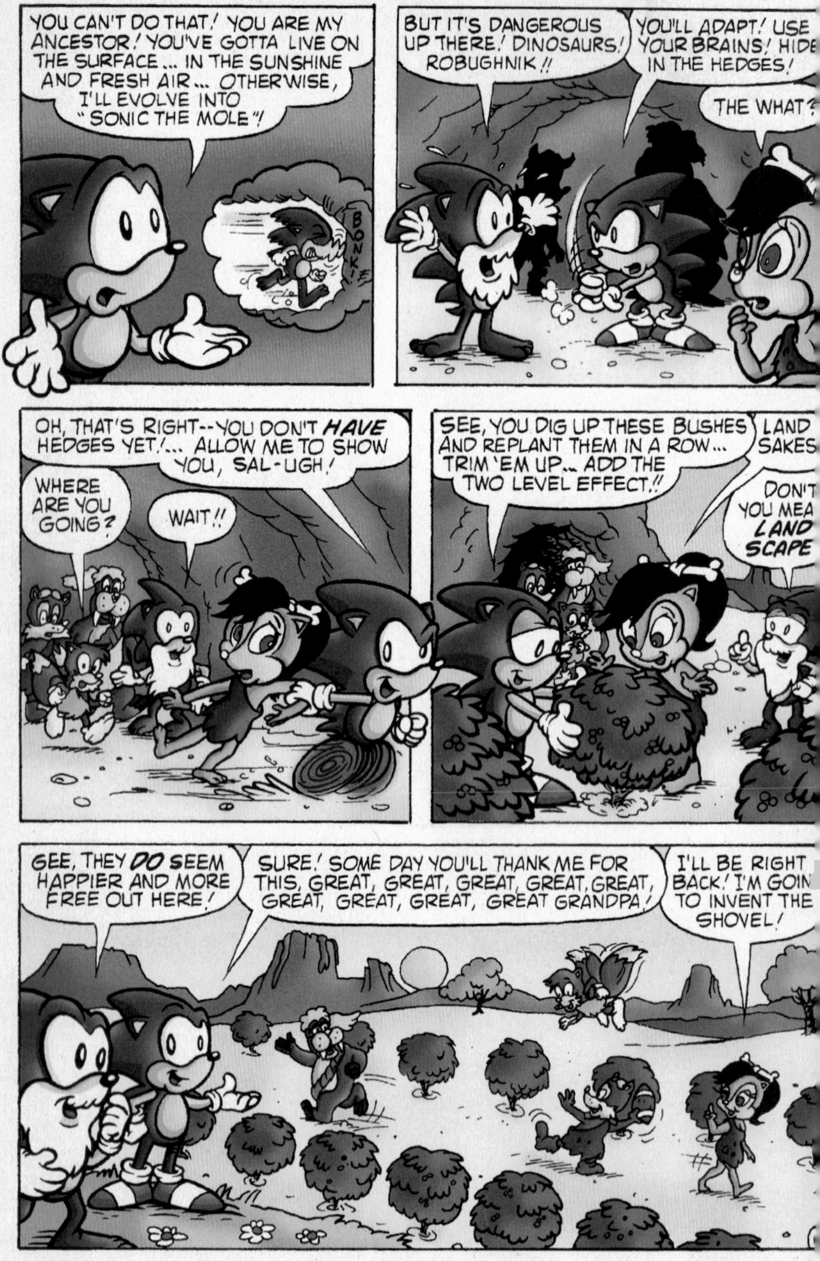
YOU CAN'T DO THAT! YOU ARE MY ANCESTOR! YOU'VE GOTTA LIVE ON THE SURFACE ... IN THE SUNSHINE AND FRESH AIR ... OTHERWISE, I'LL EVOLVE INTO "SONIC THE MOLE"!
BONK!
BUT IT'S DANGEROUS UP THERE! DINOSAURS! ROBUGHNIK!!
YOU'LL ADAPT! USE YOUR BRAINS! HIDE IN THE HEDGES!
THE WHAT?
OH, THAT'S RIGHT--YOU DON'T HAVE HEDGES YET!... ALLOW ME TO SHOW YOU, SAL-UGH!
WHERE ARE YOU GOING?
WAIT!!
SEE, YOU DIG UP THESE BUSHES AND REPLANT THEM IN A ROW... TRIM 'EM UP... ADD THE TWO LEVEL EFFECT!!
LAND SAKES
DON'T YOU MEA LAND SCAPE
GEE, THEY DO SEEM HAPPIER AND MORE FREE OUT HERE!
SURE! SOME DAY YOU'LL THANK ME FOR THIS, GREAT, GREAT, GREAT, GREAT, GREAT, GREAT, GREAT, GREAT, GREAT GRANDPA!
I'LL BE RIGHT BACK! I'M GOIN TO INVENT THE SHOVEL!

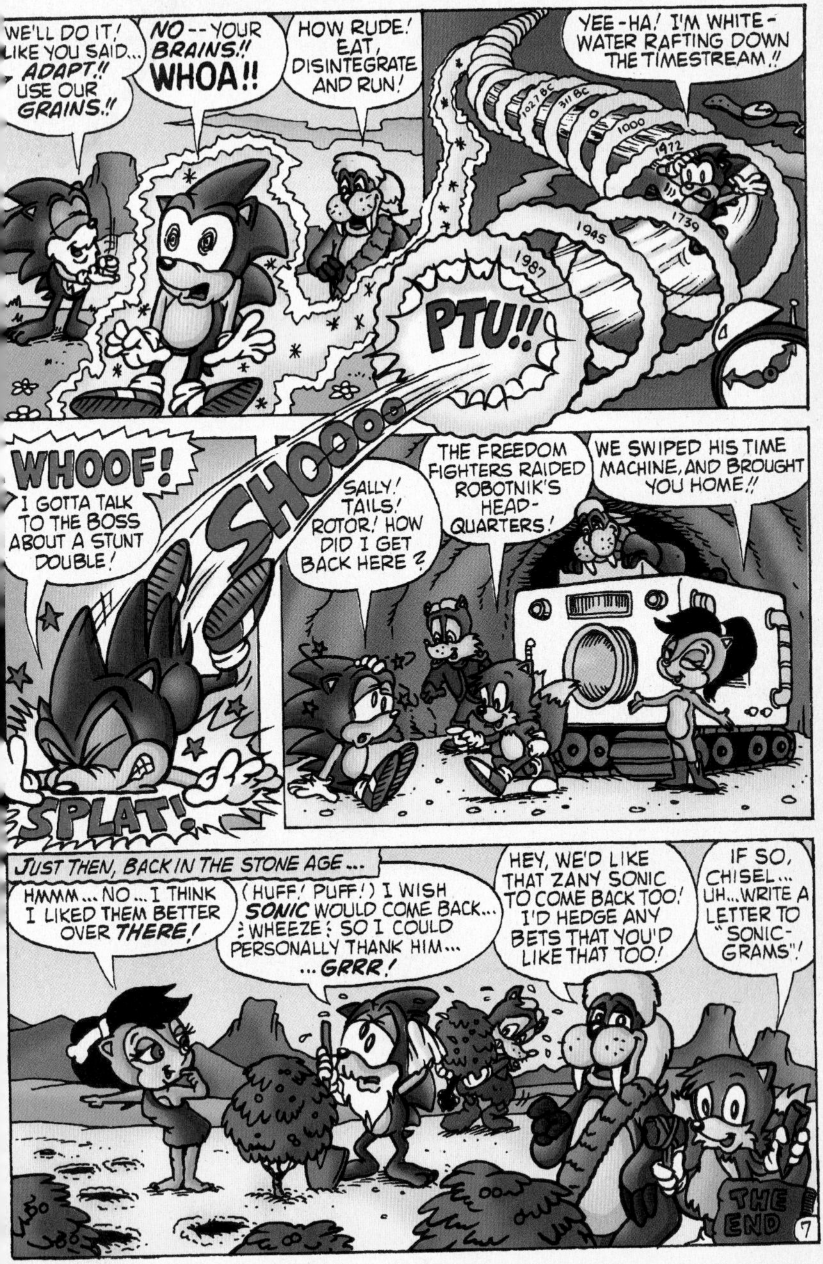
WE'LL DO IT! LIKE YOU SAID... ADAPT!! USE OUR GRAINS!!
NO -- YOUR BRAINS!! WHOA!!
HOW RUDE! EAT, DISINTEGRATE AND RUN!
YEE-HA! I'M WHITE-WATER RAFTING DOWN THE TIMESTREAM!!
1027 BC
311 BC
0
1000
1972
1739
1945
1987
PTU!!
SHOOOO
WHOOF!
I GOTTA TALK TO THE BOSS ABOUT A STUNT DOUBLE!
SPLAT!
SALLY! TAILS! ROTOR! HOW DID I GET BACK HERE?
THE FREEDOM FIGHTERS RAIDED ROBOTNIK'S HEAD-QUARTERS!
WE SWIPED HIS TIME MACHINE, AND BROUGHT YOU HOME!!
JUST THEN, BACK IN THE STONE AGE...
HMMM... NO... I THINK I LIKED THEM BETTER OVER THERE!
(HUFF! PUFF!) I WISH SONIC WOULD COME BACK... :WHEEZE: SO I COULD PERSONALLY THANK HIM... ...GRRR!
HEY, WE'D LIKE THAT ZANY SONIC TO COME BACK TOO! I'D HEDGE ANY BETS THAT YOU'D LIKE THAT TOO!
IF SO, CHISEL... UH...WRITE A LETTER TO "SONIC-GRAMS"!
THE END

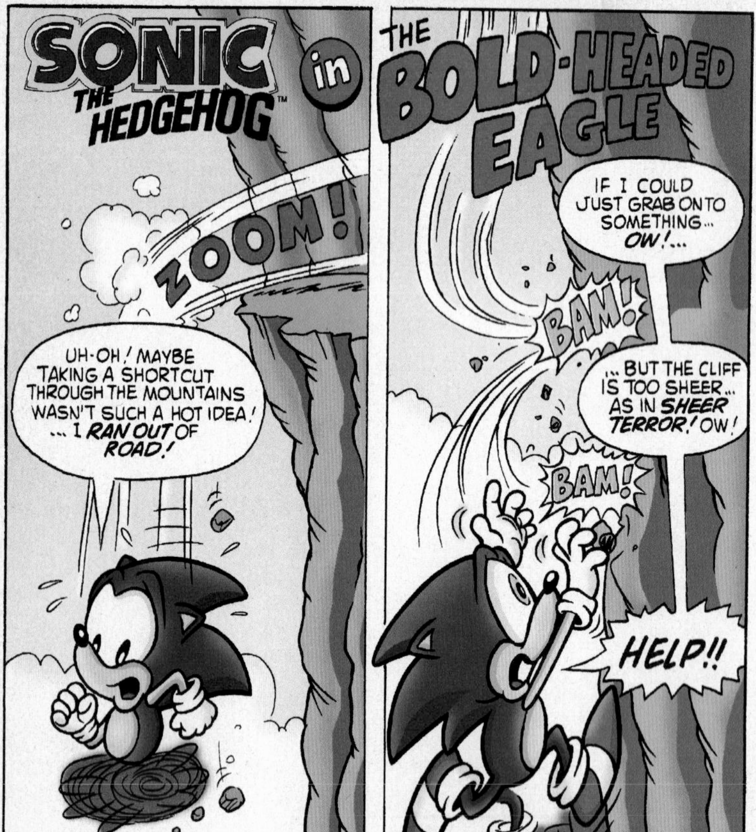
SONIC THE HEDGEHOG™
in
THE BOLD-HEADED EAGLE
ZOOM!
UH-OH! MAYBE TAKING A SHORTCUT THROUGH THE MOUNTAINS WASN'T SUCH A HOT IDEA! ... I RAN OUT OF ROAD!
IF I COULD JUST GRAB ONTO SOMETHING... OW!...
BAM!
... BUT THE CLIFF IS TOO SHEER... AS IN SHEER TERROR! OW!
BAM!
HELP!!

SCRIPT: MIKE KANTEROVICH/KEN PENDERS PENCILLING: ART MAWHINNEY INKING: RICH KOSLOWSKI

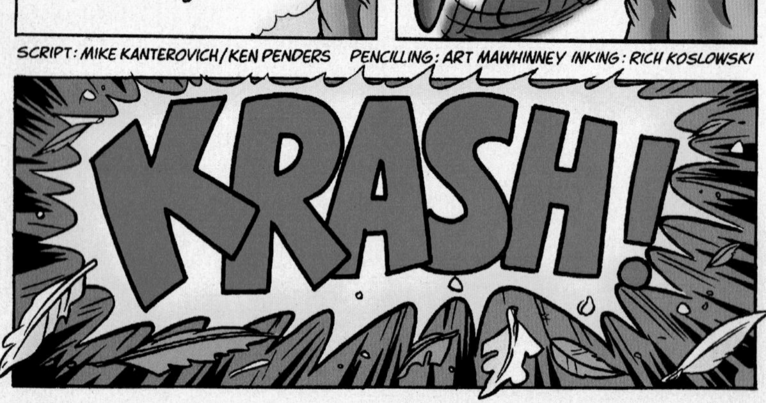
KRASH!

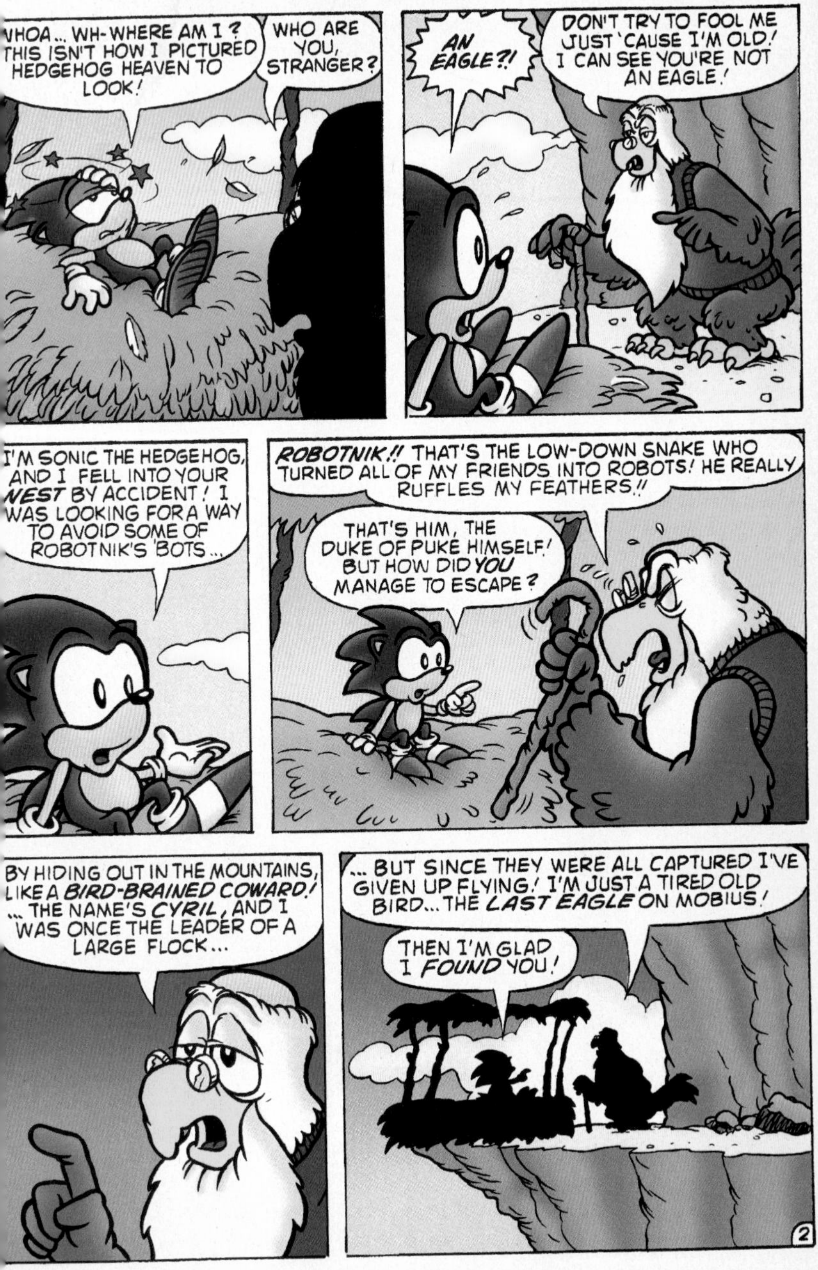
WHOA... WH-WHERE AM I? THIS ISN'T HOW I PICTURED HEDGEHOG HEAVEN TO LOOK!
WHO ARE YOU, STRANGER?
AN EAGLE?!
DON'T TRY TO FOOL ME JUST 'CAUSE I'M OLD! I CAN SEE YOU'RE NOT AN EAGLE!
I'M SONIC THE HEDGEHOG, AND I FELL INTO YOUR NEST BY ACCIDENT! I WAS LOOKING FOR A WAY TO AVOID SOME OF ROBOTNIK'S 'BOTS...
ROBOTNIK!! THAT'S THE LOW-DOWN SNAKE WHO TURNED ALL OF MY FRIENDS INTO ROBOTS! HE REALLY RUFFLES MY FEATHERS!!
THAT'S HIM, THE DUKE OF PUKE HIMSELF! BUT HOW DID YOU MANAGE TO ESCAPE?
BY HIDING OUT IN THE MOUNTAINS, LIKE A BIRD-BRAINED COWARD! ... THE NAME'S CYRIL, AND I WAS ONCE THE LEADER OF A LARGE FLOCK...
... BUT SINCE THEY WERE ALL CAPTURED I'VE GIVEN UP FLYING! I'M JUST A TIRED OLD BIRD... THE LAST EAGLE ON MOBIUS!
THEN I'M GLAD I FOUND YOU!
2

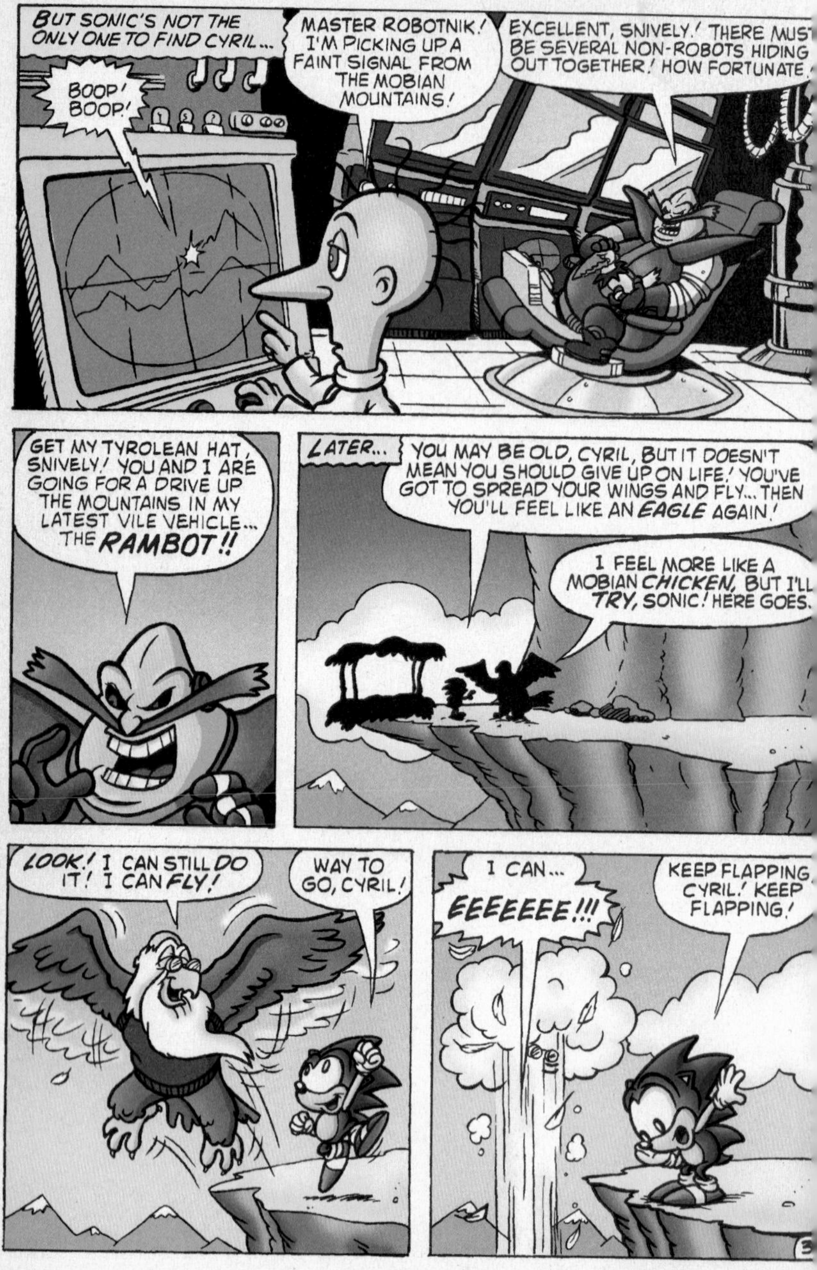
BUT SONIC'S NOT THE ONLY ONE TO FIND CYRIL...
BOOP! BOOP!
MASTER ROBOTNIK! I'M PICKING UP A FAINT SIGNAL FROM THE MOBIAN MOUNTAINS!
EXCELLENT, SNIVELY! THERE MUST BE SEVERAL NON-ROBOTS HIDING OUT TOGETHER! HOW FORTUNATE
GET MY TYROLEAN HAT, SNIVELY! YOU AND I ARE GOING FOR A DRIVE UP THE MOUNTAINS IN MY LATEST VILE VEHICLE... THE RAMBOT!!
LATER...
YOU MAY BE OLD, CYRIL, BUT IT DOESN'T MEAN YOU SHOULD GIVE UP ON LIFE! YOU'VE GOT TO SPREAD YOUR WINGS AND FLY... THEN YOU'LL FEEL LIKE AN EAGLE AGAIN!
I FEEL MORE LIKE A MOBIAN CHICKEN, BUT I'LL TRY, SONIC! HERE GOES.
LOOK! I CAN STILL DO IT! I CAN FLY!
WAY TO GO, CYRIL!
I CAN...
EEEEEEE!!!
KEEP FLAPPING, CYRIL! KEEP FLAPPING!
3

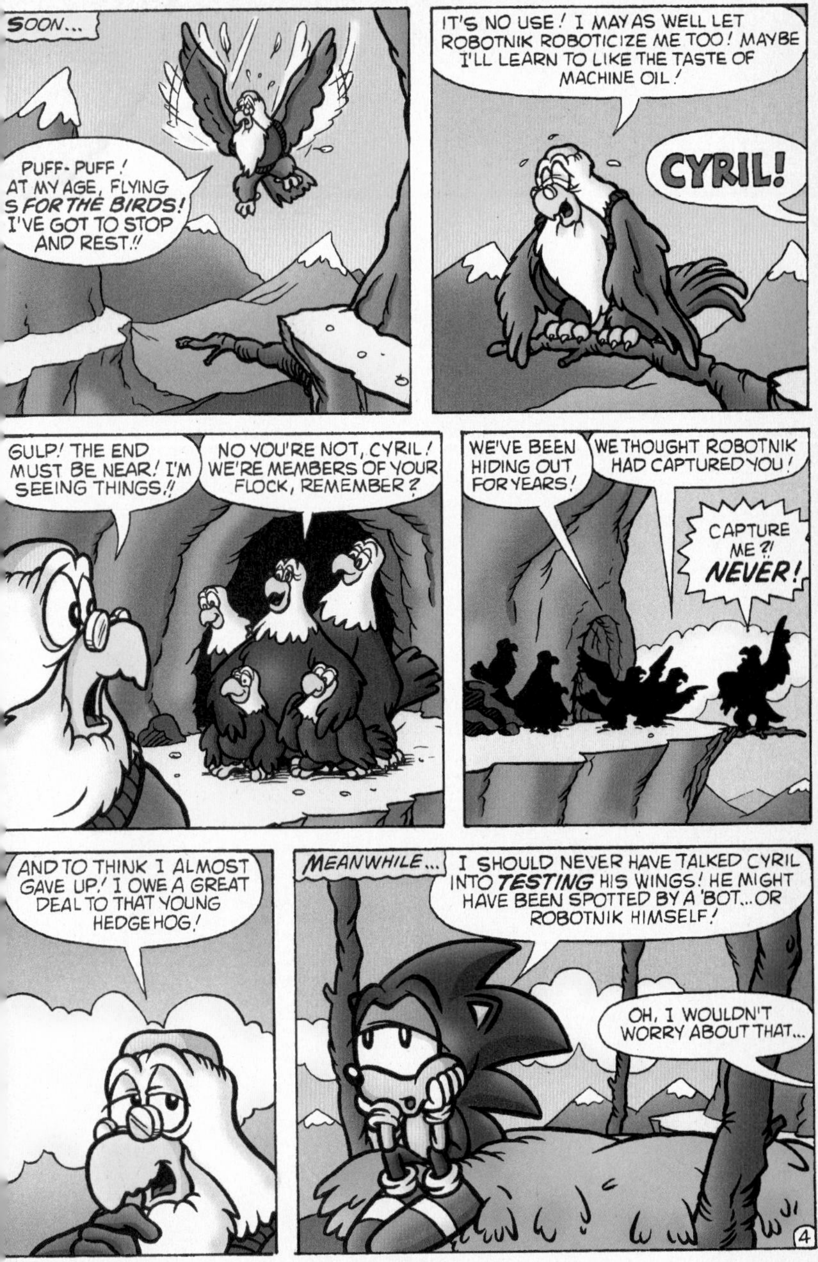
SOON...
PUFF- PUFF! AT MY AGE, FLYING S FOR THE BIRDS! I'VE GOT TO STOP AND REST!!
IT'S NO USE! I MAY AS WELL LET ROBOTNIK ROBOTICIZE ME TOO! MAYBE I'LL LEARN TO LIKE THE TASTE OF MACHINE OIL!
CYRIL!
GULP! THE END MUST BE NEAR! I'M SEEING THINGS!!
NO YOU'RE NOT, CYRIL! WE'RE MEMBERS OF YOUR FLOCK, REMEMBER?
WE'VE BEEN HIDING OUT FOR YEARS!
WE THOUGHT ROBOTNIK HAD CAPTURED YOU!
CAPTURE ME?! NEVER!
AND TO THINK I ALMOST GAVE UP! I OWE A GREAT DEAL TO THAT YOUNG HEDGEHOG!
MEANWHILE...
I SHOULD NEVER HAVE TALKED CYRIL INTO TESTING HIS WINGS! HE MIGHT HAVE BEEN SPOTTED BY A 'BOT...OR ROBOTNIK HIMSELF!
OH, I WOULDN'T WORRY ABOUT THAT...
4

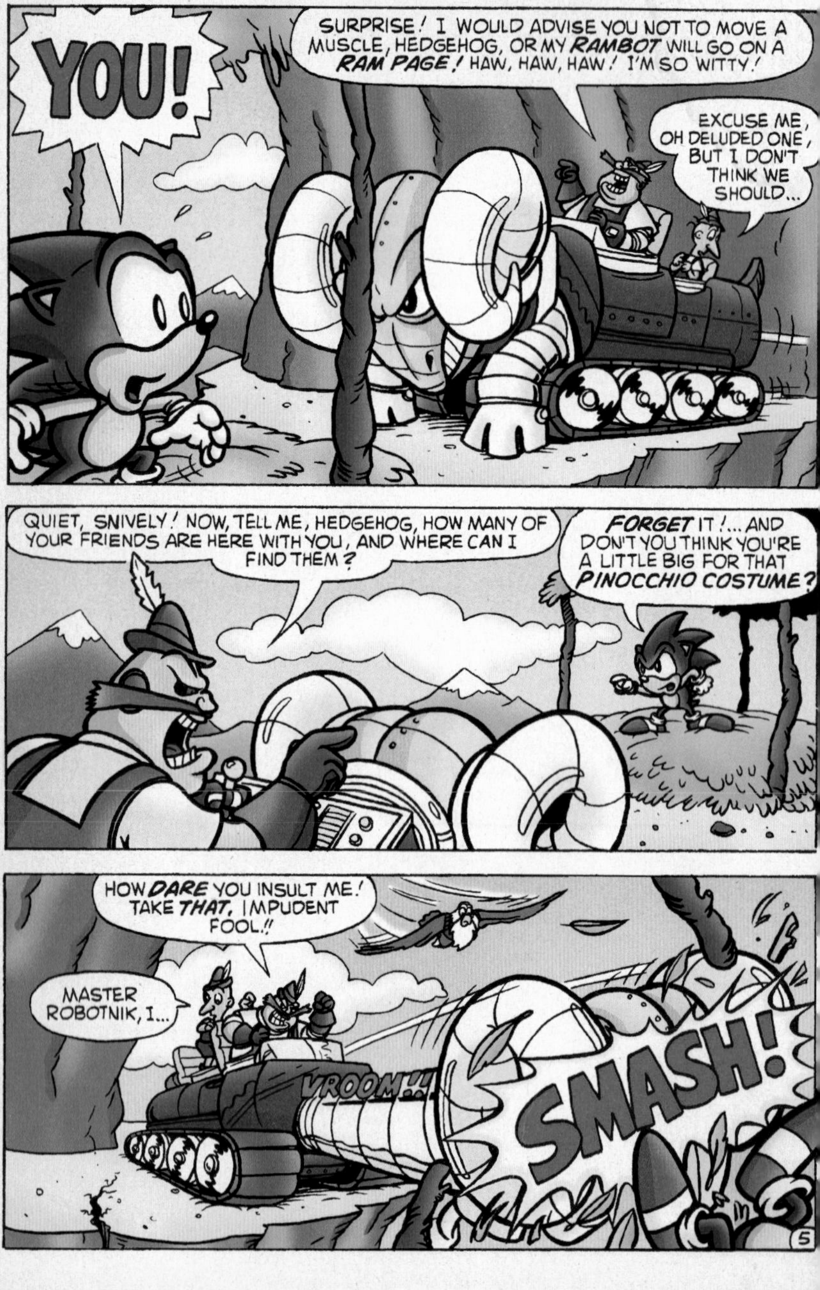
YOU!
SURPRISE! I WOULD ADVISE YOU NOT TO MOVE A MUSCLE, HEDGEHOG, OR MY *RAMBOT* WILL GO ON A *RAM PAGE!* HAW, HAW, HAW! I'M SO WITTY!
EXCUSE ME, OH DELUDED ONE, BUT I DON'T THINK WE SHOULD...
QUIET, SNIVELY! NOW, TELL ME, HEDGEHOG, HOW MANY OF YOUR FRIENDS ARE HERE WITH YOU, AND WHERE CAN I FIND THEM?
FORGET IT!... AND DON'T YOU THINK YOU'RE A LITTLE BIG FOR THAT *PINOCCHIO COSTUME?*
HOW *DARE* YOU INSULT ME! TAKE *THAT,* IMPUDENT FOOL!!
MASTER ROBOTNIK, I...
VROOM!!
SMASH!

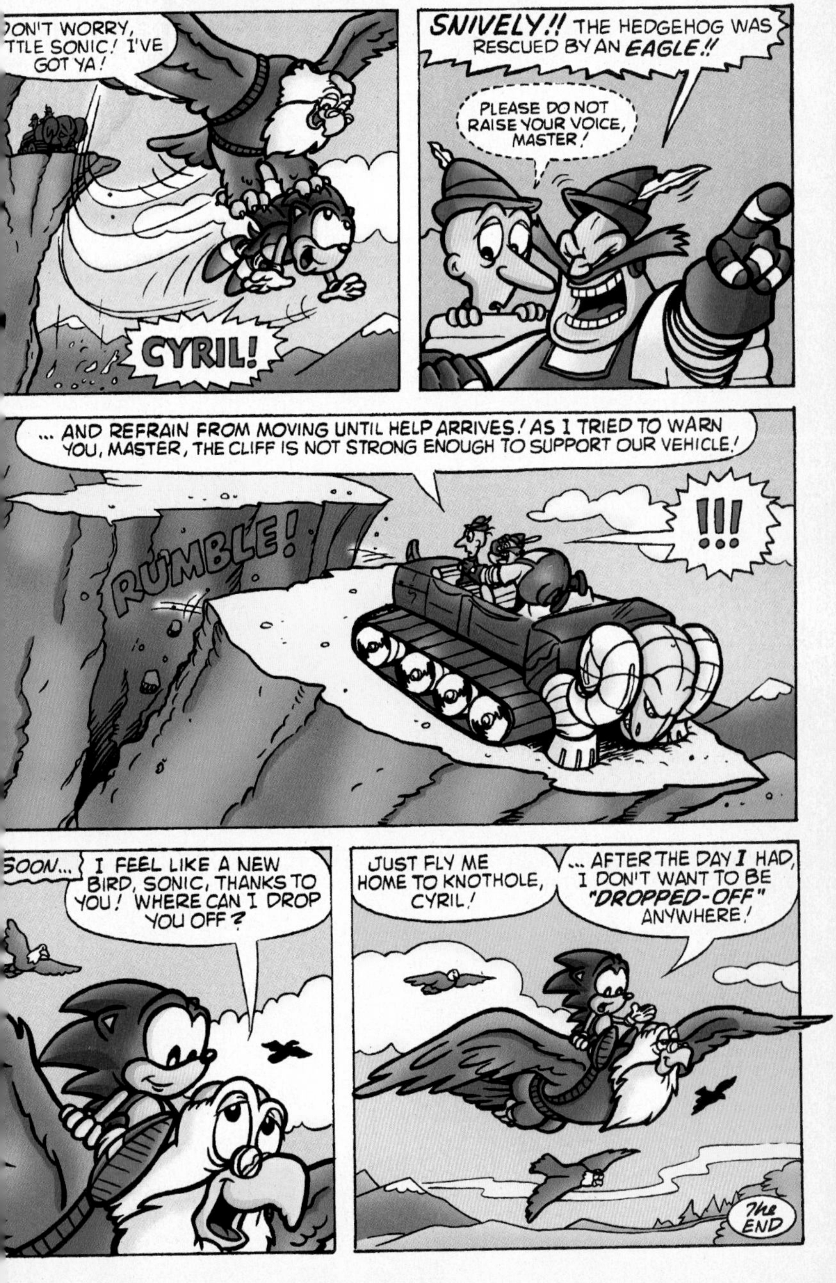
DON'T WORRY, LITTLE SONIC! I'VE GOT YA!
CYRIL!
SNIVELY!! THE HEDGEHOG WAS RESCUED BY AN EAGLE!!
PLEASE DO NOT RAISE YOUR VOICE, MASTER!
... AND REFRAIN FROM MOVING UNTIL HELP ARRIVES! AS I TRIED TO WARN YOU, MASTER, THE CLIFF IS NOT STRONG ENOUGH TO SUPPORT OUR VEHICLE!
RUMBLE!
!!!
SOON...
I FEEL LIKE A NEW BIRD, SONIC, THANKS TO YOU! WHERE CAN I DROP YOU OFF?
JUST FLY ME HOME TO KNOTHOLE, CYRIL!
... AFTER THE DAY I HAD, I DON'T WANT TO BE "DROPPED-OFF" ANYWHERE!
The END

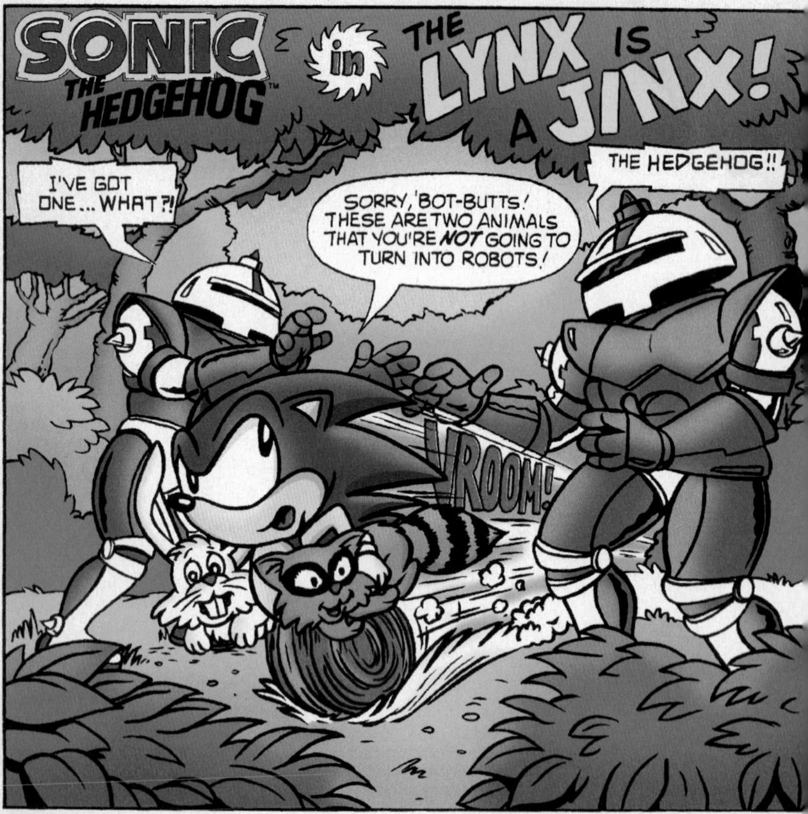
SONIC THE HEDGEHOG in THE LYNX IS A JINX!
I'VE GOT ONE... WHAT?!
SORRY, 'BOT-BUTTS! THESE ARE TWO ANIMALS THAT YOU'RE NOT GOING TO TURN INTO ROBOTS!
THE HEDGEHOG!!
VROOM!

SCRIPT: ANGELO DeCESARE PENCILLING: ART MAWHINNEY INKING: RICH KOSLOWSK

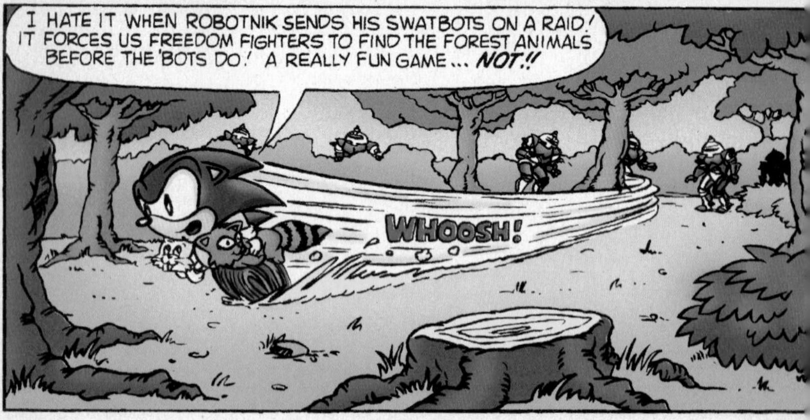
I HATE IT WHEN ROBOTNIK SENDS HIS SWATBOTS ON A RAID! IT FORCES US FREEDOM FIGHTERS TO FIND THE FOREST ANIMALS BEFORE THE 'BOTS DO! A REALLY FUN GAME... NOT!!
WHOOSH!

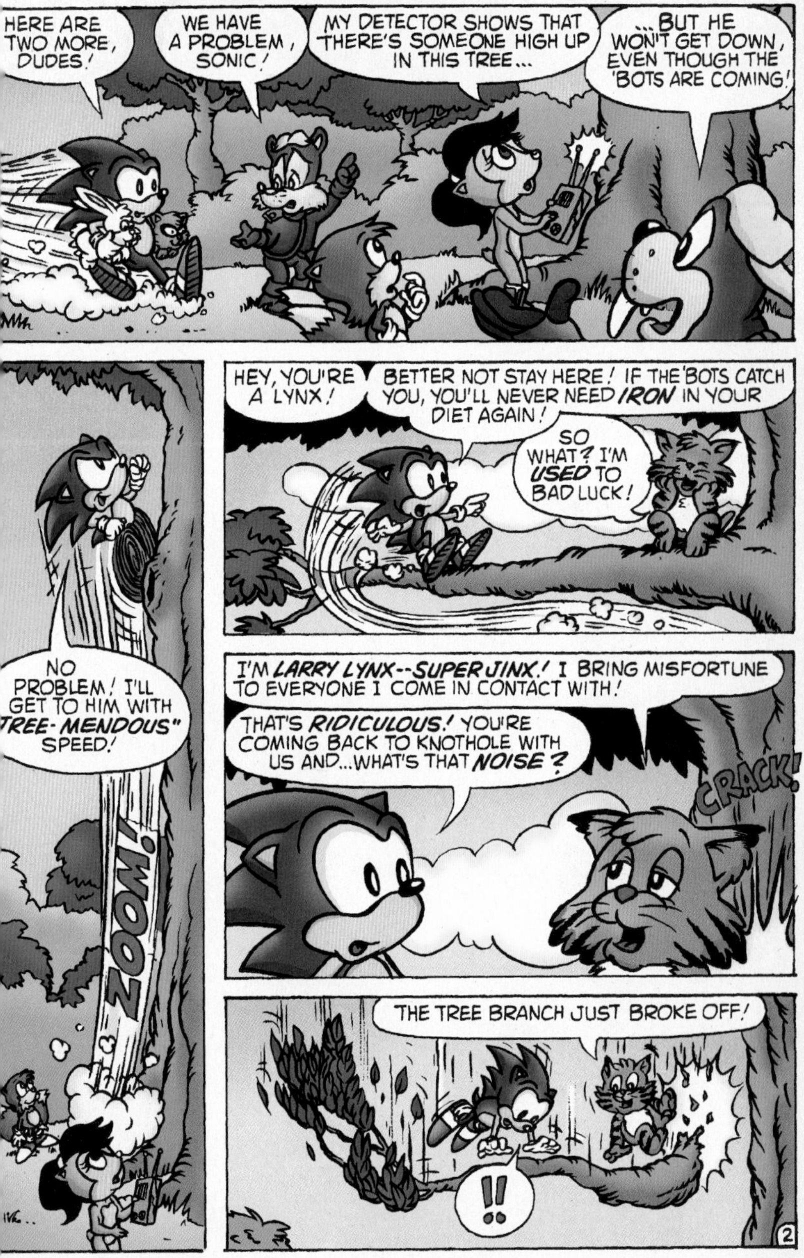

HERE ARE TWO MORE, DUDES!
WE HAVE A PROBLEM, SONIC!
MY DETECTOR SHOWS THAT THERE'S SOMEONE HIGH UP IN THIS TREE...
...BUT HE WON'T GET DOWN, EVEN THOUGH THE 'BOTS ARE COMING!
NO PROBLEM! I'LL GET TO HIM WITH "TREE-MENDOUS" SPEED!
ZOOM!
HEY, YOU'RE A LYNX!
BETTER NOT STAY HERE! IF THE 'BOTS CATCH YOU, YOU'LL NEVER NEED IRON IN YOUR DIET AGAIN!
SO WHAT? I'M USED TO BAD LUCK!
I'M LARRY LYNX--SUPER JINX! I BRING MISFORTUNE TO EVERYONE I COME IN CONTACT WITH!
THAT'S RIDICULOUS! YOU'RE COMING BACK TO KNOTHOLE WITH US AND...WHAT'S THAT NOISE?
CRACK!
THE TREE BRANCH JUST BROKE OFF!
!!
2

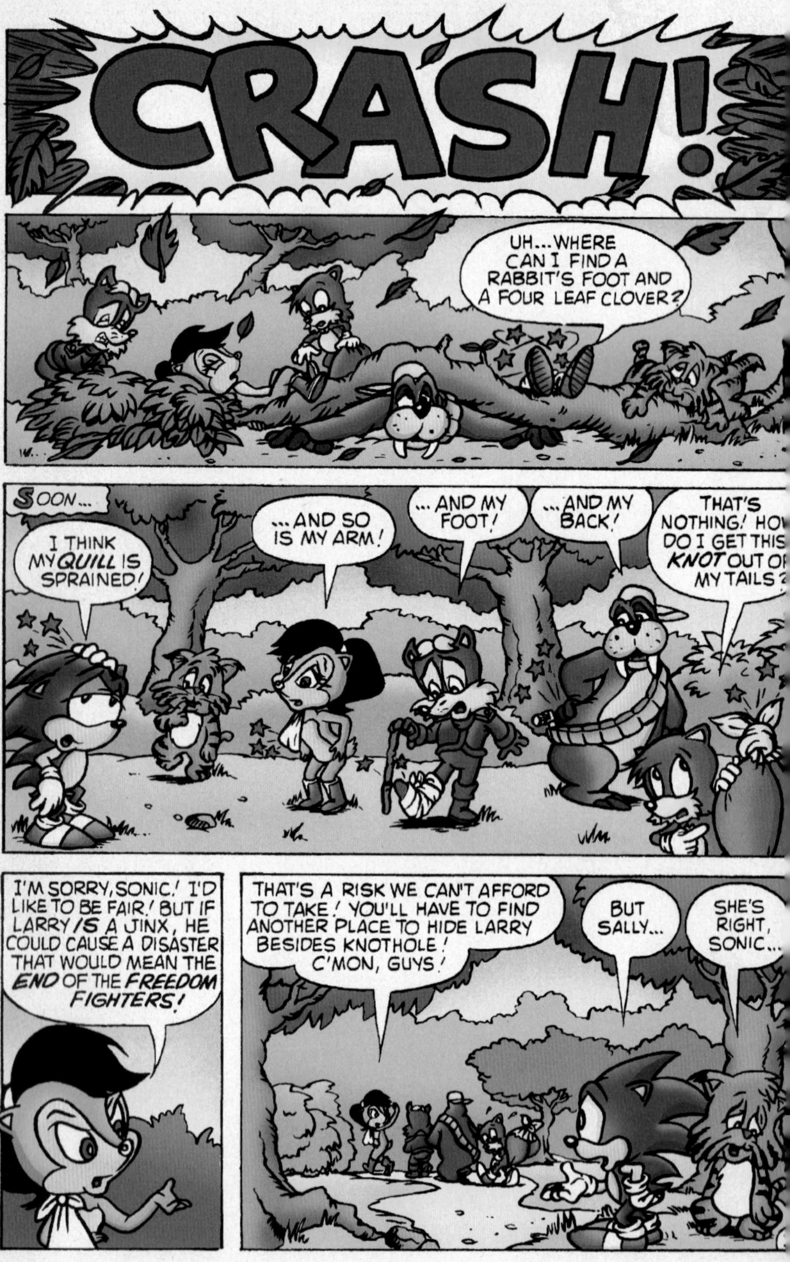
CRASH!
UH...WHERE CAN I FIND A RABBIT'S FOOT AND A FOUR LEAF CLOVER?
SOON...
I THINK MY QUILL IS SPRAINED!
...AND SO IS MY ARM!
...AND MY FOOT!
...AND MY BACK!
THAT'S NOTHING! HOW DO I GET THIS KNOT OUT OF MY TAILS?
I'M SORRY, SONIC! I'D LIKE TO BE FAIR! BUT IF LARRY IS A JINX, HE COULD CAUSE A DISASTER THAT WOULD MEAN THE END OF THE FREEDOM FIGHTERS!
THAT'S A RISK WE CAN'T AFFORD TO TAKE! YOU'LL HAVE TO FIND ANOTHER PLACE TO HIDE LARRY BESIDES KNOTHOLE! C'MON, GUYS!
BUT SALLY...
SHE'S RIGHT, SONIC...

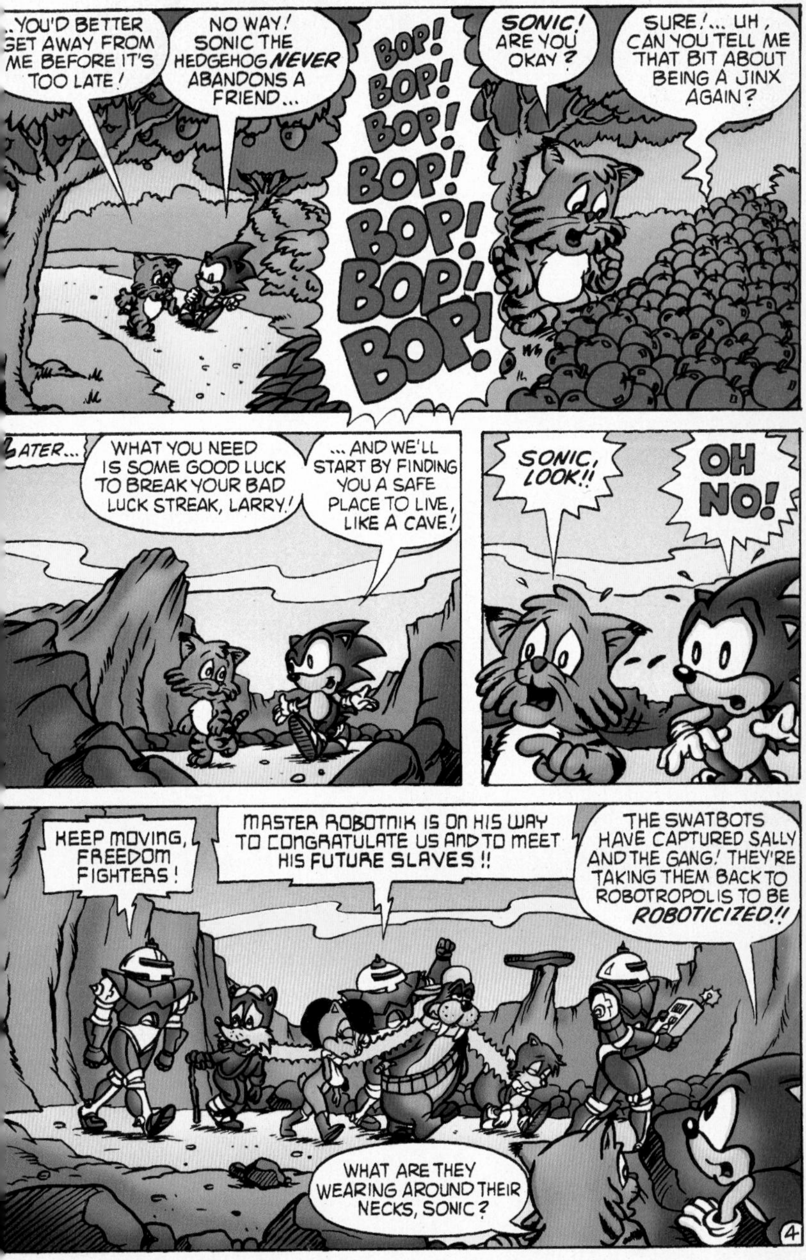
..YOU'D BETTER GET AWAY FROM ME BEFORE IT'S TOO LATE!
NO WAY! SONIC THE HEDGEHOG NEVER ABANDONS A FRIEND...
BOP! BOP! BOP! BOP! BOP! BOP! BOP!
SONIC! ARE YOU OKAY?
SURE!... UH, CAN YOU TELL ME THAT BIT ABOUT BEING A JINX AGAIN?
LATER...
WHAT YOU NEED IS SOME GOOD LUCK TO BREAK YOUR BAD LUCK STREAK, LARRY!
...AND WE'LL START BY FINDING YOU A SAFE PLACE TO LIVE, LIKE A CAVE!
SONIC, LOOK!!
OH NO!
KEEP MOVING, FREEDOM FIGHTERS!
MASTER ROBOTNIK IS ON HIS WAY TO CONGRATULATE US AND TO MEET HIS FUTURE SLAVES!!
THE SWATBOTS HAVE CAPTURED SALLY AND THE GANG! THEY'RE TAKING THEM BACK TO ROBOTROPOLIS TO BE ROBOTICIZED!!
WHAT ARE THEY WEARING AROUND THEIR NECKS, SONIC?
4

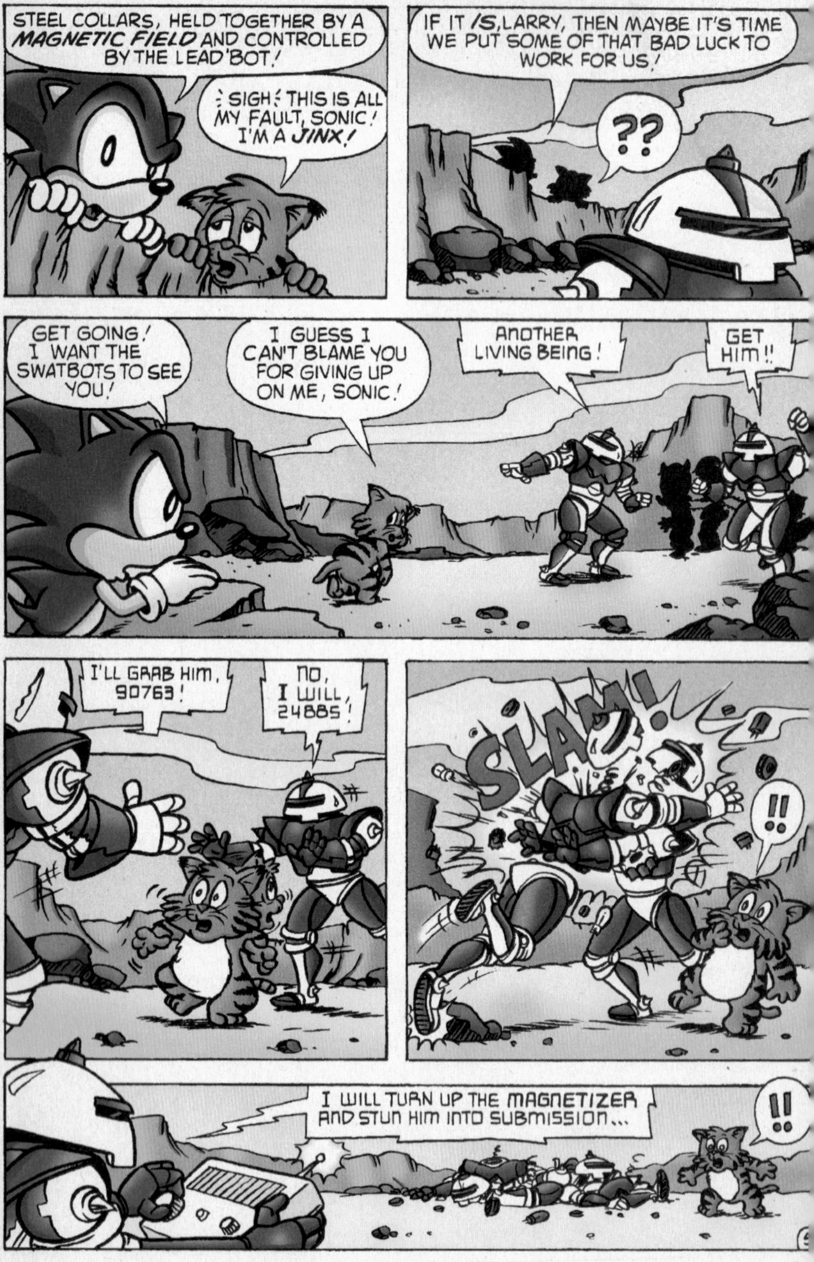
STEEL COLLARS, HELD TOGETHER BY A MAGNETIC FIELD AND CONTROLLED BY THE LEAD'BOT!
:SIGH: THIS IS ALL MY FAULT, SONIC! I'M A JINX!
IF IT IS, LARRY, THEN MAYBE IT'S TIME WE PUT SOME OF THAT BAD LUCK TO WORK FOR US!
??
GET GOING! I WANT THE SWATBOTS TO SEE YOU!
I GUESS I CAN'T BLAME YOU FOR GIVING UP ON ME, SONIC!
ANOTHER LIVING BEING!
GET HIM!!
I'LL GRAB HIM, 90763!
NO, I WILL, 24885!
SLAM!
!!
I WILL TURN UP THE MAGNETIZER AND STUN HIM INTO SUBMISSION...
!!

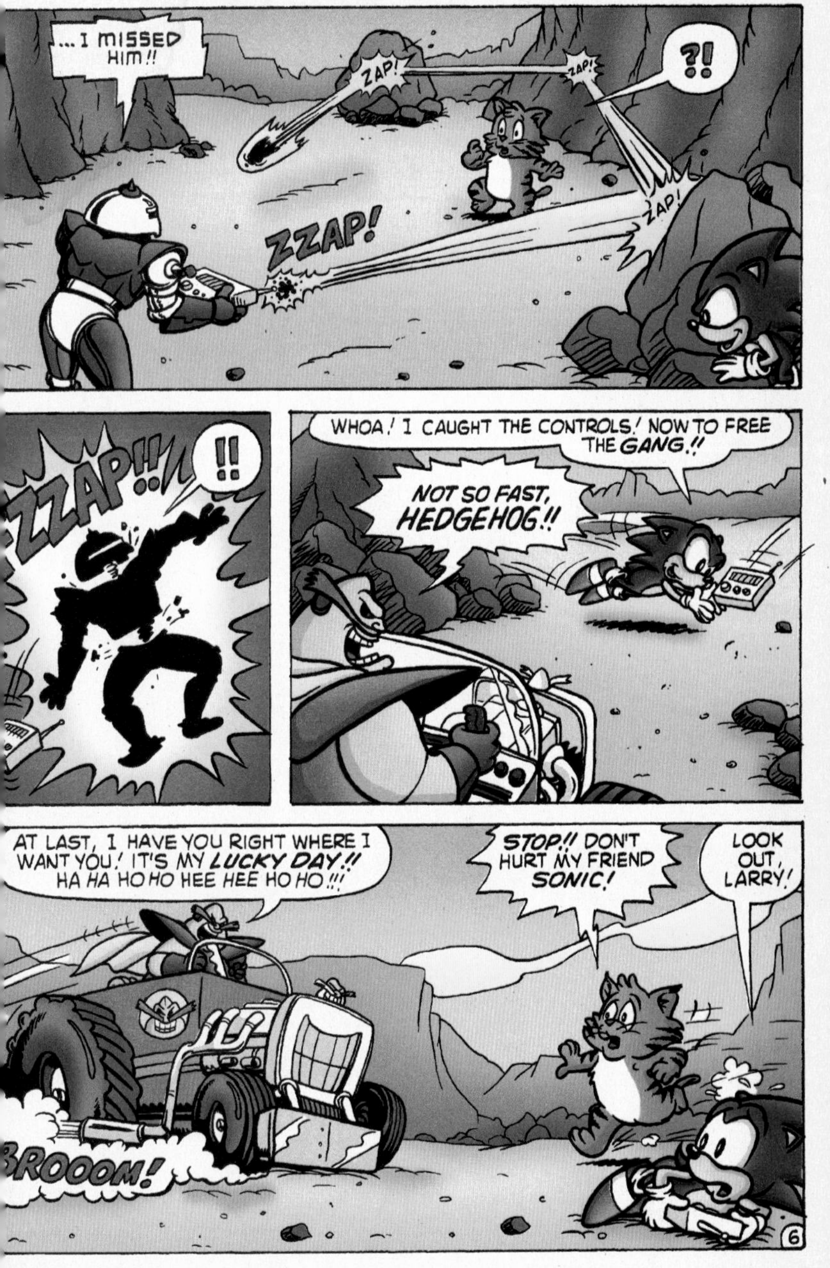
...I MISSED HIM!!
ZAP!
ZAP!
?!
ZZAP!
ZAP!
ZZAP!!
!!
WHOA! I CAUGHT THE CONTROLS! NOW TO FREE THE GANG!!
NOT SO FAST, HEDGEHOG!!
AT LAST, I HAVE YOU RIGHT WHERE I WANT YOU! IT'S MY LUCKY DAY!! HA HA HO HO HEE HEE HO HO!!!
STOP!! DON'T HURT MY FRIEND SONIC!
LOOK OUT, LARRY!
BROOOM!
6

WHAT HAPPENED?! I'VE LOST CONTROL! I CAN'T STEER!

SCREECH!!

K-BLAM!

I HATE THAT HEDGEHOG, *AND THAT LYNX, TOO!!*

MY PLAN WORKED, LARRY! I KNEW THAT SOONER OR LATER *YOUR* BAD LUCK WOULD BRING SOMEONE ELSE *GOOD LUCK!*

...NAMELY, *US!!*

THE BAD LUCK STREAK IS BROKEN, LARRY...AND I JUST KNOW HOW TO PROVE IT!

?!

BACK AT KNOTHOLE...

MATE!

LARRY'S WON *FIFTY GAMES OF CHESS* IN A ROW, SONIC! I THINK YOU'VE PROVEN YOUR POINT!

UH... JUST "CHECKING" MATES

THE END

How do they make those covers?

Pat "Spaz" Spaziante, one of the most sought after artists in the industry,
has become almost as integral to the
Sonic the Hedgehog comics and spin-off series as Sonic himself.
First starting in the office of Archie Comics over 10 years ago, he
began by doing, among other things, original
art for the Sonic comic ads, finally getting his first chance
to pencil a story and cover with issue #21.
(Don't worry: we will reprint that issue in a later volume.)

From character design, interior pencils, and some of the best
cover art of any comic, Spaz has worked on covers for various
Sonic Specials, Super Specials, Knuckles the Echidna,
and currently Sonic the Hedgehog, Sonic's newest spin-off;
Sonic X, and of course these Sonic the Hedgehog Archives.

He has left the biggest and arguably most popular artistic
stamps on the Sonic comic world. Despite the countless fan letters
that come in daily, he is still one of the nicest and most
easy going people to work with. Being so kind,
Spaz let us into his creative world for a rare glimpse
at how he creates a cover.

How do they make those covers?
Getting started:

Each cover usually has the same process.
The editor and I go over the story, in this case several stories,
and try to pick the most exciting moment or events.
With Archives Volume 3 we both agreed Pseudo-Sonic,
the first of many to come metal Sonics, showing up, and Evil Sonic,
the carbon copy of Sonic from the reverse universe,
had to be on the cover.

With most covers we go through several quick design ideas,
never mind tossing around conceptual ideas.
For whatever reason, maybe knowing we would have this sneak peek
as to how a cover was created, we got it right on the first try.

Despite the event not happening in this collection, the idea
of having the three Sonics racing was just too good to pass up.
Of course, we would have Sonic winning the race.

This is an early Thumbnail Sketch. In most cases these
are just for me, but the editor and I know each other well
enough that this is usually it until the tight pencilling stage.
At this point, if memory serves, moving Tails from the upper left to the
upper right corner of the cover, and moving the
race banner, were the only "big" changes. Tails is that little squiggle,
in the upper left hand corner for those keeping track.

How do they make those covers?

Thumbnail Sketch:

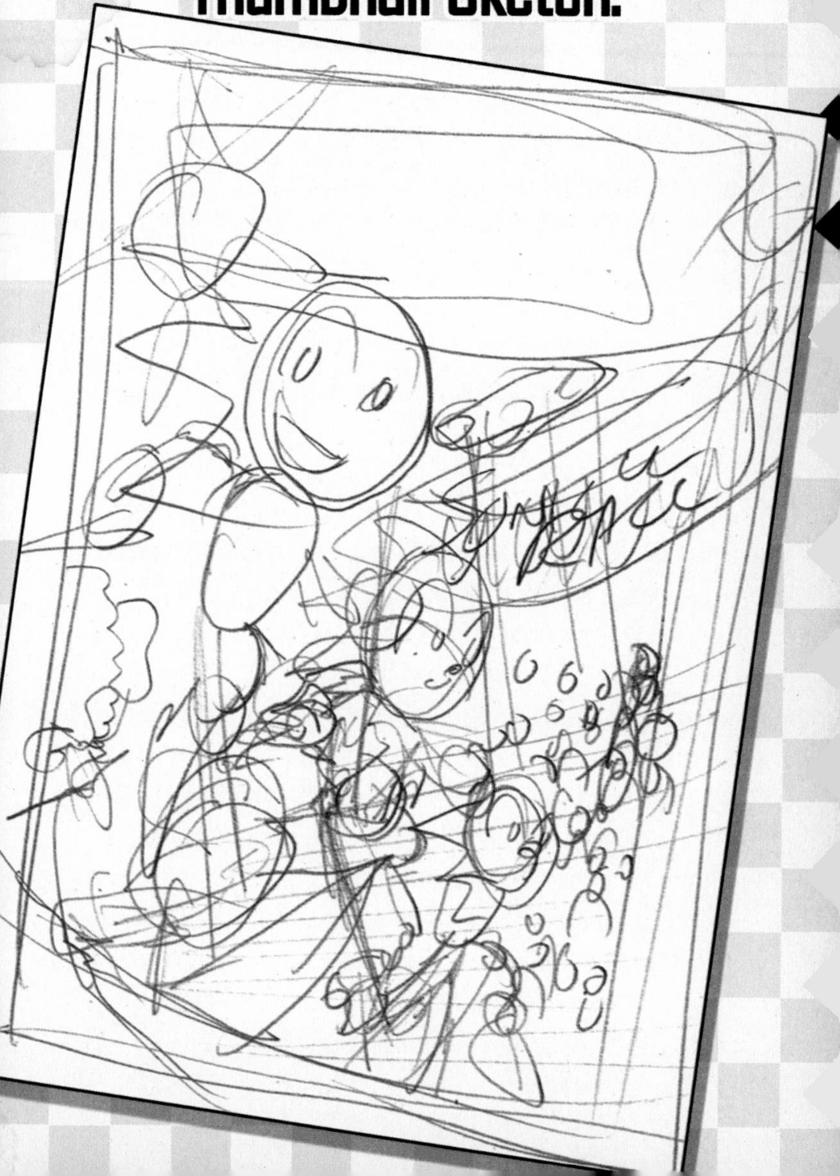

How do they make those covers?
Getting the lead out:

With a good idea of where we were going with this one,
and on the first try too, I jumped right in with the pencilling. This is
where the figures and the background are fully formed and
moved around if necessary. Things like clouds in the sky,
little bits of dust kicking up from the race,
plus the people in the stands, the race banner and
finish line all get a little more firmly
placed in the Sonic "universe."

This is also where, once approved, I will start
inking the pencil lines. At this point I will take the time
to make little corrections that I notice while inking. Usually most
people will never notice the difference. It is just a bit of
my need to make these covers as close
to perfect as possible.

For these covers, we add very little "thick -to- thin" in the inking.
In traditional inking, the ink lines will vary their thickness on the page,
or "thick-to-thin", but for the Archive covers, the ink lines
stay the same weight, like a ball point pen. We chose this style
of inking because the depth, or realism, of the cover will come
from the color. During the stages of coloring we will probably have
additional changes and improvements besides
the several made during the inking stage.

How do they make those covers?

Pencilling and inking:

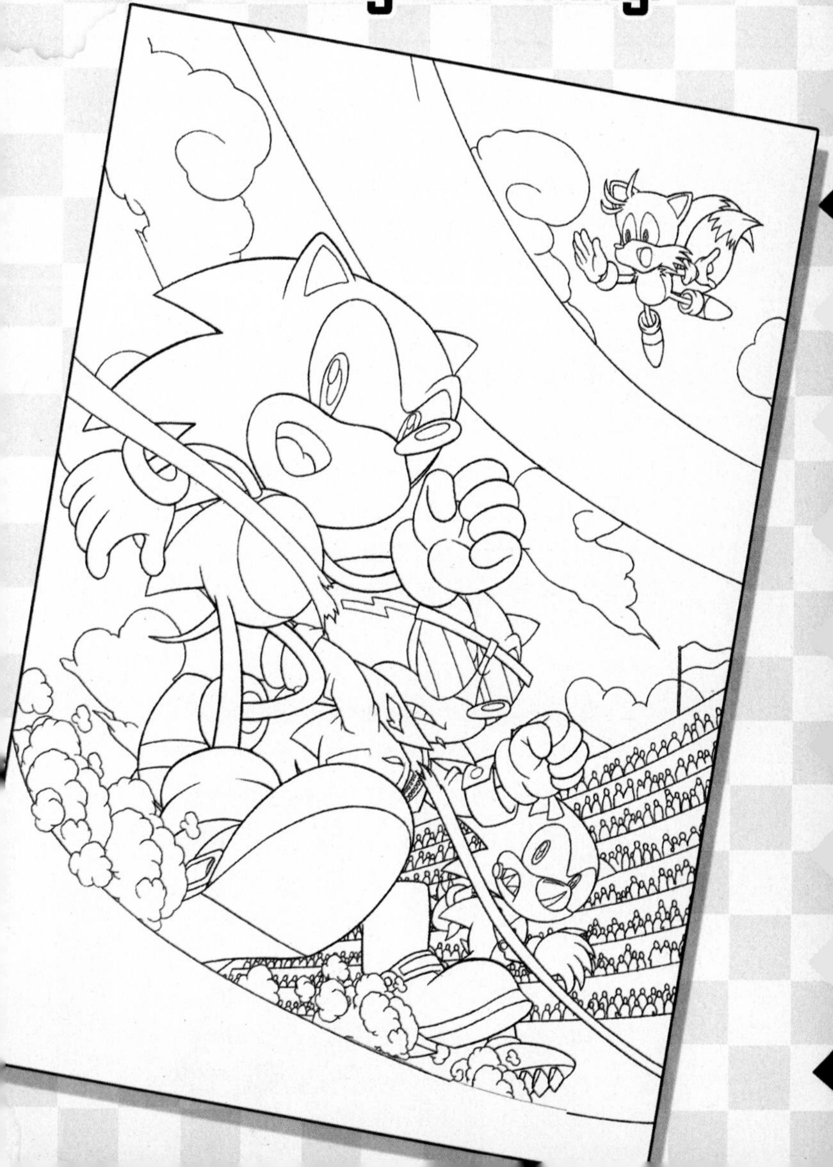

How do they make those covers?
Getting colorful:

During the flat coloring stage,
we have worked it out so that each character and
cover image is set up on its own layer.
Think something like magnets on a refrigerator.
Each area is colored and cleaned up
of any stray marks of ink or other mistakes.
Of course, we made some additional tweaks to
the cover during this stage.

At this point, we played around with several of the
cover elements. The buildings in the far distance on the left were
added in and served as a nice framing visual.
Tails moved around again,
and the "Big Race" banner was lowered and color was lightened
a little to help give more focus to the Sonics.
The logo color was
also changed and most notably the sky
was changed to a more brilliant sunset yellow.
The two reasons behind this were one, to
differentiate this cover from the first Archive
(hopefully you already have it and love it.)
and two, to again help the Sonics
pop out from the background.

This is how the cover looked before any rendering
and some of the changes mentioned.

How do they make those covers?
Flat coloring:

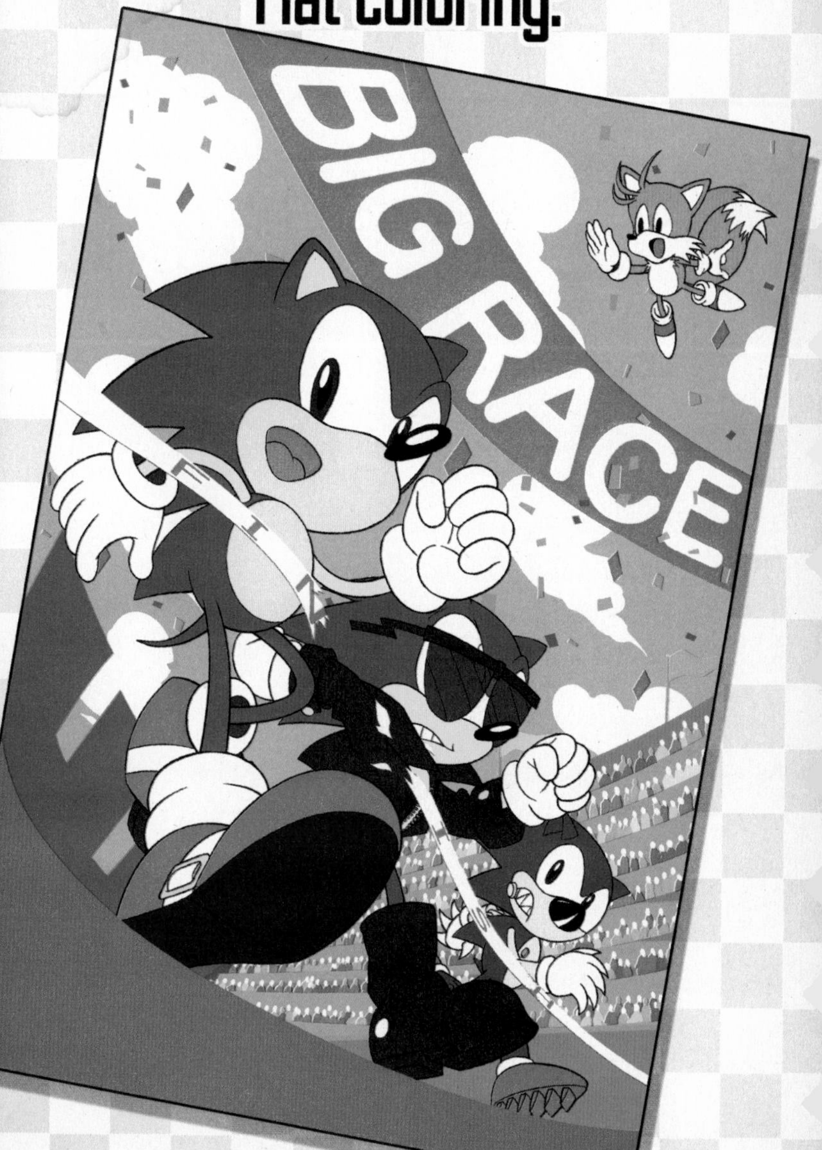
BIG RACE

How do they make those covers?
Now you know!

Here is the cover as it was handed in,
placed side-by-side with the cover that actually saw print
on the front of this collection. We decided to go with a yellow sky to
help pop out our three blue hedgehogs.

The really observant Sonic fans out there might
notice where a lot of the inspiration for the style and color of these
covers come from. Being a kid myself when the first Sonic games came out,
the promotional art really left a mark on me.

The goal of these covers was to reflect the time period
during which the comics and the video games were first introduced. It just
seemed to be the perfect place to incorporate some of
that early Sonic look of both the video games
and the comics.

Recreating the airbrush look of the time
took hours to perfect using computer coloring programs, but seems to
work nicely with the subject.

For those of you wondering, we will be continuing to
update the look of the covers as the comic itself continually evolved
its look and stories during its many different eras.

Thanks for taking some time to read about
the process of how we create a cover.

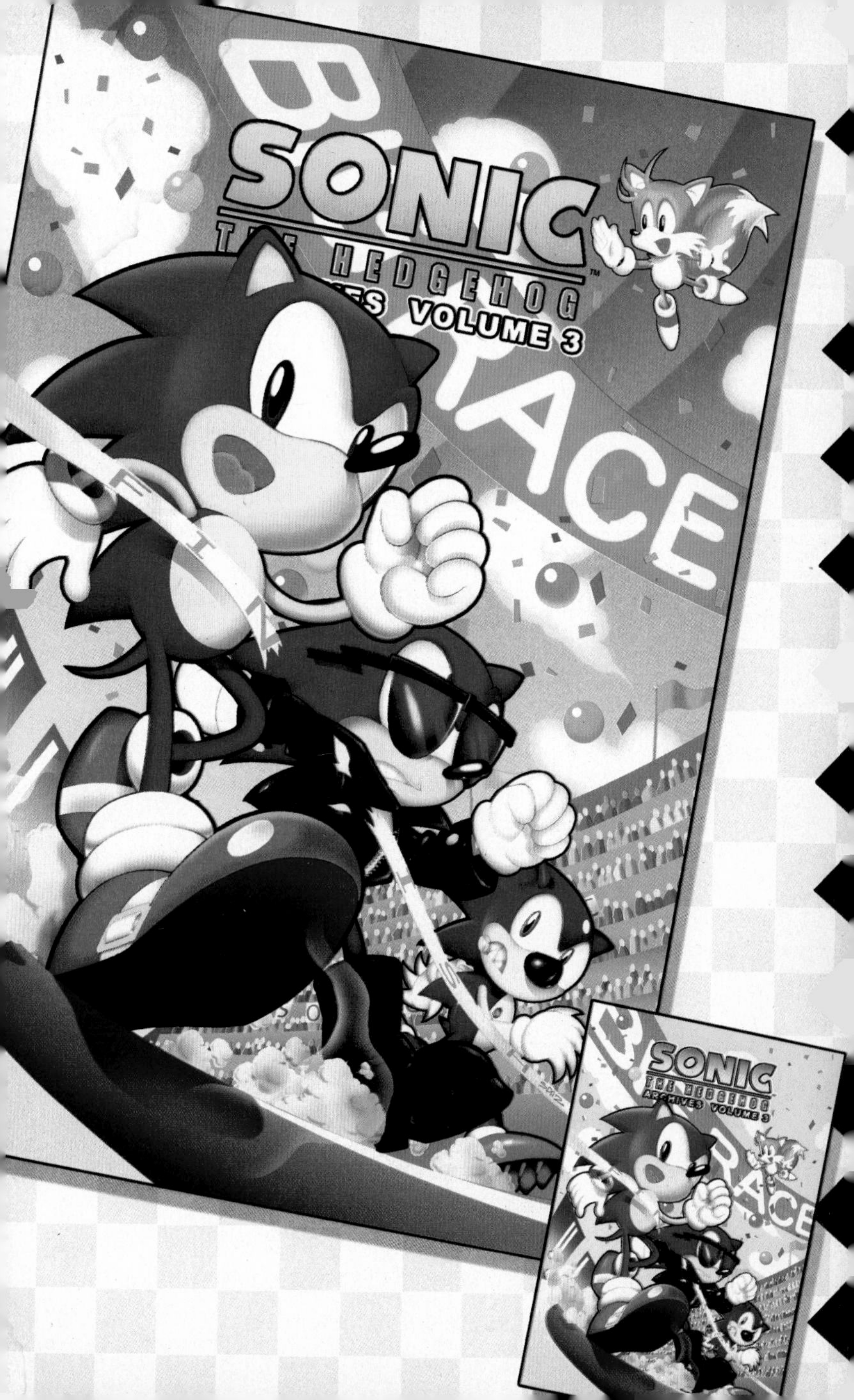
SONIC
THE HEDGEHOG
VOLUME 3
SONIC
THE HEDGEHOG
ARCHIVES VOLUME 3

How do they make those covers?

Special Extra:

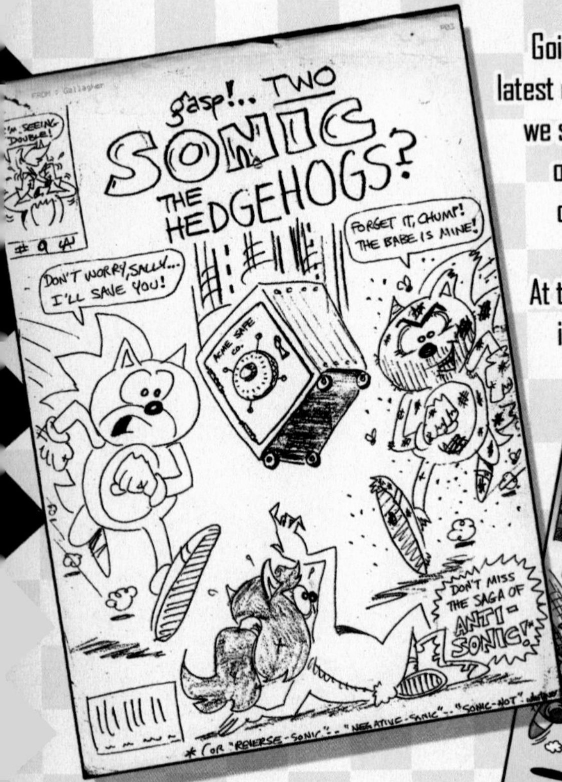
gasp!.. TWO
SONIC THE HEDGEHOGS?
I'M SEEING DOUBLE!
DON'T WORRY, SALLY... I'LL SAVE YOU!
FORGET IT, CHUMP! THE BABE IS MINE!
ACME SAFE CO.
DON'T MISS THE SAGA OF ANTI-SONIC!*
* (OR "REVERSE-SONIC" - "NEGATIVE-SONIC" - "SONIC-NOT"

Going through material for this latest collection of Sonic Archives, we stumbled on to what you see on the left here: a faxed copy of the script for the cover to Sonic the Hedgehog #9. At the time, all the scripts were in a storyboard style and not written or typed out.

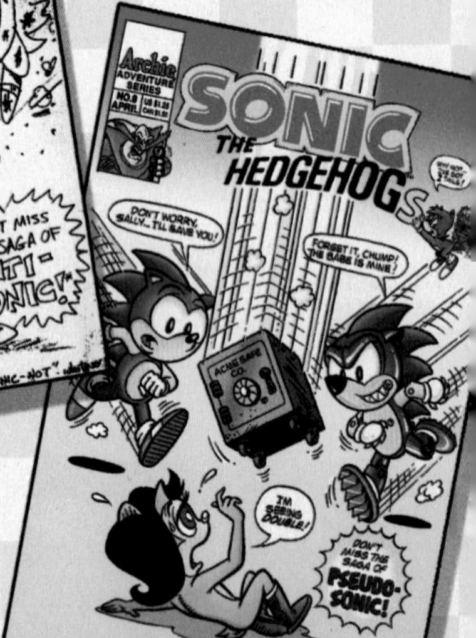
Archie ADVENTURE SERIES
SONIC THE HEDGEHOGS
DON'T WORRY, SALLY... I'LL SAVE YOU!
FORGET IT, CHUMP! THE BABE IS MINE!
ACME SAFE CO.
I'M SEEING DOUBLE!
DON'T MISS THE SAGA OF PSEUDO-SONIC!

Notice how the script was a little different from what actually printed. The character in the script is a bit more like Evil Sonic, while the final cover features Pseudo-Sonic. Also note along the bottom of the page the options for names of the hedgehog that would eventually be known as Evil Sonic, again despite the cover showcasing the first metal Sonic, Pseudo-Sonic!

Welcome to a brief who's who
of the Sonic universe.
You have just read some
of the earliest
and most loved stories from the
Sonic comic. We thought
you'd like to learn a little extra
about a few of your
favorite Sonic characters.

PSEUDO-SONIC

Pseudo-Sonic

Robotnik's baddest badnik to date!
An exact robotic duplicate of our favorite blue 'hog,
Pseudo-Sonic not only looks
exactly like our hero, but can match his speed as well!
Still, this robo-replica lacks
one thing that Sonic has: a heart! Can Pseudo-Sonic
fool the Freedom Fighters and help Robotnik
destroy Knothole once and for all, or
is he destined for the trash heap?

EVIL SONIC

Evil Sonic

What!? Another Sonic? That's right!
In a parallel universe (180 degrees from the
Mobius we have come to know) lurks a foul
being that looks, moves, and sounds like our
true blue hero. Except that Evil Sonic
has a taste for violence and mayhem
(especially against little kids and puppies)!
What dastardly plans will he have
for the Freedom Fighters?